1ST
US.
10

# BALLAD OF DOGS' BEACH

## Dossier of a Crime

# BALLAD OF DOGS' BEACH

## Dossier of a Crime

José Cardoso Pires

*Translated from the Portuguese by*
Mary Fitton

**Beaufort Books**
*Publishers*
NEW YORK

First published in Great Britain by J. M. Dent & Sons Ltd.
1986. English translation copyright © J. M. Dent & Sons Ltd.
1986.
Originally published in Portuguese © José Cardoso Pires
1982, under the title *Balada da Praia dos Cães*

Library of Congress Cataloging-in-Publication Data

Pires, José Cardoso.
    Ballad of Dogs' Beach.

    Translation of: Balada da praia dos cães.
    I. Title.
PQ278.I7B313 1986      869.3'42      86–32207
ISBN 0–8253–0416–4

Published in the United States by Beaufort Books Publishers,
New York.

Printed in the U.S.A.      First American Edition 1987

10  9  8  7  6  5  4  3  2  1

# BALLAD OF DOGS' BEACH

## Dossier of a Crime

## BODY OF UNKNOWN MAN
found, Praia do Mastro, 3rd April, 1960:

1  Male, height 1.72m. Well-nourished, probable age fifty
2  no signs of rigor mortis, no bruising
3  bullet-hole, 4mm. diameter, in vault of skull at height of left occipito-parietal suture
4  perforation of right temple (inner table)
5  rupture of duro-mater at level of injuries
6  comminuted fracture of left orbit, with bone-loss (4mm. diameter) in path of bullet travelling towards right side of hard palate
7  brain in advanced state of decomposition; greenish-grey mass, offensive odour
8  perforation of third intercostal space, with haemor-rhagic infiltration of surrounding muscle
9  perforation of pericardium
10  perforation of oesophagus
11  heart: four perforations (left auricle, left auricular appendix, pulmonary artery and bases of ventricle) Weight, 300g. Advanced state of decomposition
12  circular perforation (4mm. diameter) of seventh dorsal vertebra: entry-point of bullet, which travelled to and lodged in spinal canal
13  bullet in soft tissue of left elbow
14  bullet in stomach. Large blood-clots present
15  no indications of homosexuality, active or passive

*Circumstances of discovery.* Site, undulating sand-dunes, in one of which, approximately 100m. from road, a human knee and elbow were observed, with tissue partly destroyed . . . and thick with flies. Sand removed, with every precaution, and man's body found lying on left side, much decayed. Shoes were reversed, i.e. right shoe on left foot, left shoe on right. Woollen socks, well-worn. Wrist-watch (Tissot MM) stopped at 05.27.41. No documents, personal effects or evidence of identity. Shreds of clothing at no great distance, torn by dogs.

. . . stray dogs, and one of them, a typical Portuguese mongrel that looked as if it had yellow eyebrows, attracted the attention of a fisherman and led him to the body. A scavenger, it had probably slept on the beach, which was deserted at this time of year, among the storage-huts, iron frames for booths and awnings, and a litter of holiday rubbish — scraps of paper in the sand, a washed-up shoe, used cartons and containers. From here the buoy was visible night and day, and here the debris of the sea was cast. Crucified on a solitary pole was the popular travel-poster, in English: PORTUGAL, EUROPE'S BEST-KEPT SECRET. FLY TAP. Among these summer spectres the wandering dog had bedded down.

It was off at dawn, going north; and this, considering a scavenger's way of life, was odd, since the north was the loneliest direction. But it must have caught an urgent scent and knew where it was going — trotting on a straight line, nose to the ground, whimpering. It broke into a gallop as the fisherman watched, and vanished into the dunes.

Soon he saw it again, a thin shape howling on the sandhills through vaporous spray. Curious, he went to investigate. The howling continued, the beast did not even hear him. He climbed the dune, stooped near the dog, and saw why it was there.

Down in a hollow, dogs. Dogs round a corpse. Some of them jumped aside when he appeared, and then jumped back. Others, less easily distracted, balanced on the heap, snarling and snatching morsels from one another.

As Superintendent Otero of the Criminal Police remarked later, there was in this a certain irony. The deceased, by all accounts, had been mad about dogs.

# Investigation
## 7th May, 1960

## I

Inspector Elias Santana figures in the record of this investigation, as he figured in it personally. He was a pale man, and not of robust appearance; 1.73m tall and very near-sighted, with protruding, exophthalmic eyes. His complexion, and other external signs, perhaps indicated digestive troubles – chronic gastritis, at a guess – but the only obvious physical peculiarity was a little fingernail, long and polished (as though he played the guitar, or were a Chinese circus-magician), with an armorial ring on the same finger to set it off. He dressed usually in a check jacket, plain trousers and dark tie (suitable for the job), with a grey pearl pin. A hunter-type Longines watch in his breast-pocket had luminous hands and was attached by a gold chain to his lapel. He blinked, dim and mole-like, behind thick lenses, and meticulously combed what hair he had across his balding skull, to make the most of it.

*A curriculum vitae* might be constructed: Elias Cabral Santana, son of a District Judge. Born, Lisbon, 1909, in the cathedral parish. Attended St James's College but left on death of parents and was brought up, until of age, by his sister. A keen late-night poker-player, and sang in local operatic societies. After a spell in hospital (Sanatorio de Flamenga at Loures), joined the Criminal Police (7th Sept, 1934) for training on recommendation of the then commissioner, Judge Bravo. Nickname, Covas – 'Graveyard', or 'Big Chief Graveyard'. This because he had been twenty years and more in Homicide, digging up the murder-clues and delivering the guilty to the various assorted cemeteries that are the prisons of this country. Devoted service, much applauded (see Service Record), and carried out with appropriate taciturnity and restraint. Never known to refer to any corpse with which he is concerned as Defunct, Deceased or Dead; favours the term De Cujus (*de cujus successione agitur* – 'he whose inheritance is in question') invariably employed by his late father the judge. Encountered by chance on duty at any unexpected place or time, Elias Santana (Graveyard) will say no more than that he is there 'to interview the deaf and dumb'. This demonstrates his discretion, a healthy, natural attitude to murderer and victim, and the fact that he has no further statement to make.

Such, then, is Inspector Elias, or Graveyard, who, because an unidentified body was found – some seventy hours ago already – on 3rd April, 1960, at Praia do Mastro fifty kilometres from Lisbon, sits on his bed in his satin pyjamas, thinking, with yesterday's paper open at the crime page.

It was seven o'clock in the morning. The third-floor flat in the Travessa da Sé enjoyed a river-view, but this inner room had a small oval window onto the stairs. In it there was a bombé chest that had been his mother's, a mahogany bed-table with marble top, and a bright china spittoon. The bed-linen had the embroidered mono-gram *MT*.

Though one might have thought Elias half-asleep he was awake, face turned to the array of photographs on the chest. In one of these the judge was robed, with wife beside him. In another, the couple had with them a little girl, all frills, on her mother's lap. Another, and there they were again, plus a small boy on a toy horse against a garden backcloth with fountains; the little girl had shed her ruffles and stood holding a bicycle by the handlebars. Last was a young woman, head and shoulders, in a silver frame. Her expression was sad and pure, she had a kiss-curl, and a mole on her upper lip was more pronounced – more individual somehow – than it had been on the child with the bicycle.

Elias without his spectacles had eyelids like a turkey's, crumpled and creased, and through them, presumably – or by an inner light – he saw the faded sepia portraits of his relations as he lay there ruminating. Then he rose and went into the hall. The smell of mice was unmistakable.

He padded to the kitchen, taking the paper with him and looking in on two rooms full of shrouded furniture *en route*. ('Going round the estate', his father would say, touring the quinta at Elvas before leaving for the law-courts.) In these rooms he saw the pile of silver on a table, the sofas and outsize armchairs upholstered in damask and swathed in dustsheets; the impressive mirror and the walnut sideboard; the statuette of an angler, fishing now in an aquarium empty save for an ornamental doorknob; the jewel-case, the tantalus, and more draped sheets. A domestic morgue it was, of highly elaborate objects. And mousetraps everywhere, vacant and derided. Mice, he supposed, had to be bright to survive, but in this house they were bright enough to dodge radar if they had to.

There was a stone sink in the kitchen, and from the back window a prospect of balconies with pigeon-lofts, and washing hung out to dry. Flowers grew in boxes and pots at other windows, and weeds along the roofs where rats scampered among the television aerials.

Elias heated his morning milk over a gas as low as his own spirits, and carried the steaming bowl through the hall to his room above the Tagus. Here he could see the boats on the river, the ferries crossing to Cacilhas, the huge flame from the steelworks on the opposite shore; nearer at hand were pigeons crooning and narcissistic cats spring-cleaning their fur in the sun.

Elias dunked biscuits.

'Eight o'clock,' he said, 'and a bloody awful day we're in for.'

He opened the newspapers, addressing his remark to an enclosed glass case, with sand in it, beneath the window.

'Today's the day we receive a kick in the pants from the corpse, my friend. How's that for a novelty?'

In the cage, listening, was a lizard. Either listening or feigning sleep, you couldn't tell. He was a big lizard, the colour of the sand, and Elias called him Reptile. He lay as if permanently poised for flight, head motionless, neck extended, long back claws spread and gripping strongly.

'And you, with your reptile thoughts,' Elias told this one and only confidante, 'you could not care less.'


### VICTIM IDENTIFIED

The victim is identified as an ex-army officer, Major Luis Dantas Castro, who in December last escaped from custody in the Forte da Graça, Elvas, where he was awaiting sentence for his part in an abortive military coup.


That was it, the kick in the pants from the Great Beyond. Unseen, ghostly footsteps coming up and getting you, fair and square, when you least expected them. Getting, in this instance, the devoted Inspector Elias.

Neither his lizard nor his milk and honey diverted him from the strident front page. There was De Cujus, photographed in uniform.

Descriptions, speculations, the whiff of death to make your hair curl. Then the background stuff, stale anecdotes like gossip at a wake: he did this, he said that – poor fellow, poor fellow. *Andante, andante*, muttered the inspector (in his pyjamas), Roll on the funeral. But now the cast is augmented by

### THE SUSPECTS,

three in number – a woman, an architect and an army corporal, and none of them, as here presented to the public, much more than a smudge of print. The woman's name was Filomena. You couldn't see her at all well, but she was young, very young. And the corporal, in battledress, a mere boy petrified by the camera. The architect, too, was young; a young idealist, exalted and intense, face to face with some important decision. These were the suspects: these had done the killing, and knew its whys and wherefores. The smudgy pictures reminded you that they were ordinary people.

Wait for it, thought Elias. The kick in the pants. *Andante*. Read on.

He could have written the article, line for line, himself and read faster and faster, *andante, andante*, as if conducting an orchestra, until suddenly he thumped his hand down, with, 'There we are!' Thumped it on the paragraph piously consigning the victim to the lowest infernal regions. The man had been involved in politics.

> Once we reject the original hypothesis of a sex-crime, the available evidence points to political assassination. The reversing of the shoes is to be noted as a ritual employed by clandestine groups at the execution of their traitors.

This, then, was where the PIDE* came in, with not a moment wasted. 'And there's a pretty sight,' Elias said to the Reptile. 'Two police forces on the case and one can't trust the other – which is what I see, as sure as I'm looking at you. They're singeing my ears – Hell's Angels, the Winged Plague. Are you with me?'

He skimmed the cinema programmes, Overseas News, peaceful interracial relations, Sonotone Radio Breaks Silence, special offers, Table of Moon and Tides. People, he mused, will hold their papers up to the light, to see what's been blacked out; and what they can't

---

* Policia Internacional e de Defesa do Estado.

see they invent, which gives us two censorships, confusion worse confounded. And on we go, reading the ex-written (if there is such a word) into what we read, because we're not exactly fools in Portugal. Certainly Inspector Elias of the Criminal Police was ready to admit that the PIDE, having known of this crime for long enough, had been procrastinating before they handed the body over to the Criminal Investigation Department: a handing-over to be accompanied by the maximum unsavoury palaver, which infuriated the public and allowed the PIDE – more euphemistically, the *Benemérita* – to pose as much-maligned agents, performers of a necessary task.

The lizard lay in his glass planet, screened and impervious, a household dragon; not of the largest, but still a dragon, time-defying, prehistoric. His owner checked the thermostat in the cage, for with warmer weather the temperature had to be controlled. Often in summer, unless the humidifier was on, Reptile grew excited, dreaming of female lizards and noon sun on the rocks.

Elias looked out of the window. What would the PIDE do next, and when would they be doing it? 'The policeman who spies on a policeman,' one had been taught, 'is twice a criminal.' Ah, but was this always true?

The vapour-trail of a jet, bound on some fathomless journey, lay on the blue April sky.

'So where do you stand?' he asked the superintendent.

'The forces of the law must pull together,' was the reply, 'each in its proper sphere.' Superintendent Otero in his dark glasses – Dr Otero, with a law-degree – spoke, as Elias saw, for the commissioner. Same phraseology, same magisterial waving of the cigarette for emphasis. In our proper sphere, then . . .

'Did you say something, Graveyard?'


## Only the Superintendent

Only the superintendent called him 'Graveyard' to his face, and this by virtue of their having been constables together until Otero (kindly subsidised, it was said, by a dashing widow from the Colonias district), qualified in law. Now, qualified, he was a superintendent, with a carpeted office at Criminal Police Head-quarters, and solid armchairs and a nice portrait of Salazar on the wall.

9

'Sorry – you were saying, Graveyard?'

'The PIDE, I said. The Winged Plague, singeing my ears.'

Otero tidied a folder or two on his table, flipped a leaf of the desk-diary, as though simultaneously arranging his thoughts. This was a serious matter.

At last, his pronouncement. 'The forces of the law must pull together, each in its proper sphere. And a political killing,' he added, 'is for the PIDE.'

Ambulances careered by in the street, sunlight crept over the carpet. Behind him Elias might have seen the diagonal slash of a jet-trail in the blue spring sky, but he was teasing the wood of his chair-arm with his long nail and weighing what he heard. *Why* did the PIDE want the body? Their habit was to fan the flames and keep out of trouble, not to lumber themselves like this.

'Political police!' he said. 'They'll wash their hands in carbolic soap and look innocent before there's a suspicion of blood.'

'I must differ. That corpse was ours when they thought we had a sex-crime, but the theory's altered.'

'If blood starts smelling of politics,' Elias rejoined, 'even the flies take off.'

The superintendent stroked his coat-lapels.

'Graveyard,' he said, 'whether they want it or whether they don't, it's political. The flavour is *animus conspirandi*. It tends to conspiracy, and what tends to conspiracy is, need I say, the concern of the PIDE. Otherwise, what are they there for?'

He looked up, and from where Elias sat was a brown polaroid reflection of the window-pane and an auburn moustache above a nodding cigarette. *Animus conspirandi*. Or *anus conspirandi*, what was a syllable here or there? That sort of jargon was good for a laugh in the tame press who, clearly, had it from the PIDE. The affair was not now to be treated as a common crime, nor De Cujus presented as a dyed-in-the-wool pervert, victim of a gang of homo-bashers.

'Good God!' roared the superintendent, 'another sodding ambulance! There are days when I leave this office with my head splitting.'

The telephone rang. He answered curtly, growling into the receiver, and hung up.

'On your marks,' he said. 'They've located the house.'

'House? What house?'

'The PIDE traced a telephone-call. Place was empty, of course.'

## Hideout

This house; the house in a photograph in the *Século Ilustrado* magazine, on a wooded slope of pinetrees and acacia and apparently facing the sea. There — that must be the sea, that line in the background. And over here, the Sintra hills. Consult the map: the sea, the Vale do Lourel, the road drawn in and the house marked with a cross, 200 metres or so from the junction with the highway from Mafra — Estrada Nacional 016B, that is, on bus-routes 17, 223 and 224.

'This village, Fornos,' said Elias. 'They'd do their shopping there?'

'Probably, yes. Oh, most probably.'

Only a chimney, which you might just glimpse among the trees, was visible from the road. Obscurity, easy access, isolation — these features, Superintendent Otero told a press conference, demonstrated the criminals' attention, from the beginning, to detail. Everything was prepared in advance. (In advance of what? Elias wished to enquire. He's letting his imagination run riot, or he's had too many late nights. Brain fatigue.)

But most important was,

SCENE OF THE CRIME DISCOVERED

DEMENTED GIRL A PRISONER

The papers carried banner headlines and all possible views of the house, from the side, from the front and through the trees. Midway on the slope, it was, from some angles, photographed in its entirety — a two-storeyed building with an attic window towards the valley on the west, a garage and a terrace. On the terrace, said the superintendent, the paving may have been tampered with.*

* How the PIDE managed to locate the Casa da Vereda in the 'Dantas Castro' case is a puzzle to this day. They must have acted on information received, but of the theories current at the time only two will hold water. One is that the landlord recognised the major's woman companion from a newspaper photograph, the other that they were alerted from Fornos, where Filomena Joana did the weekly shopping. A third, and equally credible, explanation was suggested when PIDE files were investigated after the revolution of 25th April: there were in the district two PIDE agents and a member of the Portuguese Legion, an organisation which collaborated closely with the PIDE.

It could have been any local-built country cottage of the Lisbon area; a cottage lying musty and unoccupied for months, and festooned with cobwebs and crawling with soldier-ants when the shutters came down. You knew there would be a 'Welcome' tile-panel in the entrance-hall and strip-rugs on the living-room floor and an open fireplace. It contained the regulation ornamental basket of pine-cones, the decorative plates and popular souvenirs, such as the painted pottery cat (hollow; height 33 cm) on a chest upstairs. The fire-tongs, of wrought iron, were presumably from a blacksmith in the village or bought at one of those roadside stalls with wares for the weekend motorist.

These and other domestic items would doubtless figure as evidence later on, but for the moment Elias and his assistant went through the house, touching nothing, like cats in a strange environment.

It was their initial, general survey. The key to the mystery might lie in any drawer; the diligent laboratory-staff, with their chemicals and their magnifying-glasses, might perceive, on the reverse of any rug, a tell-tale stain of Prussian blue with the plain message, 'blood'. The diligent chemists were in the house. The photographer was in the house. The whole team was at work and Elias and the sergeant prowled among them, like cats, on their own reconnaissance.

Before considering measurements and detail they must note how entrances and exits were related; descend to what had been the garage, where were deposited a badly-warped ping-pong table and a mountain of empty Three Star brandy bottles; examine the bedrooms and the attic. In the attic was a heap of newspapers to be sifted, eventually, for a date, a telephone-number, a page with a paragraph cut out. Not yet, though. For now it could be left to the nibbling insects, who would expire, poor things, poisoned by the prose. Elias unlatched the window and looked, at roof-height, to the sea.

Below him the branches were thick with birds and between the water and the sky a small white light moved slowly in the dusk. A tanker, perhaps. He lingered, watching. Tomorrow would be time for enumerating clues and testing theories. Once again, the task was his – send old Bring-'em-Back-Alive – but tomorrow would do. Sufficient unto the day. And any existent murderer, tripping over his own frightened feet, was easier prey than the victim, who wasn't there to catch.

'The bare-breasted woman,' he thought, 'must have stood here.' The house glowed in the sunset. Soon the slow tanker would be level with it, and the quick nightfall of spring would awake its real, unimaginable life; the life of rats and beetles in deserted rooms, of nocturnal insects thudding against the window. Against this window, arrowed in the *Século Illustrado* because a witness said he saw a woman with bare breasts gazing from it at the sea. The witness saw; the witness said he saw. Have to check on that. Elias returned to the terrace for some observations.

The building as described in his report differed in no respect from its few and scattered neighbours. It had been rented, in an assumed name, with contents – furniture, linen and telephone – and was 150 metres from both the EN 016B and a secondary road, the Vereda do Lourel. The guilty persons had an alternative way to the main road by a dirt lane, or track, and their nearest bus-stop, for Lisbon and elsewhere, was 300 metres from the house. A woman's hand-kerchief, a ballpoint pen and three SG cigarette packets had been retrieved from the lane; articles in the house included a pair of army-issue Canon field-glasses, 7 × 50 magnification, complete with case and accessories.

'So the topless woman could have been using binoculars?' asked the reporter from the *Diáro da Manhã*, peering upwards from the terrace. Sergeant Roque, to whom he spoke, sent for the on-the-spot witness.

This witness was a mistrustful and monosyllabic stonemason with sharp, bright eyes, who wore a straw hat. Field-glasses? He couldn't say. Was the attic window not an ideal look-out for spies or smugglers? He wouldn't know. A poor village witness could not be expected to decide what two bare breasts were doing in an attic window.

'You poor fool,' said Roque – though he didn't say it aloud, merely glared – 'don't you criticise the police.'

'Come, now! You remember!' (The *Diário da Manhã* man, a zealous Sherlock Holmes).

In vain. Between detective and reporter the stonemason with the glinting eyes shifted his weight from one foot to the other as though stuck in a quagmire, and repeated his former testimony.

'I've told you what I can. On my life, on my daughters' lives, I've told you.'

# Stonemason's Statement

Witness declared that a month or six weeks previously he was engaged to clean a well approximately 100 metres from the Casa da Vereda and that, while painting the superstructure, he saw a woman's face at the attic window. The woman was standing a little back from the window, as though to avoid being seen, and was not fully dressed. At least, her breasts were exposed, and this he could vouch for, being as he was a voluntary witness, and speaking as he found.

No, he said, it was not a cold day. No, the face did not seem anxious. It stared steadily at the sea until a dog howled among the trees. Then it vanished.

Pardonably interested, witness had gone to the spot on two, or rather three, more occasions and had fleeting glimpses of the woman. Never naked. No binoculars or anything of the kind. She stared straight in front of her and was very pale, he said, in the greenish light of the pines. That was all. A young woman, with black hair.

'Black, or blonde?' asked Detective Sergeant Roque.

'Oh, black,' said the stonemason. 'It was the other, the lady of the house, was blonde.'

'You'd swear to that, would you?' grunted Elias behind him. The man jumped and Elias wandered on through the aromatic evening, with birds flying homewards overhead.

The witness shifted his feet again. In what unhappy hour had he said he would talk to the police? From the depths of his simple soul he must be regretting it. (If, instead, he were such a simple soul. The reporter, for one, strongly suspected him as a rural *voyeur*, a yokel, Marquis de Sade or Paul Pry of the woodland.)

The attic window, slightly recessed, was half-hidden from the journalist and the witness on the terrace by the door. But it was there. There it was, and every reader of next day's *Diário* would study it. (See white arrow, in sky above pinetrees.) The ground-floor window (see caption) is no less important, being that of the living-room used by the guilty persons. And when Superintendent Otero arrived he smote his brow to see his men rummaging for clues in every corner.

'Clues! Bugger me, we shall fill twenty notebooks – plus!'

To this heart-rending cry Elias paid no attention. He was mainly concerned with lay-out and orientation and, with his assistant, was measuring the path that climbed from the house to the road: 150 metres, providing you stayed upright.

Holding one end of the tape, he estimated the angle.

'Not much fun, skidding down there.'

'And raining, too,' his subordinate agreed. 'That priest had it rough, chief.'

'Priest? Who said anything to you about a priest?'

'There's the neckband, chief. Wasn't there a neckband in the wardrobe?'

The inspector at the bottom of the path imagined a night of torrential rain. From what was known so far of the escape, the priest and his companion got here at night, which was bad enough, with no visibility – but a winter's night in a hurricane! The reverend gentleman must have had a word to say. No question of the cautious step-by-step advance which priest, or soldier, would prefer in these conditions. One simply slipped and slid and hoped blindly for the best.

It would be in the small hours, the inspector calculated, and the two had a taxi. There was no alternative, they had to have a taxi, probably to the bus-stop on the top road. The path was then in front of them, but the priest was relying on the girl to find it. 'Mena!' he called her in the stormy dark.

They plunged into the steep track, swerving to opposite sides. Her name was lost in the wind – Mena! Mena! – in the noise of crashing and scrambling as they hurled themselves onward by flashes of lightning. Somehow, somewhere, her hand met his in the scything downpour and they lurched together through mud and briars and stony ruts to a wall and a door and the miracle of a yielding lock; a light-switch; and they were in this very house, Casa da Vereda (see police-report). The girl and the priest in the tiny entrance-hall, safe from the gale, relieved of fear.

Talk about *Babes in the Wood*. Only the robins were missing.

Elias had seen them both in the police photographs and, clearly and vividly, could see them here. The priest, black from top to toe and dripping wet, like a jungle-cat out of the rain; and she, gasping for breath by the door, squeezing her hair dry and becoming gradually, utterly still. She was exhausted, standing in a watery blur, but her eyes shone as she looked at him. He stooped, and shook his greying, rain-dark hair, and looked at her. They looked and looked, then sprang at one another, showering water along the wall, mouth on mouth, greedy for smell and touch, coupling with no sound but the woman's stifled, retching sob. 'You . . . you. Yes, oh, yes!' Truly her voice, after ten eternal months.

Ten months (March–January, see official records) they slaked and cancelled now in one another; rolling, avidly, no holds barred, against the tablelegs and over the rugs that scratched their skin to fire. And when they were done at last, and aware of their surroundings, they were in a strange room, illuminated feebly from the hall.

Wet, naked, warm, relaxed, they lay side by side. Would they light cigarettes?

'The times I've thought of this!' She smiled gently, miles away.

'And me. I thought I'd have forgotten how to.'

'You did?' She lifted and balanced her arms, let them drop and smiled again, to herself.

Once more they heard the storm, but as survivors swept to a secret refuge by the rain and wind. Naked, their clothes all over the floor, they were sheltered, unafraid, secure.

The priest, chaplain, whatever he was, bent above the woman. Her flesh was white – serenely, incredibly white, even in the shadowy room – and she had dazzling teeth.

Her body, as shown in the photographs seized in her apartment, was magnificent. Firm, resilient, faultless. Elias had admired it especially in the picture of her in a bikini by a swimming-pool somewhere, with a row of peacocks on the grass behind her. And the man, the tempest-driven fugitive, leaned on his elbow to contemplate this serene beauty of strong, lovely thighs and swelling pubis. He stroked her skin, and the curve of her neck and breasts. Were the nipples golden and soft that morning, or ridged and prominent? Slowly and heavily his hand went over her, and rested on the thick, crinkling hair, fragrant and dark in the pale bikini-triangle. Elias imagined a splendid pubis, ardent, generous.

The floor was hurting the man's knees and elbow but he stayed where he was, enchanted. The rain and wind howled. Clothes were strewn as they had fallen – a shoe, a crumpled dress – like rubbish washed in from the sea. The neckband shone, whiter than white, in the glimmer from the hall.

'A priest!' Mena was laughing. 'Never in my wildest dreams!'

16

# Wardrobe Department

From among the laboratory items, Elias picked the neckband.

'A priest!' My God, how did they know we needed one?'

Otero reached over the desk and examined it with care. On a sweat-smudged label was written *Minerva Wardrobes*. No genuine priest, he said, would wear that; it was over-starched, stiff and uncomfortable.

'It rates a high score, though.'

'Oh, yes?' This was news, but who could tell?

'Women, I mean. Bedding a priest is definitely top marks. I presume,' explained Elias, 'that priest equals father, equals God, equals sin. What more could some of them require, all in one go?'

'You will read these depraved books, Graveyard.'

'That's right,' said Elias.

The whole of the laboratory report filled the superintendent with dismay. 'Clues, clues – you can't stir for clues. Why not leave visiting-cards and identity-papers while they were at it?'

'Exhibitionism, maybe?' suggested Elias, helpfully.

'No, no. There are just too many clues. Those fingerprints – when did you see such a gallery? The villain who plasters the wall with bloodstained fingerprints is either off his head, or he's having games with the police.'

'Might have been an illiterate villain, practising his mark.'

'These damn jokes, Graveyard.'

Elias took an indigestion tablet, mechanically, as if at an appointed hour, and yawned.

'To think – this time tomorrow one will be at Elvas, exchanging compliments with the military. There was an artist in a Boris Karloff movie,' he added, 'whose hobby was dead men's fingerprints. Made a fortune, photographing them in colour.'

Otero was signing the day's mail.

'Picasso of the cemeteries, as it were.'

'I'm serious. Dactyloscopic art, he christened it, to impress the public. The trouble was, though, he photographed a spare hand at the morgue, and it belonged to the second body Frankenstein was made of.'

'Dear me.'

'Well then, of course, Frankenstein was after him.'

'Don't tell me. He wanted royalties.'

'He wanted the hand, he wanted the hand. He had problems – neat strangling isn't easy when your hands don't match. So he's chasing Aquatints, or whatever his name was, to get at the hand and have a matching pair. Very keen on symmetry, Frankenstein.'

'There you are again. You're being humorous.'

'Forget it. It's my ulcer.'

Otero scrawled his signature.

'Ah, the ulcer.'

'My super-ulcer. Plays me up on even dates and at the equinoxes. Not otherwise.'

'How fortunate,' Otero congratulated him. 'But if I were you, Graveyard, if I were in your situation, I should be inclined to nurse it. There's no bicarbonate sold that'll be much help in a case like this.'

Elias stretched. It was late in the afternoon, when most of the headquarters would be reconnoitring the bars in and around the Praça Conde Redondo.

Otero put his papers together.

'First, we're in for more interference from the press than we've had in our lives before. Then, this mass of evidence at the house. Evidence of hasty flight, you believe; they were in a hurry. But I do not commit myself. I shall wait, and I shall see. We have too many clues. The blood, the fingerprints, the major's notebook, labels in clothes – there's a significance, don't you think?'

'Everything in the line of duty is significant for me,' Elias assured him as he rose to go.

[*Manuel F. Otero*. The son of peasants in north-eastern Portugal, Otero was acquainted with the religious life, as his remarks about the neckband show. After nearly nine years in a seminary he entered government service as a clerk in the Civil Court of the local capital, Vila Real, whence he joined the Criminal Police as a trainee. Qualified with distinction as a detective constable and was promoted, with an 'excellent' grading, to sergeant. He had 1) initiative, an imaginative approach and the ability to work in harmony with colleagues; 2) ambition, demonstrated by his reading Law at the University as a constable, though his finals were affected by duty-absences from Lisbon, and by entanglements with low-class women living apart from their husbands; 3) an inferiority complex and consequent problems of adjustment, with pretensions to elegance. He now regarded the red-brown hair which had earned him nicknames at school – Carrots and Fireball – as a gratifyingly sophisticated attribute. Prone to a sort of routine apathy, as though feeling his time might be better employed in legal practice; and with the latent, unavowed anticlericalism of the ex-student of theology.]

With Elias gone, Otero sat spinning the neckband – dog-collar, as the Criminal Police would call it – on a biro. The Policía Judiciária (the Judite, in Lisbon argot) spoke either in underworld slang or the language of the Criminal Code, but with 'dog-collar' they had the right word. A white dog-collar was what it was. *Domini canis*, dog of God.

Or a ring? A token of chastity, worn round the neck?

Token of chastity, sacred wafer with a hole in the middle, it spun on his pen into an orbit which enclosed the earth's entire priesthood. Rigid figures, hands crossed on their breasts and cassocks billowing, priests gyred and whirled. Straight upwards, heavenwards, revolving one above another, they soared to life eternal. Our planet was traversed by flying priests in dog-collars and we, poor erring mortals, couldn't see them.

But this dog-collar, subsiding onto the superintendent's table, bore an address and, securely wrapped in a parcel, was carried by the hand of the law to a theatrical costumier's in the Parque Mayer quarter. The man had a toupée, and was an obvious homosexual.

'And do you happen to recognise this?' enquired the Criminal Police.

## A Toupée, Tête-a-Tête

The costumier said yes, he did. It was on the books as having been hired out by his firm, Minerva Wardrobes, for some charity performance.

To whom, he could not tell. Out on hire was out on hire. Full stop. You give the customers what they ask for, money in the till and *au revoir*, ducky. This wasn't a solicitor's office, and this costumier was too old, and had too much on his plate, to remember every stray tom-fool who walked in here for a fancy dress. 'And pity me – I should be dead in a week if I tried to.' He flapped his wrists as though shooing from him some totally unprofitable annoyance.

But the police held their usual trump-card, and as he retreated to his sewing-machine the hand of the law plucked forth a woman's photograph and laid it on the counter.

'Oh, her!' Glasses were pushed onto the forehead like the goggles of a pioneer aviator. 'God bless you, yes. A priest's soutane, with the neckband.'

So that settled that, and the name didn't matter, for it was on Otero's desk, in an official report from the military prison at Elvas: Filomena, Mena for short. Filomena Joana Vanilo Athaide (sic).* 'They put that in a confidential document!' snorted Otero. 'Shit.'

From the window he could see the trams toiling up Rua Conde Redondo, with passengers clustering on like flies. Itinerant traders were chivvied by unsympathetic policemen. He saw the snack-bars, and the shops full of electrical gadgets and kitchen equipment. 'Soares the Tobacconist', traditional figure, was at his door to scan the passers-by – those multitudes, those swarms of flies, bumbling and buzzing. They bought their packets of government-stamped paper, they hastened to the Town Hall and the administrative pigeon-holes on which their lives depended; they rushed to the Judite for a writ, or a certificate, or one thing or another. The ambulances; the police-vans, and – fly-trap again – the cake-shop, Açoreana's, at the corner of Rua Gomes Freire. This was Conde Redondo on a regular working-day; a steep street that led to the prison and the Miguel Bombarda lunatic asylum, to brothels and barracks and more than met the eye. What a load of shit! The world, altogether, was one great corpse, glistening with the flies.

Silhouetted in his office-window, the superintendent was thinking that the deceased could, to quote Graveyard, deliver a kick in the pants at any moment to any member of the Homicide Department. The phrase was humorous, one realised, but the more vexations beset Covas the more acidulous were his jokes, and he had hit this nail on the head. You investigate what you see as a perfectly normal corpse, and, without warning, wham! I'm a political corpse, take that! The dazed investigator is then as deep as

* Pencilled correction by Superintendent Otero: Should be Van Niel, not Vanilo; her mother, now dead, was the daughter of business people in S. Africa. (according to our records), age 23, unmarried. Permission (exceptional) to visit Major Dantas Castro on such and such dates, under regulations obtaining at the Fort. Signed, etc. etc.

deep can be in political mire, with Subversive Crime splashed over the front pages and two-column speculation on a cadaver with its shoes reversed. 'Communist Ritual', said *A Voz* and the *Diário de Manhã*; 'this detail betrays Communist ritual'. And journalists go on and on. The blonde spy fascinates them. She may be dotty, she may have been kidnapped, but press and public demand the naming of traitors – traitors who, having bartered our Indian possessions to the enemy, now threaten lives and property at home. Otero considered himself as in the mire. Might-have-been priest, might-have-been lawyer, it was a police officer in the mire who stood here to survey the electric trams. And, priest or policeman, where was the difference? One embraced the law if not the crucifix. Still his days were given to missals – missals on official paper, full of death and recantation and the function of Justice. He still interpreted texts and testimonials, though not as articles of faith (far from it). Nor did he handle them as a nit-picking lawyer would; he paid attention to trivia between the lines, angled for informants and wallowed in the bloody element of Cain. He waded in a lake of blood, fishing by flashlight here and there.

'And this time the blood's political. Group S for Subversive, which couldn't be worse. Shit!'

(The superintendent's all-purpose key-word. He often employed it – 'Shit up to the eye-balls' – when totally impeded by calamity or intransigeance.)

## Elvas, Oh Elvas

It was a lengthy trip, with Detective-Sergeant Roque, across the Alentejo to the Forte da Graca, and in the train Elias sang the song, 'Elvas, oh Elvas, that looks at Badajoz.'

'Quite a coincidence,' Roque observed. 'Have you family there, chief?'

'In Elvas? No.'

The inspector hummed his ditty to complement the scenery, then broke off and added, 'Elvas, for me, is where I learned my tables and had my first girl. It is inhabited by sergeants these days, you will find.'

Telegraph-poles at intervals. At intervals he consulted his pocket-watch, smoothed his sparse hair, or shut his eyes – the habit of cat-napping had sustained him through the late nights of his youth – and did not relinquish the brief-case on the seat beside him. Roque, opposite, was immersed in the sporting pages.

Further south, Elias opened the brief-case for a quick revision of the documents which included, with his notes, photographs confiscated from Mena's flat.

He had spent a morning in this small flat on the Estrada da Luz, over the road from the Zoo. It was in a state of organised chaos, and had a neutral feeling, as though unoccupied for months already. Necklaces dangled from a doorknob. There was a menacing, straw-framed African mask, and space on a shelf where the record-player had been. Below, in a rack, were albums of Mahler and Albinoni, the Luba Mass, and long-players of Sinatra and The Platters. A dehydrated plant trailed from a china pot and the photographs were pinned to a cork panel on the wall above the bed. Mena in Paris (situation established, as the superintendent said, by a urinal in the background); Mena skiing, Mena in a candlelit restaurant (her companion was snipped from the picture), and on the grass by a swimming-pool. No photograph of the major came to light, despite a thorough search.

Mena by the pool was the inspector's most vivid impression from the flat. Head raised, facing the camera, she seemed to leap from the glossy print, cool and self-possessed. Her thighs were, to Elias, a perpetual marvel. Behind her were cherry-trees in flower and, he thought, peacocks.

Peacocks?

Peacocks, peacocks. Imperial peacocks; an attendant, irridescent frieze, copper and blue-green, poised in their coronets, each spike of which was starred with feathers. And so skilfully had the photographer caught their nature, proportions and colourings, that the touches of blue and green were there, even in black and white.

This image Elias entitled 'Woman with Peacocks'; woman attended by royal birds. (He knew, later, that, as did the royal birds, she wore a golden anklet, but she was not wearing it here; here she was barefoot and had no jewellery.) It was his image of her, whether he sat in the train, or in his office, or communing with Reptile; and when he produced the photograph, for identification, to the guards at the fort one at least would say, 'Are those peacocks then?' You could bet on it.

Or maybe not. Maybe they wouldn't notice any peacocks. Landscape-detail, for a guard in a military prison, consisted entirely of stone walls. Wandering stickily about, the hand busy through a hole in the trouser pocket, he would notice only the girl's body, and her air of distinction. Some of them might recall the husky voice, or the direct, unhurried gaze. 'Yes,' they would confirm, 'that's her.'

Meanwhile Elias hummed, and passed his hand, with its long fingernail, over his coiffure. The train ran on, ran on, running towards his childhood and he with it through the country, through the country, the land of gold-brown earth. Through the country to Elvas, with Spain across the frontier.

(– walks by the river he remembered, and the frog-hunts;
– the deranged barber who climbed to the summit of the aqueduct, and the breathless crowd that gathered. (Would he fall?)
– his father at the courtroom window, in judge's robes; and ladies drinking tea beneath the arcades of Rua da Cadeia after mass on Sundays;
– cutting caricatures from the *Álbum das Glorias*, with the housekeeper's little girl;
– and the two of them trying to milk a hornless nanny-goat; and he remembered Senhor Vairinho, the schoolmaster;
– the invasion, on St John's Eve, of filthy village prostitutes from over the frontier;
– Elvas, oh Elvas, that looks at Badajoz.)

The early-spring heat was no surprise to Roque, for Elias had warned him that you either boiled or froze in Elvas. He saw what might, (no disrespect, chief), be compared to a model town in a Christmas crib, with the tiers of the old stone aqueduct before it. And high on a hill the prison, the Fortress of Our Lady of Grace, was posted above the border, and the smuggling-traffic, and allied activities.

'Well, well – and here we are in Elvas!' marvelled Roque before the sentry-boxes; and both were impressed, when the high, sweet bugle-call floated from the barracks and hovered in the streets at sunset as the garrison flag came down, to see polite citizens remove their hats, and a reverential few stand still. 'Now, what about that?' said Elias. His junior then admired the famous Pousada and the square with the lawcourts, and was entertained to Spanish television and *churros* in a café.

Next morning it was time to do what Otero had told them to do, and they tackled the uncounted hairpin bends to the fort. They stopped once, to view a monument by the road, commemorating some magnificent, unspecified deed or other

THIS MEMORIAL
WAS PLACED HERE
THAT MEN MIGHT RENDER THANKS
TO THE GOD OF BATTLES
GOD OF VICTORY

From the monument it was a short distance to the pillboxes, wide ditches and towering walls of the prison and the end of the climb.

Within, hordes of men on a punishment squad ascended and descended, each with one of the notorious 'watercasks' on his shoulders, fetching water to the top of the fort and pouring it into a bottomless tank. Most had a mixture of uniform and tattered civilian clothing, with rags on their feet instead of boots. 'Riff-raff,' said the duty sergeant, in evident scorn of this slovenly attire.

'The torment of Sisyphus,' Elias declared. Not as bad as you'd imagine, said the sergeant. The guards were as lenient as could be on the uphill-loaded-downhill-empty circulation, and strict only as to the quantity of water carried. The casks must not be full, since swilling water made the uphill journey worse, and that was that; it was in the regulations. He sprang to attention as the commandant approached.

This officer, on learning who they were, conducted Elias and Roque to a large room named, as they saw from a plaque on the wall, in honour of one Major Marques Maria. Its ashtrays were the tail-sections of grenades. In this room, with the standard and the portrait of Salazar, they sat to hear

## The Report:

'The escape, of the major and others, accords with conventional pattern: conjectural collaboration of civilians; aid, undoubtedly, from members of and sympathisers with the Movement to which the escapees adhered; theft of weapons and equipment; subversion of an NCO; and flight of all parties.'

The commandant read in short, staccato bursts. He could have worn a monocle with fine effect; he had the face for it.

They were then shown an attached memorandum on those involved (ref. escape from this Fort on night of 31 Dec./1 Jan. last): a) Major Luis Dantas Castro, age 47, married. Detained by order of the Military Court, sentence pending on charge of incitement to mutiny. b) Renato Manuel Fontenova Sarmento, age 25, unmarried; profession, architect. Performing his military service with rank of 2nd Lt. Detained for similar reasons. c) Corporal Bernardino Barroca, age 23, unmarried; clerk in Administration Department of the Fort. Further comments on internal discipline, in dandruff-ridden bureaucratic style, culminated with The National Interest and the commandant's signature.

Next was unfolded a map of Central and Southern Portugal. And here we are at Elvas, in the centre of a mesh of lines and dots. South to Reguengos the commandant traced the road on which Mena drove a Volkswagen on the night of the incident. Major Dantas, we have since learned, was disguised as a priest; the architect had civilian clothes, the corporal his army greatcoat and boots. Alandroal, Terena, Reguengos – 70 kilometres; say, an hour. The commandant's finger jabbed at the map. In the dark, and a foul night, gentlemen.

Then the choice – the main road to Lisbon through Évora, or east in the opposite direction, into Spain? Neither. They take a by-road, a dead-end by the look of it. It is a dead-end – very rugged, very narrow, and it peters out here. Obviously, though, they knew of this: a track, like a stone staircase for goats, blocked practically solid, but leading to the frontier. The commandant's finger accompanied them ten, fifteen, hard, hesitant kilometres east, and flicked up at the abrupt blue cut of a watercourse. The Volkswagen was suspended over a sheer drop, rain lashing at the headlamps.

The priest in the passenger-seat, station of danger, and his mistress at the wheel. Guns and prayer-books, praise the Lord and pass the ammunition, thought Elias, a devotee of paperbacks and the late-afternoon house at the cinema.

He and Roque, in a jeep with a driver from the Guarda Nacional Republicana, verified the commandant's description and saw the sheer drop for themselves. At the edge of this bare slope, with the frontier in sight, the fugitives were stranded. Praise the Lord and pass the ammunition; films again. 'Films are full of priests, and plots depend on fallen women', as St Teresa in a vision disclosed to

Al Capone. Cowboys and hit-men and characters in spaghetti Westerns – all priests, and all of it old hat. It was a very ancient ruse.

Reconnaissance revealed, by a stream at the bottom of the deep gully, the skeleton of a Volkswagen, calcined but recognisable. It had, they inferred, been set on fire.

Elias, with no more to do, went and sat by the jeep. The driver waited; the sun shone; there was a smell of spring, and the stream splashed over the stones below. Stones . . . stones . . . Roque mused, with Spain before him in the golden light; a wilderness of stone at the back of beyond. A match in the petrol-tank, the big explosion, two skips and a jump, and they're off this section of the map, with a fiery farewell. Not bad, if you asked him; a brilliant notion.

Elias had captured a beetle. Caged in his fingers, it buzzed with its feet. How and when had they turned west, into Portugal? Or had they ever left it? He would have bartered his magician's nail for the answer and there was no answer save the country silence with its mysterious, myriad noises – the water, the bleating of a goat, a shout echoing clear in early-morning quiet. Was the burned-out car, so close to the frontier, a red herring, or was it not? With two fingers he prodded the beetle, his long nail stimulating the mandibles. Yes, or no? If yes, then letters sent by the major from Paris were equally meant to confuse the issue. Written in Portugal, they would have been posted in Paris, for the PIDE to intercept. Another old trick. But these were suppositions, not for the report.

'You may have noticed,' he said – to Roque, not the beetle – 'a railway-halt in the neighbourhood. Isn't that right?' he asked the driver.

'At Brejos,' the man replied.

'Five kilometres, would it be?'

'Less. Three, more like.'

Elias jettisoned the beetle.

'A halt, Roque, is not here by accident. If you follow me.'

Roque wasn't dumb. He followed. The major and co. had boarded a train.

'That's it. Instead of fleeing to their Spanish brethren our friends bought single tickets in a sleeping-car. And we, my boy, had better see if the time-table fits in . . .'

('The criminal who has a bonfire *en route*,' commented Otero, with

26

the report, 'is either afraid of the dark or hoping the light will get in our eyes.' He read on.)

... then proceeded to the one-platform halt above-mentioned. This is neglected and overgrown, functioning solely for the communities of Murtal and Ventanas, former supply-centres for the pyrite-mines, now derelict.

Calculating time and distance, and allowing for the circumstances, Elias and Roque had decided their theory was correct.

The branching of the railway at Vendas Novas presented another possibility. From here the major and the girl might go on to Lisbon, while the architect and the corporal journeyed by road – a minor road, for preference – to Barreiro or Montijo. A check with the GNR at Vendas Novas confirmed the simple strategy: two bicycles had been stolen on that morning of *sauve qui peut*, and pieces of them found in a pinewood, the Mata dos Cabedos, fifteen kilometres to the north.

Elias and Roque therefore visited the pinewood in a taxi, stopping to question residents and shopkeepers on the way. Meeting with neither material, information nor anything that was relevant, they extended the search and

... from near the wood, to an estimated distance of 700 metres, various bicycle parts and accessories were recovered: one chain in an oak tree, another from surrounding undergrowth; a handlebar with plastic grips and a wheel, complete with tyre, were in a dilapidated hut in which the (presumed) criminals had sought shelter.

After that, where? Through the uncultivated countryside, north up the river to Lisbon. But there were dozens of roads to Lisbon. Elias and Roque, poring over Central and Southern Portugal, soon marked so many, and in so many directions, that the result was a glorified palmist's chart, a Hand of God with the fatelines of the entire human race . . .

('The conventional escape-pattern,' said the commandant, 'presupposes external assistance.')


### Inspector's Report (continued)

... dozens of roads, which would multiply their options (i.e. those

27

of the corporal, the architect, the major and the girl), given the cavalier attitude to transport. Vehicles were appropriated, and burned or wrecked when finished with. (Elias had seen the remains of the bicycles.)

Roque suggested that the fugitives were 'merely hiding their own shadows, as you might say – trying to cover their tracks.'

'Merely!' was the magisterial response. 'A shadow, my dear boy, is the bane and penalty of every creature living. He has to make it, and it affords him no protection.'

'Good Lord,' said Roque, 'how true! Even a dog lies down in case anything uses its shadow for shelter. That must be why.'

'Dogs piss against the wall, and thus they are identified.'

'The same with these types, then. They try to destroy their shadow, and it stays on all this scrap iron.'

'Now you're talking. About dogs, though – their shadows vanish, but the shadow of piss does not. And that no villain has yet managed to conceal. If you follow me.'

There was little more (it seemed) to delay them. It was late, and they decided to eat in a workman's café on the road back to Vendas Novas. And here, as they sat down, Elias exclaimed, 'Aha!'

Behind the counter, on a cask, was a pair of bull's horns, mounted on bicycle handlebars and labelled, by the proprietor, 'Mine.' Roque, though dubious, nevertheless enquired, just to see how they got here. Oh, those? A pedlar brought them from Vendas Novas.

The inspector, at table, smiled. Not, as he was to acknowledge, because he doubted the proprietor, but at the expectation of miracle ingrained in his profession. For who but Sherlock Holmes would have wafted two detectives from Homicide to the very eating-house that had bull's horns on the handlebars of one of the stolen bicycles? The hell with the handlebars. On with the report.

Soon after this, on Sunday, 10 April, the police, on an unexpected tip-off from a switchboard girl at the Novo Residencial hotel, apprehended Mena, who had registered there on the Saturday night. She was sitting in her room with a suitcase packed, as if waiting for someone.

She had gone previously to her flat on the Estrada da Luz, though it was sealed by the court, to destroy papers and burn such photographs as the police had left there. A caricature of herself, pinned to the wall, was apparently burned with a cigarette-end; as was the charred fragment of a letter to her father – 'the most horrifying things have been happening to me . . .' Similar fragments found in the hotel room were no more than repetitions of this broken sentence.

The switchboard-girl had recognised her from newspaper photographs, and an accounts-clerk said there was a telegram to Lourenço Marques on her bill: to her father, the police assumed. Inspector Elias Santana (absent from the arrest, attending to his family vault in the cemetery of Alto do São João) was convinced that the PIDE had hatched the tip-off. It was Superintendent Otero, with Detective-Sergeant Silvino Saravia Roque, who came to the hotel in a police-car.

On arrest Filomena Athaide – Mena – said nothing but, 'Must you?' when they handcuffed her. On the drive to Headquarters she kept her hands on her knees, looking at them.

She was put straight into solitary confinement, with none of the normal admission processes, such as photographing or fingerprinting. This effectively minimised the number of those who saw her. The strictest conditions were ordered by the commissioner, in the interests of the enquiry.

The inspector saw her an hour or two later – a girl with her hair in a pony-tail, wearing mules and a full skirt, and not in the least like the pictures he had. He at once began the first interrogation, which was held in the superintendent's office and lasted through the night and into the next morning, with Detective-Sergeant Roque at the typewriter.

Roque and the inspector had their map of Central and Southern Portugal. Vendas Novas, yes; but before Vendas Novas?

'Shall we go over it again?' said Elias.

Night or morning, what does – what did – it matter? They were closeted with this girl who smoked and smoked, and who was infinitely detached in the blue, curling haze.

Elias sucked a pastille.

'Well, then – the road, the car. You set fire to the car. Brejos, Vendas Novas. And at Vendas Novas the bicycles are sitting there when the corporal and the architect leave the train. It couldn't have been more convenient. We are correct, I think?'

'Yes,' Mena agreed. The inspector's thick glasses glinted above the map. The portrait of Salazar was on the wall.

So, they had the bicycles. Main roads would have been less hazardous – amazing, to Elias, that this had not occurred to them – but naturally the rain would slow them down. Onward, though, as fast as they could. Forward, bent double, with everything and everyone against them – destiny, and the clock, and the ubiquitous GNR of that region. They sheltered in a hut. We've seen the hut. And underneath a footbridge. Could that be this double line over a stream? And then, they told Mena (and Mena was telling in her turn), they even ventured into a bar for a nip of brandy. Ah, yes? And when was that? Which bar? Which bridge? Where, precisely?

'A complete statement is required,' said Elias.

Yet the account was vague, the route uncertain. Mena did her best with the map, but they were frightened men, pushing doggedly on, and what she said was what they had said to her. Roque at the end of the table typed her every word. Sentence by sentence, kilometre by kilometre, the typewriter ploughed patiently in the wake of revolving bicycle-wheels, on the road, by-roads, uphill, downhill, through the puddles. Tring! went the bell, crash! went the carriage, next line, on again. A puncture. Another puncture. Destruction of bicycles in a pinewood. But was that not before the bridge, before the hut? Silence from the typewriter. 'Where are we, exactly?'

The corporal and the architect lost their heads, lost their sense of direction, walked at random. Then a lorry loomed at them out of the dark, spitting clouds of spray, a huge ghost with two shadowy figures in the cabin. They hailed it, and swung themselves in among boxes of fish and ice, under a lead-heavy tarpaulin. Forty, fifty kilometres, who could guess? They could not, squashed between the frozen fish and the leaky tarpaulin, with their teeth chattering and the rain coming in. On a quay, at dawn, the cover was rolled back.

'That would be Barreiro.' Elias had his pencil on the map. 'Next, Lisbon.' The pencil crossed the Tagus.

But beware, take heed. Lisbon over the water is a crouching beast, and it bestrides the country. *Achtung, achtung.* Drenched and grey and sleepy it may look, but do not be deceived. You'll run into a web of traffic-patrols, police-patrols, the Legion, the GNR; posts and barracks, each with its official portrait of Salazar and its files of photographs of political suspects on the run. The perimeter is thick with danger-spots, Lisbon ringed with a talkative forest of radio-masts and haloed in photographs of the wanted, with Our Leader on the wall, presiding.

The corporal and the architect weighed the risks. They must have caught the early-morning ferry and rung the Casa da Vereda from a telephone-box. Between ten and eleven o'clock (see statement) they were greeted at the house by a woman who hugged them thankfully.

'A woman with blonde hair?'

Mena exhaled cigarette-smoke.

'Correct,' she said.

No more for the time being.


# II

Elias had interrogated Mena in the basement cells and was back at his desk, by a glass wall-panel that gave onto the untenanted main office, with rows of bare tables under fluorescent lights.

The commissioner's directive, relayed via Otero was: strict confinement, no communication.

He was re-reading the notes, re-studying the all-important photographs, with what he called his Book of the Dead before him – his dossier of the crime, with confessions, transcripts and first statements. He hummed tunes from a Spanish *zarzuela*, but what he heard was Mena's voice, and what he saw was Mena, with her cigarette. In two or three interrogations he had more or less unravelled events. Under his breath, the operetta tune.

[MS note by Detective-Sergeant Roque: The corporal did not visit his mother (underlined) after escaping. This woman, Florinda Barroca, of Rugial, near Paredes, was unco-operative when questioned by the GNR corporal in the village, Joaquim Pinto, who collaborated with us. He attributes her attitude to the subversive temper of this region; says that her brother Bartolomeu, or Bertolomeu Pardo (underlined) is a known political activist, and that the corporal could safely have gone home without his (Pinto's) knowledge, since no one would have denounced him. End of statement.]

Elias had been through the stuff already, and he skipped a bit, with occasional re-readings (it is the re-reading that matters), organised his thoughts and glanced appreciatively at his long nail. Occasionally the thoughts were spoken aloud, and the long nail listened. Why not? For the little finger-nail is the nail of divination, and to it he had recourse at every doubtful juncture, personal or professional.

Beyond the glass panel were the metal-topped desks and typewriters in rows. Really, they could be in an aquarium; the continual hiss from the neon tubes could be that of a domestic fish-tank in the night. He might yet be spared to see oxygen bubbles rise against the glass and policemen floating by, wide-mouthed, flicking their tails.

He pulled out a desk-drawer crammed with magnesia tablets, herbal remedies and whatnot. He had in there a propelling pencil with a calendar on it for 1953, and a paperweight with a miniature lace brassière inside. The books – *Personal Magnetism, The Protocols of Zion, Daily Life Among the Assyrians* – had been supplemented by Jack London's *The Sea Wolf* in a Portuguese translation by Guerreiro Boto, published by Europa-América, of Lisbon. Automatically this copy opened at a page with the signature

*Bernadino Barroca*
*Nº cabo 3976/57*
*F. G. Eheas 12-5-1959*

The inscription struck Elias as a sort of general farewell on the eve of a journey to nowhere, and was his starting-point when he embarked on these wide oceans. Mena was forgotten – and at this hour would be chain-smoking on her bunk – while he sailed with Captain Larsen over the millpond water, through unclouded night, between ice-banks with colonies of seals. 'A bell-buoy, and we're a-top of it!' Captain Larsen, Sea Wolf. A sailor in greasy rags, clinging to the gaff; and the rookery of barking seals, half fish, half dog. Intelligent faces they had, whiskers, and melting canine eyes and fishes' tails: to the average dog, domestic and untravelled, a seal might be a siren, a mythical bitch of the ocean.

Elias read casually, as if killing time before renewing the interrogation, but there was more than the story to think of – there were the underlinings. Passages had been underlined, in pencil, by the corporal.

'We're dead men, I know it,' was one of these. And another, emphasised by a cross in the margin: 'He led a lost cause, and he was not afraid of God's thunderbolts.' When had Barroca reacted to these alarm-signals? Reading on his bed in barracks at Elvas that day in May or later, re-reading at the Casa da Vereda? With what hideous presentiment had he underlined the words, and why? Elias combed the narrative for an answer – this voyage of Captain Larsen, wolf by name and wolf by nature, in contrast with whose wolfishness the seals appeared more doglike. Not that hatred of mixed blood was explicit in the text, but the text had much that was implicit, and prophetic; much whose relevance was not restricted to Captain Larsen and his adventures.

It had these underlinings, for example.

Above and beyond the printed page, the inspector imagined wind and rain, and the refugees in Casa da Vereda. Their transistor radio was on his filing-cabinet, in its plastic bag from the laboratory. The arguments they must have had around it!

'We listened to the radio,' Mena told him. 'It was our only link.'

Elias moved the transistor to his desk.

'Then we'll see what it has to say.'

It promptly emitted a loud goo-oong! and a solemn voice intoned the 3 a.m. news. This is Radio Lisbon. On Public Security Day, the forces of Law and Order have paraded, before unsmiling staff officers on a flower-decked rostrum. Outdoor Mass for those fallen in the performance of their duty, peace be to them, with their

33

truncheons. Bemedalled tracker-dogs, and guards with rifles at the trail, and the Home Secretary's speech on public order. Security of life and property is his theme, and unremitting warfare is declared on agitators 'who, in foreign pay or inspired by libertine notions, attempt by any means to disrupt the Student Body and the Labour Force, to deny Faith and Morals, and to challenge Authority.' Unquote.

Elias dozed, blinking.

His mind was on the past winter, and the refugees from Elvas cooped up by rain and fear in the conditions Mena spoke of – the cold, the gales, the smoky house, the isolation. Their radio would not then have been reporting baton-swinging parades, or outdoor Masses for deserving policemen, with ranks of sweet children in procession. ('Suffer the little children to come unto me,' said a voice in his ear: the infamous Captain Maltês, with visor, riot-shield and baton, on one of his student-hunts, to which there was no reference on the News.) President Thomaz was on the News, attending a fox-hunt in the morning and a Te Deum after luncheon for the conversion of the Hindus. This concluded the bulletin, read, most probably, by the announcer who spoke in the living-room of Casa da Vereda three months earlier. (Though his tones may have been hoarser, because of the cold weather.)

It was a bad winter, with floods at Santarem and shanty-towns washed away; and hidden in Casa da Vereda, four fugitives intent on a transistor in a stifling room (the wood must have been damp, and the chimney wouldn't draw in that wind), with a sulphurous yellow light burning. Not for them the chill neon brilliance of Criminal Police Headquarters, but a sinister, lunar glow.

Goo-oong! And after the news, the Official Commentary. Threat to Portuguese India, the galleon foundered with its ballast of statued Viceroys, a Lisbon announcer breathing fire and retribution. The architect stood up.

'Nothing about us yet.'

Elias switched off. And what there was about them they would never hear, for by then the major would be listening to God alone, and the others have been panicked onto a different wavelength.

' Calm in the inspector's office; flailing rain at the Casa da Vereda.

The major said, 'Corporal! You're biting your nails.'

Corporal Barroca lowered a grubby, inelegant hand. The sad, mulish countenance Elias had seen in the police photograph; the clothes Mena had described – greatcoat over the shoulders, twill trousers, army boots.

'Three days, and that telephone hasn't rung!'

'Patience, Fontenova, patience. Silence can be an offensive, remember.'

That's the spirit. Hang on and keep smiling. Elias looked at his glass panel. How many such evenings did they spend, in the grip of winter, with the major pacing the room, as was, it seemed, his habit?

'Depend on it, if the commodore doesn't ring, he has his reasons. And you know what a fuss there is in the Assembly, over Brazil.'

'That won't last. They'll all kiss and be friends any day,' the architect replied.

'Once, maybe. But unfortunately for the government, Galvão is in Brazil.' (Mena had indeed mentioned Captain Henrique Galvão; it was in the notes.) 'For the future, where Brazil's concerned, they have him to reckon with, and he'll mobilise everyone against them, make no mistake.'*

'Yes, but where do we come in?'

'Us? For God's sake, where are your wits? We're part of the whole operation.'

The fire smokes, the major strides, the glowing cigarette moves to and fro.

'And then – is he in Brazil, Fontenova? Officially, yes. Officially he can't leave – but has he left? Can you be sure? I'm not saying he has, I'm only asking.'

Fontenova craned to see through and over the billowing smoke, The major's cigarette was here, and there, and lost to view; he was a disembodied voice.

'It's a question of calculating risks. Even if he didn't sweep the country, his presence in Portugal would pay enormous political dividends. The world sees him as the big gun, and by God, he is.'

By now (see notes) the voice was at the far end of the room. The major sat at the table with Mena, in a dressing-gown, behind him: haggard from lack of sleep, one hand on his shoulder, the other, with a cigarette, at her side.

'No guarantee, as I say, that he's here. It's a mere probability,

* Galvão, an opponent of Salazar, in January 1961 seized the Portuguese liner *Santa Maria* in the Caribbean, intending to attack the colonies in West Africa.

among many probabilities.' He reached for the girl and clasped her to the back of his chair. 'But what if he were? That would be awkward for the bastards.'

He was caressing Mena as he spoke. 'Tactics of surprise, they'd call it.' His hand strayed from her haunches to her spine. 'And we have the advantage. They don't know when to expect what, they're shit-scared and they can't win. Not against water-tight planning, with every detail thought of. What are you gaping at?'

'Me, sir?' (Voice of the corporal).

'Yes, you. I'm speaking, and you stand there gaping – at what?'

No reply. For a second Mena's eyes met those of the architect.

'Barroca,' the major continued, 'the telephone is dynamite; get that into your thick skull. Goggle if you must, but do not touch. Dynamite, Barroca. Must I tell you again?'

The architect, by the hearth, was looking across at the window. (But the internal shutters would be over the windows, in that weather. Fontenova was trying to procure himself distance, and space.)

'I woke once, and I thought it was ringing.' Mena was talking for the sake of talking. 'I was dreaming, though.'

Fingers on her thighs. 'Worse, you had a hallucination.' Flanks, buttocks, through the dressing-gown.

'Hallucination?'

'There are auditory hallucinations, I believe. And you –,' the major jutted his chin at the corporal – 'you're at the stage of hearing telephone-bells. You do nothing but goggle at the thing. The telephone's a trap. It's becoming a nightmare.'

He laughed. His hand roved on, between her thighs, and Elias forgot the corporal, who faded into the smoke. The architect said, 'Yes, becoming a nightmare.'

'I'm going to bed.' (That would be Mena.)

'The man's entitled to look.' The hand still strayed and stroked. 'Look at what he fancies, when he fancies, no crime in that. It's his damned shiftiness I object to. Shifty. Idling round the telephone.'

Heavy footsteps from above. The corporal in his room was tramping a regular beat, as though on sentry-duty, inviting weariness, inviting sleep. Then the noise stopped. Was he reading?

Was he reading *The Sea Wolf*, which the inspector had been leafing through a moment before? Quiet ensued. No talk, no footsteps. The rain beat at the house unceasingly, unregarded; the wind blew in squalls and rocked the trees. General Winter, scourge of the weak and ally of the strong – who said that? Major Dantas, or his revered Liddell Hart? Or could it have been Clausewitz? The arrogant Clausewitz, Shakespeare of the barrack-room?*

The architect sat at the table, opposite the major.

'We're in a pretty mess if Gama e Sá has lost the number.'

'Names, Fontenova – no names! If the commodore isn't in contact, there will be an explanation.'

'Oh yes, yes. Patience, patience. But we don't know where we are until he rings.'

'Patience, Fontenova, patience.'

This was a reply, an echo, for Elias. In that house, time and people were recurrent and re-echoing. Mena, leaning on the major's chair, a misty echo, a nocturnal projection, with her cigarette.

'All in due season,' Dantas said, 'and through the proper channels. The commodore is simply abiding by the rules.'

'The commodore! If you ask me, he's wiped his arse with the telephone-number.'

'You'd bet on that?' The major smiled.

Debate, debate. The radio silent and a pack of cards on the table. Drawn game? wondered Elias in his office. But the architect was shaking his head. He did not accept this non-communication of Dr. Gama e Sá. Sorry – the commodore.

'But if he has lost it, Dantas? Or if he's under observation? There could be a dozen reasons, I don't have to tell you. And who's to let us know – how do we find out if anything's wrong?'

The major bent forward. 'With me,' he said emphatically, 'nothing goes wrong. Nothing, Fontenova.'

The smoke billowed between them. (Don't confuse the voices, Elias told himself; but there were no voices.) They sat and eyed each other. The logs crackled and the sparks flew. No sound from above where, Elias would swear, the corporal was reading and underlining awful warnings in *The Sea Wolf*. Unless he had his ear to the floorboards.

---

* '. . . the ignorance of these intellectuals on military matters can depress one beyond words. A few days ago Fontenova said Clausewitz was 'a barrack-room Shakespeare, who learned his tables from the scoreboard on a shooting-range.' He never read a line of Clausewitz in his life. Damned effrontery.' From the major's notebook, found at the Casa da Vereda.

Then the voices were audible again, though fainter and difficult to distinguish.

'Nothing goes wrong. Nothing, I tell you!'

'And, Dantas, there's my list.'

'Oh, God – you and your supporters!' And, 'I'm sick and tired of that bloody rubbish.'

'Dantas, you've seen the list.'

'Supporters you call them?'

The argument, patchy and conjectural, was nevertheless fairly accurate, according to Mena, nonchalant among her cigarette-fumes. Ah, but had she actually heard it? Where was she at the time?

'Give the word. I can start contacting them as soon as you say.'

'I tell you, it isn't worth the effort.'

'But why should we waste them? Why?'

'It's all you can talk about, your bloody list, your bloody contacts.'

'Have it your own way. But where's the harm in trying?'

The major shrugged. 'That rabble of students! Students. Can you swear they're none of them in the Party? Or Communists, or PIDE recruits, or parlour pinks? No, Fontenova, I stick to my opinions.'

Early morning, and the lights in both offices were fading in the ashy whiteness from the windows. Elias was ready to ring down the curtain and send the disputants to bed.

The disputants disappeared.

He, too, quitted his desk.

[On the record of Mena's evidence was a note: 'the witness soon saw that the major detested the corporal. Says that one night, in discussion with Fontenova, he berated the corporal, who retired to his room. Has no exact recollection, but says that Dantas more than once alluded to Captain Henrique Galvão; also that the architect referred to the unsatisfactory conduct of 'the commodore' (Dr Gama e Sá), and to a list of potential adherents which he had submitted to the major. The latter was, she said, taking certain liberties with her during the discussion, in order, she thinks, to embarrass Barroca and to see what the architect would do . . .']

# III

Interrogation of Mena by Inspector Elias, 'We'll just run over this again . . .'

The Criminal Police cell was less than eight feet square, with a spy-hole in the door. The hour might be three-thirty, or a quarter to eleven. The sunflowers might be open, or the owls still hunting. No use asking. It was an isolation cell, underground, with a tiny light in the concrete ceiling, where hours were unrecorded. (Mena had no wrist-watch. Anything that could serve as guide or reference was confiscated automatically.) One saw neither moon nor sun. Whether she were asleep or awake, Elias might walk in and say, 'We'll just go over this again . . .'

The technique was that of 'invasion of personal territory,' and sleep was among the territories invaded. The first time, in the office, Elias had set the stage, with chairs and tables where he wanted them. He sat in a corner, Mena in the middle of the room; at each question he manoeuvred his chair, inch by inch, towards her, encroaching, as though by accident, on her shrinking island. Inch by inch was enough. He leaned slightly forward, to hear her, and dragged his chair with him. He stooped for something he let fall, he went to the window, and the chair, as he resumed it, was, quite accidentally, nearer. Pretext after pretext, question after question, until suddenly he was breathing 'police' all over her. Invasion of personal territory.

(After grilling a suspect, Elias had been known to say, 'I waded in there until he split at the seams.')

But Mena was not thinking of personal defence. She had not been waiting in a hotel room in order to 'collaborate' – police jargon for 'supply information' or 'succumb to interrogation'. It was from herself she wanted to escape. It was because they were driving her yet further into herself that she said, 'Must you?' when they handcuffed her.

But interrogation has its rules. The inspector had seen that his proximity was repugnant to her, making her less willing to speak. The commissioner's instructions, moreover, were for solitary

39

confinement. For these reasons, and for reasons of his own, and though, as he acknowledged, she had told him the essentials on that first occasion, Elias thereafter came to the cell and kept his distance. She would be on her bunk. He would turn a chair and straddle it, facing her, elbows on the chairback as if on the ledge of a balcony.

Always in the cell (the instructions were definite) and always unannounced. At any moment she might awake, heavy-eyed, to the shock of his presence.

It is terrifying to see a detective by the bed when you wake, and she was terrified. Whom had she betrayed in nightmare or delirium? And if he evinced no interest – 'Relax, you didn't say a thing' – the implication was that he was in control, she must have spoken. And if not this time, then, inevitably, another.

Could you, she wondered, dream smells? Not people, or conversation – smells. Dream the scent of jungle-grass after rain, of lemons and bananas stored away from the light? Or the childhood smells: Lifebuoy soap from the shops in Salisbury, and school exercise-books that smelled of brand-new paper. A doctor's hands, and fresh bread from the oven. Her father, his pipe and his Aqua-Velva. And suitcases of hard, shiny leather, that was crumbly inside. And honeysuckle; the scent of honeysuckle round the house in the dark. Could you dream smells?

For weeks and weeks she had been smoking like a furnace and stupifying herself with Valium in a battle with insomnia. At the Casa da Vereda she would lie by Dantas, as the storm crashed and raged, and stare towards a pottery cat in a wig on the chest-of-drawers. The wig was Mena's disguise on her clandestine outings – ash-blonde, with platinum highlights; unseen in the dark, but she couldn't forget it was there. Yet, strangely, on the night of the crime she slept. After the shooting and the blood, sleep fell on her with the force of a sledge-hammer; thick, animal sleep, for a single night. After that she fought sleep, fearing to dream of the dead man.

'Oh, no, no, no! The psyche' – Elias tapped his forehead – 'the psyche has its defensive mechanism.'

But now, when she didn't need her sedatives, and Dantas no longer troubled her dreams, she was again afraid of sleeping; afraid to wake with this figure, this shadow, with its restrained mockery, bending above her.

'Only a couple of questions,' the shadow would murmur. 'We'll just go over it again . . .'

[Memorandum from Superintendent Otero: a) prisoner to remain anonymous, save to investigating officers; b) rigorous solitary confinement until we have the basic evidence needed for our dossier. This with minimum delay.]

Fast, that is, very fast, Don't dilly-dally. The Law prefers things cut and dried, this is not the kind of situation it is happy with. And there is the PIDE, all-cognisant and almighty, able to whisk the prisoner away from us when it wants to. (Though Elias believed that PIDE would not butt in before the Judite had solved the murder, and caught the murderers, for them.)

After the second interrogation the inspector had the threads of the solution in his hands; he had only to weave his web. With what he knew, and did not divulge, he could have written 'case closed' and forwarded the papers to the court any day. As for Mena, she had wound up her old life with a total confession. It was to finish with that life that she destroyed every trace of it – letters, photographs, diaries – at her flat before, as the police said, 'cutting her own throat' by getting arrested. Then, finally to free herself, she related what she had done, witnessed and experienced, in its entirety, to the detective with the disgusting fingernail. Once, twice, ten times she told him, in the chill, abstracted voice of those who suffer, and admit to, horrors.

The behaviour-pattern was not new to Elias. This basement world was never without someone tearing himself to pieces over a dead-and-gone victim; spilling his own last drop of blood in purgation and speaking, not of his present, too-appalling persona, but of a former, different being. It was a divesting process, in which the past was viewed with incredible accuracy. 'A man who thinks of suicide will come to suicide, and a murderer is actually killing himself.' This axiom, though not – as it sounded – scriptural, was the inspector's conclusion, more or less, afters years of struggling with fatality.

Mena talked, therefore, as though she had left herself, and others, far behind. She was hollow. In a way, she was dead.

But confession, Elias averred, is the beginning of truth, and the peacock girl, as he called her, was not to be spirited off, at this stage, to some godforsaken prison. She might have more to tell him; he would work at it while he had her there.

'Just a couple of questions, if I may.'

Mena looked at him, dazed, from the pillow. He was straddling the chair by the washbasin, sad-eyed, bespectacled.

'One: you remember, perhaps, what books you read while you were at the house? Two: when did the corporal first turn against the major, and why?'

Go on, go on. I'm listening.

She bought a novel by Simone de Beauvoir on her second visit to the lawyer. There were the *Reader's Digests* in the attic. Oh, and a book about the battle of Elvas, historical, but he brought that from the library at the fort. ('He' invariably meant the major.)

'But you read *The Sea Wolf*?'

'Oh, yes. *The Sea Wolf.*'

'And the major?'

'What?'

'Did the major read *The Sea Wolf*?'

'He wasn't a novel-reader.' Well, had the architect read it? After she read it, or before?

Mena couldn't say, but he might have done. The corporal, yes. He'd lent it to her, anyhow.

'And he first turned against the major, when?'

'The corporal? I told you. How often have I told you? He agreed with us to start with. It was later he wanted to go to France.'

'No. Not later. They promised originally to get him to Paris after the escape. Is that correct, or not?'

She clutched the sheet under her chin and shut her eyes.

'Oh, that's right.'

'And then?'

'You know,' she said. 'You must be sick of hearing.'


## *Bernardino Barroca, Deserter, Whereabouts Unknown*

It was a sickening story, to which Elias scarcely listened. He scarcely had to listen, for it was all on his little scraps of paper, all in his notes for the record. But confession is music to a policeman's ears, he cannot have enough of it. He needs to confirm and reconfirm, check the notes and check again. How was the corporal suborned? How had they stolen the weapons? How did they escape?

The Barrocas of this world were tough nuts. (The inspector's phrase, not Mena's.) Selfish, morose, imbibing grievance with their mothers' milk and graduating to a diet of revolt and opposition. Very poor material, they were. And this specimen, a boy who knocked birds and rabbits on the head and crunched acorns in his teeth, was driving a tractor without a licence when his military service came round. Year by year, furrow up and furrow down, he rode the tractor, while he and his nine brothers saw the land depopulated as the neighbours emigrated one by one to France. So much Elias learned from the excellent Roque and his men whose information, as they sought for the corporal high and low, was from old people in Barroca's village, for the young would have nothing to do with them.

'You say the major knew the corporal before – before he was in the fort. You are positive of this?'

Dantas always said so. On some provincial posting, though where she had no idea. But Barroca, arriving with his new stubbly hair-cut, beheld in Captain Castro a warrior angel. Captain Castro, King of the Castle, living proof that any toffee-nosed officer could have another side to him. A friend in combat and a nursemaid in barracks; one to whom recruits were orphans and grass-widowers, unloved and underfed. That was Captain Dantas Castro.

The recital was overlaid for Elias by boyhood recollections; the sentinels and barracks and bugles in the Alentejo, the soldier-songs about deserters:

> Oh Beja, dreadful Beja,
> Misfortune and despair.
> It was at three one afternoon
> I joined the army there.

That prophetic stanza was written on the corporal's palm as surely as his name was Barroca. Nor was misfortune long in coming. It descended at Elvas, in the Forte de Graça, when, with two stripes up and a third in sight, he again and for the last time encountered Dantas. Dantas under escort and stripped of his gold braid: the fallen, rebel angel.

'Tell me more,' said Elias.

Mena lit a cigarette and inhaled. Her expression hardened.
'Well, he would have stuck to the major, then? But he understands the lawyer is cooling off; he stays in his room and studies French, which the architect teaches him. So far, so good. What next? Was he included in the discussions, or not? Did he ever talk to the major, or ever attempt to leave? All this is most important.'

The enormous fingernail sawed slowly, deliberately, above the bald cranium.

'Well?'

Mena took a deep breath and, hardly hearing her own words, repeated her story. Oh, God, that nail! Her mind was torn between the burden of memory and the moving claw. Forwards, backwards; one incident, another incident. Forward, and back. Sleepy-seeming, yet vigilant for her least hesitation or contradiction, the inspector assembled his picture of Barroca. Barroca the farm-boy, taciturn, cunning, suspicious and limited, true son of the Alentejo. Small wonder if the major's more extravagant projects lost their appeal for him. He was an infantry corporal, not a conspirator. If, as Mena said, he sat upstairs and studied French, it was partly because his private war-aim was to reach *la douce France*, not to be involved in futile revolution at home, and partly because the fewer secrets he shared the better were his chances of dismissal as a harmless dolt if captured.

Backwards, forwards. The nail was the beak of a lone bird on the bald, bureaucratic pate.

She remembered Barroca reciting elementary French exercises, *voici le lit, voici la porte, elle est en bois*, and his being interrupted by a shattering bellow from below.

*Garde-à-vous, caporal!*

This was a summons from the major. The news-bulletin was due, or he required the corporal at the card-table. The corporal obeyed.

The radio, the cards, the fire in the living-room; *les jeux sont faits*. Three men at a table, and a woman interminably smoking. (And dragging on her cigarette in a way that seriously distressed the inspector. The cell was instantaneously thick with smoke, and the tin plate that served as an ashtray overflowed.)

'It wasn't a living-room,' Mena said, 'it was a ward for insomniacs. And the four of us smoked like chimneys.'

'And have you learned what shit-scared is in French, *caporal*? Or deserter? *Qu'est-ce que c'est un déserteur, caporal?*'

These shafts, though launched at Barroca, were for the architect. (Perhaps, in military speech, two-target shooting, thought Elias.) Major Dantas was plainly not the man to pardon Fontenova for his individual-tuition programme. He felt, so to speak, cuckolded; deceived, as an officer, by a fellow-officer who got together with an NCO over a dictionary and an elementary French reader.

'*Ça va*, my dear corporal?'

The barrage was renewed at every opportunity. When Barroca was sitting in the card-game, or bolting his food, or when, one morning, he presented himself unshaven.

'Aha! we are growing a beard! The complete intellectual!'

The cards were the worst, with the gambling and the cut-throat revenges.

'They were deadly serious. It was all deadly serious – heads down, hardly a word. And high stakes. And these cracks he was making.'

'Growing a beard, are we?'

Dantas, lounging in his chair, appraised his cards. Alas, though, for the corporal – beards were against the regulations. By whose permission was he growing a beard? 'Has he your permission, Fontenova? Well, then, I'm sorry, but you'll have to apply your razor, corporal. *Vite, vite.*'

Elias said, 'The corporal had quite a knack for the cards, I presume?'

'He played as seldom as he could,' Mena replied. 'And when he won, it was in IOU's.'

These were the currency, written out in full, or scribbled angrily between deals, either for a given date or payment on demand. 'Corporal Barroca. IOU one raincoat and one suitcase. Signed, Dantas C.' (The police had this example, and whether the C here stood for Castro, or Cem, which meant a hundred, or Commandant, or Condor, which meant a vulture, or for Cavaleiro, who could say?)

'And tell me,' said Elias, 'when you read *The Sea Wolf*, were any of the pages underlined?'

Mena did not answer at once.

'Pages underlined?' she said.

## Large Sums of Money at Hideout
### (Headline, *Diáro da Manhã*, 14 April, 1960)

Money. Where had this money come from? Persons, states or organisations had financed Major Dantas, and who were they?* A resolute national press published, in two-column articles, demands for explanations. It hinted at hirsute gentlemen in Cuba, saw Russians agog in baggy trousers behind the Iron Curtain, and heaven knew what in the woodpile. There was, in addition, the enduring enigma of the blonde spy.

'Hoards of money, now,' Otero groaned. 'Another of their rumours.'

'Gospel for the readers, though,' Elias reminded him. 'We've rung round, in hopes they might correct it.'

'No, no, a letter. This calls for a written letter.'

'Letter or telephone, there's the Censor to reckon with.'

'The Censor – always the Censor. Spare me, Graveyard, spare me, I shall compose a communiqué, and see if they change their tune.'

'Oh, yes? And how do we frame this communiqué?'

'As an official request for a new and accurate statement of the facts.'

'And have you considered the PIDE?'

'The PIDE?'

'The PIDE, the PIDE.'

'The PIDE will be pestering you,' said Elias, 'about these IOUs. But where were we? The card games. No cash bets, you're sure?'

None. She told him again what she had told him before. And the major and the architect betted most because – did she have to say again? – the corporal played less frequently. He wasn't downstairs much, and on this score the major had objected violently.

'Objected violently? When was this?'

'One night when he was drunk.'

'The major?'

Mena raised a hand to her face, and looked between her fingers at a patch of mildew she had noticed that morning in a corner of the ceiling. It was a horrid grey-brown colour, and the shape, of a

---

* 'My single contribution of 3500 escudos was for purely humanitarian reasons, with no political motive.' Dr Gama e Sá to the court, 9th November 1960

lizard. A motionless, weird lizard overhead, with pads on small spreading toes. She sighed.

'He was very drunk, that night.'

He had been drinking, by himself, in the living-room, as he wrote the three letters she would deliver to the lawyer.

'The letters from Paris?'

'Those, yes.'

He spent hours drafting and redrafting them, but finished at last and put them in the envelopes. (Mena had bought these envelopes – more or less square, she indicated – shortly before the escape; also paper with a French water-mark. Dear God, the chase she had for that!) Having sealed them, he shouted for her and the architect (she was to visit the lawyer next day), flew at once at Fontenova and stunned him into silence.

'You can stop wasting your time on language-lessons. That corporal stays with us.' Orders, and no argument. 'He's not stirring from our sight. We should be mad, he knows too much. He drops his bloody French, and let's get back to normal.'

He then spoke his piece against the mercenary attitude in the Forces – all for the good life, stuffing their guts, and to hell with anyone else, to hell with the revolution; against sloppy humanists who adopted the same opinions; against son-of-a-bitch Christian piety, creeps, cowardice and the deserter's instinct, or whatever you wished to call it. Mena's recollection was incomplete, but she had gathered that Barroca could cease to batter his brains over French, because Barroca wouldn't need it. Henceforth, said the major, France was here, in the Casa da Vereda. By way of illustration, he seized the envelopes from her and brandished them at Fontenova.

'Paris-on-the-Tagus, Fontenova. *Paris-sur-Tage*. The PIDE finds these, and where are we? We are in Paris!'

He sat, puffing clouds of smoke, to judge the effect of this declaration.

'For God's sake, it isn't a tragedy! What's wrong with it?'

The architect turned to go.

'I'll see to Barroca, then.'

'Barroca, shall we say, is seen to.' Another great gust of smoke, as to disperse any notions persisting in Fontenova's head. 'No one leaves this house alone, you can tell him, unless he leaves it for the cemetery. And while you're at it, he can wipe that sulky expression off his face.'

Dantas then apparently forgot both the girl and the architect and huddled, brooding, in his chair.

'Cowardly sods,' he muttered, 'can't abide them. Nothing I hate more than a cowardly sod.' It was at this point, Mena thought, that the architect retreated.

'And you?' enquired the inspector.

She? At the first opportunity – to a hot bath, her Valium tablets, sleep. She was running the water, with a bathroom full of steam, when the major, at the top of his voice, began to sing. He was singing a soldier-song, she said, loud enough for the corporal to hear.

'A soldier-song?'

'*Auprès de ma blonde*. It's French.'

'Ah, yes. Yes. I am familiar with it from the films.' Elias cleaned his spectacles on his handkerchief.

You could barely see for cigarette-smoke, and somewhere in the fumes a gesticulating figure waved three envelopes with a sort of malign glee.

## Oddments Department

In the hushed room with the high window, where the lizard lived, one could, aided by material from the oddments department, envisage Mena as she was before imprisonment. The inspector's oddments department was his folder of remnants, a medley of this and that from the interrogations. Among them he burrowed like an ant and they helped him to solidify the characters involved. Late at night he sieved it through, and the live individuals emerged from photostats and reminiscences and marginal notes.

*Testimony of the concièrge Emilia (still suffering from the shock of events):*

Says her health is impaired, though this is difficult to credit. Has known Mena, 'the young lady in the fifth-floor left,' for years – since her father came, with friends from Africa, and bought the flat from the landlord. That is, the landlord's godson, it was in his name. And never had there been anything that would lead you to suspect the Senhorina . . . Not that she was nosey; she, Emilia, hadn't a nosey nature. We all have our problems, and what folk do with the front door shut is their affair. Yes, well the young lady.

Who in this world would have dreamed —? She wouldn't. She knew the major, yes; knew of him, that is, and saw him now and again. You couldn't say he was a nice man; not a nice manner with him. But there you are, you choose your friends to please yourself and he wasn't the only visitor. There were university friends. A boy they called Nelson; and Norah, and Cristina. Cristina not so often. But never a sign of anything going on, that she would swear to. And the place, they would see, hadn't been disturbed since the young lady went. At least, not until the police were in, and you know what they're like. She went to live in the Avenida de Roma, or somewhere, with the major, more or less, and Emilia was in charge. 'Emilia,' she said, 'you're in charge. Attend to the bills and the telephone for me, and carry on as if I were here.' And nothing was disturbed and nothing was missing until the police were in, they had her word for it.

*Interview with Marta Aires Fontenova Sarmento:*

1) Declines to make a statement, on plea of ill-health.

2) Must, however, protest at the inhuman and intrusive conduct of the police. Regards it as an outrage. They (the police) are quite aware there is no law to make a mother testify against her son. Repeats, she is receiving no visitors, on medical advice. Has had to have telephone disconnected owing to the intrusions and the low, vulgar curiosity.

(Marginal note by Inspector Elias: More to this than anonymous calls, which the monitoring-system had detected. It was to prevent our tracing her son should he ring. Only her lawyer, or one of her son's friends with whom she was in contact, could have advised her to have the telephone cut.)

*Conversation in bar at Estoril (18th April, 1960, 0.30 hrs. approx.)*
*Extract:*

An engineer named Martins, an habitué of this bar, was discussing press-reports of the Praia do Mastro crime with an unidentified companion. They referred to the father of the victim's mistress as 'Chico', or 'Chico Ataíde.' Martins 'thought it was peculiar' that Chico had not flown to Lisbon as soon as he knew his daughter was implicated. The other said that 'Chico was in a mess in Durban' (informant thinks it was Durban), though not, for a change, with women.

They joked on this subject, and on the immoderate behaviour of the major and Ataíde in Lourenço Marques. 'In six months they laid a lot of married ladies (actual phrase employed); and best of luck.' The unidentified speaker was evidently familiar with Ataíde's domestic arrangements. Separated, he said, or at any rate living alone, and failed to superintend his daughter properly, beyond providing a generous allowance. And how sad – this ironically – that she should have been grabbed by one of her father's chums. Most painful situation. The engineer said, 'OK for the major, though, he could have fared worse,' and, 'the old, old story. Let's make hay, Papa's away.'

After some business dicussion they reverted to Ataíde, agreeing that 'it was a bloody knock for him, enough to smash anyone.' By then they had a fair load of whisky on board and there were confused references to 'jealousy.' The engineer kept saying, 'God – a man catches his daughter in bed with a fellow his own age, he's jealous on two counts! Pretty unacceptable, you must admit.'

Totally unacceptable, the other agreed, but – edging towards Martins – that was not why Chico hadn't come to Lisbon. 'Chico Ataíde,' he stated emphatically, 'has plans to join that daughter of his abroad. I tell you, these rich sods are organised. One fine day, it's France for them.'

A telephone-call from Luanda for Martins cut short the conversation. As they separated he told his friend, 'And I'd have beaten the daylights out of them, if it had been me.'

> Signed: *Tony Clemente*, senior barman.
> Hotel Continental, Estoril.
> *Martins*, Engineer.
> STI Ltd (Admin.)

*Statement by Aldina Mariano*:

Aldina Mariano, assistant analyst in the regional Health Centre at Rastreio, lived with the architect from January to November, 1955, he being then nearly twenty-one and she seventeen. (Report submitted by Detective-Sergeant Roque.)

Was with her godparents in Lisbon until 'something happened' (unspecified, but almost certainly an abortion), over which they treated her unkindly (coercion and physical assault), and she left their home. Had been in the Santa Barbara Hospital, and it was there she met the architect.

The man she met previously was in medical advertising, married, with a contested divorce pending. The liason had to be concealed, rendezvous were infrequent, and afterwards (after the abortion, presumably), this man consulted a friend of his, saying he could not assist her openly for fear of repercussions on the divorce, especially as her godfather was blackmailing him. His friend – the architect – was a tactful and conscientious negotiator. He dealt with the blackmailer – who made much of the girl's being under-age while the seducer was both richer and of higher social class – and, having extricated the other from his responsibilities, shouldered them in his stead. Extraordinary, but true, and with the result to be expected: the acquaintance ripened, and Aldina and the architect moved into her rented flat near the Avenida Almirante Reis, he continuing meanwhile to visit his mother daily.

'. . . eight months together, all those memories,' she said. 'But he was – oh, strained, from the beginning. As though he were fulfilling a task, or something. He had a friend – still has – from his schooldays, who's a Jesuit; he and I got along fine. Father Miguel said – and I think, looking back, he was right – that Renato had an awful driving urge to prove himself, he couldn't choose the easy way. He wasn't trying to prove anything by living with me – that's an exaggeration – but every minute, even when we were really close, he had to be protective. Amazing, isn't it, what you don't see until afterwards? I was an object to be protected, and now I see how much that hurt me. It honestly did. I was young to have forebodings, but that's what I had; I wasn't comfortable, or happy. Then it was over. It had to be, you couldn't alter that. But it was eight whole months out of my life and I can't just bury them. And without him I might not have pulled through – you have to live it, I can't explain. It was Renato Fontenova who encouraged me to study and get on, though we'd split up by then, and so I have this job. I owe him that, you see. I'm alive, and I'm independent, and I shouldn't be, if I'd never met him. And I'm telling you all this to keep the record straight. I said I hadn't seen him since he was in prison, and I haven't, nor for months before. But I ought to tell you, too, that if he'd knocked on my door I shouldn't have shut it on him. I don't care what it would have cost me.'

## Appliances

Elias was in the Largo do Caldas. 'Where she paid off the taxi.'

Mena paid the taxi, not on such a bright, sunny morning, but in winter, three months earlier. She came by bus from Casa da Vereda to the Duarte Pacheco aqueduct on the city-boundary, and tried to hail a taxi in the Campo de Ourique. He could see her: dripping mackintosh, dripping scarf over her wig, the procession of dripping windscreens going by. One may more readily push an omnibus through the eye of a needle than find a taxi on a rainy day.

['Witness,' said the record, 'did the journey as instructed . . . by taxi to the Largo do Caldas and thence on foot to the office of Dr Gama e Sá, arriving there at ten-thirty approximately'.]

She would thus avoid the Rua da Conceição, the too-famous road from PIDE headquarters in Rua Antonio Maria Cardoso to the Aljube gaol; a mile or two from cell to torture-chamber, the death-run, you might say. But Elias wasn't in Largo do Caldas to reconstruct Mena's route on her first trip to the lawyer, though heading, indeed, for the same office, to investigate that gentleman's statements. He was there because it was near his flat and on his way; in the line of duty, as they said in the Force. He knew it through and through: the barber's with the flyblown mirror and solitary chair, the sound of cabinet-makers, unseen in rear workshops, the big house with the barred windows, where you saw a small light wandering at night; and the pigeons preening along its roof you saw on any sunny morning. It was across the square that there was plenty to look at and ample food for thought, in the orthopaedic shops on the slope of Rua Madalena.

Today, thanks to Modern Science, dead portions of the human body can be reanimated, with motive power, natural shape and expression restored. Signed: *Professor Hasaloff* (Vienna).

At each shop-door of that steep street, as if under the starter's flag in some impromptu rally, stood an invalid chair. From above, these shining conveyances might have been poised to roll downhill and, gaining speed and height, soar crazily and vanish over the roofs of Lisbon. At day's end they would be taken, like pets, indoors, but the showroom lights burned on in shrine-windows stocked with ex-votos and permanently illuminated for the benefit of the stroller, who could admire dramatic corsetry designed, one would think, for a torture-chamber, metal collars, and an exhibition of prostheses and trusses. In one window Professor Hasaloff, framed in what resembled a velvet reliquary, delivered his revivalist message on the subject of dead portions of the body.

And, a magnet for Elias, there was the motor-car with the severed hand. It was a fixture, this ancient Oldsmobile, parked always to an inch, in front of the shop, with a sticker in the back window – *Orthopaedic Appliances, Free Estimates, No Obligation* – and the hand. A foam-rubber hand, brown and clayey, its furry wrist projecting from a sleeveless cuff; equipped with wrinkles, nails, hairs in the pores and a wedding-ring on the appropriate finger. The tyres of the Oldsmobile never sagged, its paint was free of the caked dust seen on abandoned vehicles. Was it a car that set forth when no one was watching, whose hours of departure were unannounced and whose destinations unavowable? But it was always there. Was it a doughty survivor of days when the dust was caked indeed, when commercial travellers proudly trundled their merchandise on the circuit of shabby provincial towns? Orthopaedic Appliances, Estimates, No Obligation. And the hand, though no more than a glove-puppet to fit on a flesh-and-blood hand which had hair, nails and skin-pores of its own, the unassociated hand was there too, clamped, in sign of possession, loyally at its post. The Oldsmobile belonged to it.

When in the Largo do Caldas Elias couldn't resist the attraction and had to go and see. He might then walk through Rossio, the Praça dos Restauradores and the insalubrious Parque Mayer district; or, as today, towards the river, in the opposite direction. Down the Rua Augusta, with its traffic-lights and windows of clothes and filigree jewellery and souvenirs, the money-changing establishments and impressive banks, to the baroque glory of the triumphal arch – gateway of Lisbon, gateway to the Tagus; a huge stone span, benevolent above the crowds and the commerce, inscribed *Ad Virtutem Maiorum*. Ten-thirty by its great clock, which regulated Lisbon life.

Here we were, then. At the corner Elias paused for a moment, though the lawyer's office was only a few steps further on – right, into the Rua do Ouro, first door, with shoeblacks at the entrance. The customers sat with their newspapers among the smell of polish. The cries of lottery-sellers, the screeching of brakes and the slap

53

and snap of the polishing-cloths faded as Elias climbed the stairs between flaking stuccoed walls. The office was in another world of carpeted silence, horse-hide chairs and soft, indeterminate shadows. The doors were padded, and there was an aroma of cigar-smoke. Seated at a huge, bare mahogany table, the inspector proffered a document.

'We should be glad to know about this letter, Senhor Doutor. Whether you recognise the writing, and the signature?'

Slowly two hands advanced, with flashing rings and brilliant nails. Above them was the sheen of silk, and an enormously broad chest resplendent against the horse-hide. And the head – glasses agleam and skin aglow, trim beard fresh from the after-shave and the hot towels.

'Ah, yes.' The lawyer perused the letter once, twice, without hurry, stroking his chin. 'Yes, this would appear to be written by Major Dantas Castro.'

'To his defending lawyer; and from Paris.'

'As I see. As I see,' nodded Dr Gama e Sá, still reading.

## Dear Friend, and Lawyer

What he read was a diatribe against the treacherous poltroonery of generals, with their stars and their gold braid. But thanks, to begin with – overdue, I fear – for your invaluable assistance, both as lawyer and friend. Sincerely and without flattery, I see in the patronage of someone of your acknowledged standing a much-appreciated honour. Dear friend and lawyer, Dr Gama e Sá (addressee); your skill and learning, I feel, match the humanity of your spontaneous support; and your unshakeable devotion entitles you to an explanation – unnecessary, perhaps – of the escape from Elvas. I would not for the world have it thought that my motive was either despair or lack of confidence in the conduct of my defence. No smallest doubt as to your capacities, Dr Gama e Sá, my esteemed friend. Nor was it a flight, but an adoption of new ground for the struggle, as I shall shortly demonstrate. Traitors, be warned. Major Dantas knew of those who swaggered in their headquarters, decked in gold braid earned by the efforts of comrades with whom they had entered into agreements of honour. He was not ignorant of developments, though in exile, for Portugal was in his heart. Nor

54

did he forget the monocled major, so lost to decency as to command the escort taking him, Dantas, and other officers to prison. Long reckonings; enough said. In the prevailing climate of subservience, when the government's chief weapon is corruption, neither I nor my fellow-prisoners could expect justice in the courts. This I wrote at the time, foreseeing (as you yourself foresaw, Dr Gama e Sá, my dear friend), the postponements, the interventions, the pretexts for adjournment. You were frank about the position, and I am grateful to you. But in my opinion the silence had to be broken by a big scandal. My plan was favourably received; by gaining public attention it would both benefit the prisoners remaining in the Fort, and arouse the conscience of honourable serving soldiers. And Major Dantas could vouch that such existed; the military establishment was not entirely demoralised, as would be evident. He guaranteed it, there was no need to amplify. At the age of forty-seven, distant from home and kindred, he had, nevertheless, the support of other exiles and soon he would return, he swore it. He feared no difficulties, since any difficulty was preferable to the poltroonery rife in Portugal. The letter concluded with more lively gratitude to the writer's dear friend and lawyer, who could reach him at PO Box 300, Paris VII.

The lawyer passed it back.

'No one but a lunatic would send that through the post.'

He lit a cigar and his huge chest expanded as he puffed. Elias saw him, in his beautifully-appointed office, as every inch a Habeas Corpus man.

'Incredible – the only word for it,' said the inspector.

Had Mena, three months previously, sat where he was sitting? Seen cigar-smoke curling from those fingers, with their diamond rings?

'The letters, then, are new to you?'

'Letters? Letters? Am I to infer there were more?'

The inspector ('always give it a beat before replying') glanced at the door, luxurious with sound-proof padding and gilded wood. Mena, again.

'Oh, very possibly, I should imagine – wouldn't you? And similar subject-matter?'

Habeas Corpus was relaxed in his chair.

'My dear sir, anything's possible.' Cigar-smoke was propelled into the distance. 'But the risk,' he said in an undertone, 'the risk!'

And Elias could see Mena in the blue haze as clearly as if she were there by the door.

'What a letter to write! And in the present state of the country!'

Mena, dripping and frozen, just inside the room, with a small pool of water at her feet and a cold blonde halo in a ray of sunshine from the window. The three white envelopes she held were almost luminous, and water deluged her unceasingly. She seemed to generate it.

'I beg your pardon?' said Elias.

'I said, it was a risk.'

'A calculated risk, maybe. There is nothing to show you this letter was actually written in Paris.'

'Show me? What has it to do with me?'

Another long smoke-trail. Had he seen her too?

'The major did not leave Portugal, doctor. It's not – shall we say? – the newest of schemes, to have letters posted abroad.'

'Oh, and naïve, to put it mildly. He should have realised the police have their connections in Paris. They can check, they can check.'

Habeas Corpus, cigar pendant between his lips, put his hands on the table. Beringed fingers lit its mahogany surface.

'Good, then, good. Nothing else, inspector?'

'One more point – the money problem. After his escape, did the major ask you for money at all?'

'I last saw the major when he was in prison. In my professional capacity.'

'The major, or any agent of his?'

'No, no, no.'

'By telephone, perhaps?'

Habeas Corpus smiled. 'A risk occasionally,' said the smile, 'but, my dear sir, enough's enough.' The inspector sat, dim and unresponsive as the doctor deposited his cigar in the ashtray. Delay; caution.

'He knows perfectly well' – he adjusted his spectacles with, Elias thought, the merest flicker to where Mena would have been. 'Perfectly well, it is safe to say, how strict are the conventions of political life. There are proper channels. There are accepted rules.' The voice altered slightly, as though directed not at Elias but beyond him, to Mena's wavering face. 'A little tact, a little circumspection! And if he doesn't know, he ought to. One does not accost

56

people in this fashion, whoever they are, much less people in public life. You cannot march in here, demand and collect.'

He rose.

Elias rose, and said that this was true. 'Surprises excepted, of course.'

Again he waited, half out of the room, for a reaction, then added, as an afterthought,

'It occurs to me, though – and quite amusing, you'll agree –'

'What?'

'Why, the girl-friend, Dr Gama e Sá. The major's mistress. She could walk through this door of yours any day!'

The vision was disposed of with a graceful gesture.

'A surprise one would not wish on one's worst enemy, my dear fellow!'

'And a very nice chat we've had,' Elias told himself, as he descended the rickety stairs.

In the street, past the shoeblacks on their perches, it was raining. This pleased him. On the day of her visit it was raining. Look round and she would be there, a mute, bedraggled water-nymph, midway up the staircase.

From the entrance he regarded the traffic and the scurrying pedestrians. The men having their shoes cleaned sat, each with a shoeblack squatting before him and one foot raised as though in blessing, engrossed in their newspapers, oblivious of the winning lottery-numbers written on a mirror in shaving-soap, *With Best Thanks to our Respected Clients.*

It was an April shower, pelting unheralded in sunshine; something for the tourists to talk about. Until it was over, Elias enjoyed weak coffee and toast at the Café Suiça and observed the pickpockets, though he had more urgent tasks, such as going to the pawnbroker's.

['. . . from the office of Dr Gama e Sá the witness, still in the above-mentioned disguise, went to a pawnbroker's at no. 118–F, Praça da Figueira (mezzanine floor) and pawned several items of personal property. This she did to supplement the lawyer's meagre donation of 3500 escudos. His letter, in which the sum was specified, she destroyed. Interrogated as to contents of this letter, had an idea that it referred, by alias, to military supporters. Remembers only Rio Maior, or Rio Grande, who was a colonel.

Also to the despatch of money, maps and forged papers, viz. three identity-cards, one passport and a driving-licence. These to be supplied by Dr Gama e Sá on receipt of a pre-arranged coded telephone-message.' – Official record.]

From the Suiça, then, into the Praça da Figueira where gipsies congregated twelve months of the year – a throng of black-shirted hawkers, rolls of material under the arm, watches cradled in the palm, and a swarm of children at the women's skirts. Elias shouldered through them and found the name-plate he wanted. To forestall misunderstanding, he showed his police-card with the pawn-ticket.

The clerk was a sour, grizzled man, pocked with blackheads on lip and nose, and resembled the sort of gherkin you see in an *hors d'oeuvre*.

'Single loan?' he enquired, without a spark of interest, and produced the pledges.

Gold-plated lighter and cigarette-case, antique pin-brooch with diamond, one gold chain. Total, 10087 escudos, net of tax.

Elias lifted the chain from the counter, trickled it through his fingers, wrapped it on his wrist. A pretty enough bracelet, but on a woman's ankle it would be a love-token. With the grizzled pawnbroker for audience he toyed with the gold chain, slipping it across his knuckles, drawing it up and dropping it into his hand. Slowly he swung it to and fro, examined it over two fingers, then over his wrist. His eyes grew dull behind their lenses. The diviner's nail was dull.


# IV

'In these dark days for Portugal we, officers of the Armed Forces, have decided, for the honour of the Army, to lay the following facts before the nation:

1) Our comrade, Major Luis Dantas Castro had, as his service record shows, earned the Medalha de Mérito, together with other

awards and commendations. He was a dedicated, brave and gallant officer.

2) He received a Catholic education, and was a student supporter of the Christian Democrats. As a soldier he was indifferent to politics until, resenting the subservience exacted from People and Army by the totalitarian régime of Salazar, he took part in the military rising, with dozens of fellow-officers and civilians. Arrested and detained in the gaol at Trafaria, he behaved with spirit and dignity, protesting against the interventions of the PIDE in the case. Transferred to the Forte da Graça at Elvas, he contrived an escape, in company with Renato Manuel Fontenova Sarmento, a militia lieutenant, in civil life an architect.

3) The body of Major Dantas was discovered 'by chance' and, as the press has indicated, in equivocal circumstances. The nation has a right to ask, *Who killed him, and why?*

4) Major Dantas escaped from Elvas with the object of rejoining his companions who had remained at liberty and of reorganising those involved in the abortive rising. He had contacted, for this purpose, prominent members of the Armed Forces; and it is therefore imperative to ask, *To whom may his death have been convenient?*

5) The killers buried the body in a shallow grave, and for this ineffective hiding-place they chose a beach, thus lending colour to the theory that the major had fled to Paris and from there returned to Portugal. But he never left Portugal. *In whose interest was this theory advanced?*

6) Our late Comrade was killed because it was necessary to eliminate a brave adversary, and as a warning to his companions in the struggle. *Who killed him?* We do not have to tell the nation who kills the opponents of Salazar, and the serving soldiers of this country have a Comrade to avenge.'

Signed: 'F.A.I. – Frente Armada Independence,' this text was a photocopy, rubber-stamped by the Investigation Department of the PIDE and annotated – by the commissioner, probably – 'DOCUMENT A' in capital letters above the stamp.

DOCUMENT B: an original, type-written communication to the Commissioner of Criminal Police, Lisbon. 'We have neither freedom nor a free press, yet the country has no faith in your "penetrating" investigations into the Praia do Mastro affair. The PIDE continues its nauseating crimes in secret and all you do is conceal the evidence.' Signed: A Portuguese Citizen.

DOCUMENT C (original): a postcard, in capital letters, addressed to The Criminal Police, Lisbon.
THE MAJOR WAS ASSASSINATED IN RUA ANTÓNIO MARIA CARDOSO. THE PIDE DID IT.

DOCUMENT D: photocopy of an article in the Brazilian newspaper *Tribuna Popular*, of 13th April 1960 (page 2). Stamped, PIDE. With it was the front-page headline, and a column-wide photograph of Major Dantas in the sweater that was on the murdered body. He had an engaging smile.
    'Rio. From our Special Correspondent. Left-wing opposition circles here in Guanabara accuse Salazar's police of having murdered Major Dantas Castro, whose body was found recently on a beach near Lisbon.
    'After a spectacular escape from prison, where he was detained before trial, Castro had been living in France and planning armed resistance in Portugal. According to the official version, the crime was committed, for political reasons, by his mistress and two companions, after dissension over his clandestine return to the country. Rival opposition groups were also implicated.
    'Independent and usually reliable sources say that Dantas was killed by the PIDE, Salazar's special police, at a rendezvous with pretended opposition sympathisers. The woman and two men are untraced. Journalists have encountered the very cautiously-expressed belief that the three were confederates of the PIDE and that the crime had, therefore, been arranged well ahead.
    'Details are currently open to more than one interpretation. Thus the escape, while hailed as a sensational triumph by the opposition, has undoubtedly relieved the government of the prospect of a public hearing, with awkward revelations by the major of corruption and unrest in the Salazarist army. Such a theory, advanced by some of those interviewed, would imply that the PIDE had prepared the escape and instructed the two servicemen with Castro. Logically, it would be these two who afterwards urged the move to Paris where, through him, they could penetrate and report on the opposition network abroad . . .'
    'Load of rubbish, any way you look at it!' Superintendent Otero

dismissed the collection to a corner of his desk. 'Documents? You'd have to be round the bend to treat that political garbage as a file of documents.' (Who, for instance? The commissioner?)

He tapped a cigarette on his case. There was a lustre of splendid starched shirt-cuffs, the bright Dupon lighter clicked into flame and between leisurely inhalations he eyed the garbage with distaste. A typical, venemous batch. Accusations, crack-brained, feeble nonsense, grievance and denunciation – typical of what the political enthusiasts were pushing beneath the honest toiler's door, to poison the community. Talk about sympathetic ink – this trash was printed in sympathetic shit and had to be read against the light. Worse, it bred. And for that very reason the commissioner (far end of the corridor, opposite) shot it straight from his office to that of the wretched superintendent: Superintendent Otero, in his executive capacity, the qualified lawyer who could – and had to – sign things.

But everybody knew, though nobody said, what the Great Man was. He was a *moscardo*, heart and soul. 'Gadflies' the PIDE were called, *moscardos*, and the commissioner had been a notable gadfly, with various flights, or stages, in the PIDE, in the Censorship, and probing the secret recesses of the nation. His own business, one might say. But a large gadfly has a wide range, and will augment the general muckheap.

It was a beautiful sunny morning, as seen from Otero's window, but that did not mean the muckheap wasn't active. On the contrary, the sun on the compost multiplied the maggots and the unwary citizen could survive only by standing on tiptoe, shit up to the eyeballs. And, being subversive, it stuck. Ripples would be unsafe, causing inflow. The least tremor or complaint, and political shit flows into the poor devil; flows into his entrails and rapidly sets. He is then a rigid statue, a curiosity for amateurs of sadism.

'Keep calm,' Otero told himself. 'One must keep calm.'

## In Whose Interest?

In whose interest was it to delay enquiry into the major's death? That of the PIDE, first and foremost. They, evading the avalanche of accusation and denunciation themselves, were nevertheless urging on the sorely-tried Criminal Police, whom they inundated with documents, photostats, and confidential rubbish galore. Meanwhile, Detective-Sergeant Roque and party were miles away, scouring 'the far bounds of Spain and Portugal' for the corporal and the architect, and lucky they would be if their quarry didn't shoot them. But if and when they were restored, successful and undamaged, the PIDE could annex the prisoners. Could and would, the greedy bastards. Mena, the architect, everything and everybody, in one fell swoop, immediately.

'Oh, let them,' thought Otero. 'Let 'em. And I hope it stays fine for them.'

No one, reading the Dantas case attentively (archive in the Cascais District Court), could fail to notice the almost complete absence of the PIDE from its entire eight volumes. Yet, from start to finish, they were there – iron feet in velvet slippers; iron feet which, just now and then, went, very forcibly, in. Save for the material on these rare incursions, and a few of the statements, memoranda and other details, the account was assembled, item by item, by Inspector Elias, in consultation with his magic fingernail. It was he who arranged and wrote it, for it was he who held the interrogations and he who wrote the notes – the official version, and that he made for himself. A hidden recorder, he wrote down what happened, and why; and had he been a medieval chronicler he could have added, 'those who read may give full credence to what the book says.'

As chronicler of the crime, however, and as an investigator, he was seen by the regular police-reporters as one whose position was, professionally speaking, vague, and whose methods were idiosyncratic to a degree. But his superiors relied on his extensive experience of murder, were happy, though puzzled, that he did not compete for promotion, and allowed him considerable latitude.

Elias had a basic text which he, at any rate, ascribed to Moses. 'In the midst of the storm, be calm and undismayed. Seek your signs in the barren desert where is neither serpent's egg nor camel's skull; soon, on that road to truth, all will be made clear.'

Characteristically, he maintained that this was counsel from an age when the Lord, in consideration for His police, would Himself resuscitate the dead. He probably heard it, as a schoolboy, from the naval chaplain who taught history at St James's College. Years later, coming upon it in an old exercise-book, he had copied it on the office typewriter (used at interrogations) and kept it in view under the glass top of his desk: the detective's golden rule.

'In the midst of the storm, be calm.' Legends grow around policemen and after a year or two in Homicide anyone has his dramatic or – heaven forbid – his uninspiring, nickname in the underworld. Within the Judite and adjacent territory Elias was 'Graveyard' and impervious, they said, to all but dead men's voices and out-of-date tunes. But if he seemed to drift through life in a fog, he was observing and interpreting constantly. The interpretations were grounded on what he saw and what he was told. As Cardinal Savater, Minister of the Court of the Sacred Rota, said (in his *Memoirs*, vol. 11, published in 1907 at Saragossa), 'despite attempts to undervalue the personal myths attached to the able investigator, we should accept that any exaggeration has its grain of truth and any reputation is, in some measure, deserved.' Elias was an excellent illustration of this argument. The air of comatose disillusion was his Inquisitor's mantle behind which, calm and undismayed, he would confront his suspects. The Dantas case was an example of his power of self-effacement in interrogation and of the disconcerting suddenness of his knockout blow.

Any magistrate, with the narrative before him, could appreciate the skill and precision of the inspector's method with evidence. Yet an attentive re-reading of the files, and a date-analysis of Mena's confessions, might convince him that it had taken Elias no more than a day or two to arrive at the facts.

Only the wilfully blind would deny this. Soon after the initial sessions with Mena the notes were suspended ('interrogation terminated at an early hour of the morning; to be resumed as convenient'), and later were sporadic, with a thinner spread of information relevant to the crime. This being so – in whose interest was it to delay enquiry into the major's death?

According to Detective-Sergeant Roque, who had been with Otero at her arrest, Mena admitted everything at her second interrogation; and though present at the first only, he could see the inspector would make short work of it. He saw too that, once the crime was intelligible, he wanted to dig out all there was to know. Fair enough. Elias was a thorough-going man with a delicate investigation on his hands; anything and everything she could tell him he wanted to hear, and – fair enough – he wanted more than that, and no prize for guessing. But nobody could really throw much light, as Roque said, since Elias questioned her privately and out of normal hours.

It is obvious, in 1982, that the inspector, in possession of the truth, was, as it were, exploring the margins of the case for further angles and clarifications. And what was he seeking? An inconsistency in her confession? Or to postpone revelations as to the major's death while the two fugitives were still at large? Otero said, 'We can never be certain what evidence he had, merely that he was patiently amassing notes and photographs in that jealously-guarded oddments folder. Until he closed the file – which, to judge from the notes, was when the corporal and the architect were caught – he continued to glean and garner.' From the assorted oddments – a melting-pot in which the essence of the crime was distilled – Otero expected that Elias would evolve a couple of dozen missiles – statements and confessions with which (and the requisite firing-squad and ceremony) to despatch Mena and her two associates.

But when the trial came on and he examined those eight volumes, the superintendent saw the point and recognised the value of this solid and highly-condensed report. It was concise, free of unintentional repetition, impeccably set out and argued. How much material must have been discarded to achieve such a result! And what, the Superintendent wondered, might that material be? Had Graveyard a separate archive on Mena, which he was preserving quietly at home?

Of all creatures on earth, only Reptile could have answered him.

## Memento Mori

And that man down there, chewing a crust – with a skull at his feet, I shouldn't be surprised – (Elias could not see for sure), consumes his snack at the rim of the grave which will consume him, in due course . . . The man leaned on his spade, chewing and deliberating, and in his shadow and that of the cypress trees slept a congregation under marble, with crosses to say who they were. This was the everlasting resting-place, and heavens! how it grew: the cemetery, the tombstone garden, increasing hour by hour as the gravedigger dug on. He could number his flock like a shepherd, and ate his bread at noontide with an uninterrupted view of the river, while they lay in the hill in the sun.

The inspector sat on a folding-chair at the door of his family vault, a flask of milky coffee by him. He had cleaned the urns, draped each in its lace-trimmed white cloth, and repositioned the photographs – lamented parents, lamented sister. He had swept up with a little stiff brush, dusted this and that, and done the flowers, and now, at peace in an alley of tombs, was reading the *Diário de Notícias* for today, Sunday, 17th April. The gravedigger was halfway down the slope, a visitor or two walked between the crosses, and beyond them shimmered the silver-scaled waters of the Tagus.

Why this height? Why did cemeteries tower above the living? Elias attributed their elevation to fear of the plague in days gone by: the hallowed soil of churches, or the wind, alone would combat fumes and putrefaction. The fresh wind on the heights dispelled them.

A butterfly fluttered past, then another. Signs of spring among the monuments. From their winged dance Elias looked at the gravedigger again; at him and his hillside, that shroud of earth on the slope of corpses, with flowers growing among flat stones. Then, as you climbed, the family vaults began: a township of tombs, avenues of obelisks and cypresses, of dim religious windows and gates with sculpted guardian angels; of ornate facades and family names and the letters R.I.P. Names and letters recurred in the *Diário de Notícias*, whose obituary page, column after column of crosses, was like an additional shroud. The phrases in the paper were repeated on the vaults, and *vice versa*: Rest Eternal, grieving friends and kindred. The photograph one saw in the paper was here suitably framed above the mortal relics.

Heaps of chrysanthemums faded on stone thresholds, and veiled ladies attended to things within. Elias knew by sight those whose dead were in his neighbourhood, but he exchanged no greetings. He came here to relax, and gather himself together. He would watch their advent, and see them chatting mournfully at the portals of death, but did not budge from his picnic chair.

He was ensconced in it when a bitch, harried by a rabble of yelping dogs, appeared at the top of the funereal alley – a diminutive sheepdog bitch, trotting fast and aimlessly, trailed by a snarling escort with a limping setter in the rear-rank. Hither and thither she trotted, carrying her scent with her, and when she halted for a few seconds the escort encircled her, panting, with lolling tongues. Some lurked in narrow lanes between the tombs, or nuzzled her hindquarters in hopes of trying their luck if they could make her stand. Some in desperation mounted the nearest fellow-pursuer, while the setter scratched his belly with his lame foot and regarded them confidently from a distance.

Elias threw a stone and the horde dispersed, howling, downhill, bolting in a tangle of legs. He returned to the *Diário de Notícias*, which was more and more of an undertakers' gazette. Deaths multiplied day by day, and not just on the page of black crosses, with announcements of Masses for the dead of a week ago and advertisements for the Magno Funeral Service. There was Vigil at the Unknown Soldier's Grave in the monastery of Batalha; disturbance in India and collapse in Goa; Perpetual Fond Remembrance; and President Thomaz, looking as dead as any of them. A printed cemetery, pure and simple. The President, in double column, could have been a decrepit medical specimen, an ancient penis tricked out in Admiral's uniform. Caryl Chessman, last words in the electric chair; and, say seismologists, another earthquake soon in Agadir. Street-accidents; St Christopher cannot be protecting everybody, everywhere; Giant Conger Landed at Sesimbra – a macabre stage-prop, hacked and gashed and drooping on a hook, with a queue of spectators eagerly comparing heights. *Memento Mori*: thus would the principal of St James's introduce any discourse on the illustrious departed, and Elias and the other pupils, with their school smocks and exercise-books, would respond in chorus, *Pul-vis-est* (slight pause) *Et-in-gloria-tran-sit*. (Amen).

To the sexton leaning on his spade the bitch and her attendants, diminished among the flat graves and stone crosses, were a wave of comma-shaped sterns. There was a fine dust of butterflies in the sunlight.

Once, in the Vasca da Gama aquarium, Elias saw a conger-eel, midget though it was compared to the giant in the newspaper, sever a man's hand. It was a violent snake, snatching at chunks of fish as its keeper told spectators that congers, being both ravenous and lazy, may be devoured by the spiny lobster, a gourmet eater with horrifying tenacity of purpose. Weeks and months are dedicated by this lobster to exploiting the greed of the conger, which lies stupid and somnolent in an underwater crevice. The one grows fatter and fatter as the other feeds and monitors it, and the last visit is paid when the eel is too swollen to wriggle away; huge claws, empty now of offerings, sink into the succulent, patiently-nourished flesh.

There was commotion from below, where the sexton was chasing the curs with a bucket of lime. With lime in their eyes they fled uphill again, baying with terror, and one or two streaked past Elias like maddened creatures, dragging their muzzles and tongues on the ground.

## Afternoon and Evening of the Inspector

Elias planned a day at home, with a cinema after supper, and sat meanwhile at his window, watching the boats crossing to Ginjal, and cats on the roofs. There was a football match on the radio; a neighbour in pyjamas fed his pigeons. There was Reptile ('who's a pretty boy, then?') and the big gummed envelope with the remnants folder, from which he pulled a cascade of oddments – statements, jottings, photographs, even bits of poetry.

> '*Storks, with their tapping beaks,*
> *The long beaks tapping, tapping at you . . .*'

Mena's poems, in her large handwriting, the i's dotted with tiny circles. The pencilled lines, it seemed, were addressed to someone sound asleep, whose sleep and very being were penetrated, tapped at, by her poem. There were other scraps, and other, less intimate, verses; notes and memoranda from the evidence, and photographs. Two photographs in particular, the girl with her peacocks by the swimming-pool, and two hippopotamus-hunters on a river-bank. And oddments, and more oddments. A postcard of the Peruvian fertility-goddess; another, from Taormina, with the message, 'Men are never impotent, women can be incompetent.' (Captial letters. Apparently no signature was necessary, and the card, with rust-marks at the corners, must have been pinned to the wall for ages.) A member's pass to the Twenties Cocktail Bar. An opera programme from the São Carlos with a telephone-number, triple-ringed. All of this was surplus from the flat in Estrada da Luz, though none of it would be used in court. Not the documents, nor the photographs, nor the photocopy from a magazine (*Erotika*) found between the pages of a menu from the Ariston Palace Hotel, Barcelona – an extract which demanded further study, for on it was a scribble from the major of which something could be made. *Andante, andante,* said Elias. We shall get there in the end.

*A Landscape*:
Cloudless sky, and molten light (high humidity) falling vertically onto the river. Hippos bathing in muddy water (no reflections). Time could be midday (no shadows). At the top of the picture, the river melts into the horizon; flowing from left to right, as indicated by position of small canoe anchored in the shallows. The hippopotami, seen through a magnifying-glass, have grotesque faces, and flocks of small birds fly above them.

Distant smudges in the grassland beyond are revealed, under magnification, as swamp. Two hunters, one in a topee, the other with a camouflage service-cap, sit on a trailing tree-trunk. One, with sunglasses, has a black moustache, though the short beard is flecked with grey. The other frowns, with an ironical expression, against the light; binoculars are slung from his neck and he is smoking. Each man holds a glass – Dimple whisky, to judge from the distinctive flattened curves of the bottle beside them – and neither looks at the camera.

Ranged behind and smiling into it are six negroes, barefoot, in shorts and flapping shirt-tails; one grips a rifle in each hand, brandishing it aloft by the barrel. This divergence of gaze and interest separates natives and visitors into two groups. The hunters, the foreigners, are there for the wild life and nature; the negroes to be photographed as part of the occasion. The wonder for the white men is the exotic setting, for them it is the camera.

Scene angled at 45° to axis of river. Framed on right by two enormous trees, hiding the water; cut off abruptly on left, at edge of grassland. Black and white, 18 × 24 cms.

On the back was written, *Foz do Save, Mozambique, 2nd Oct 54.*

(Supplied for reference to the Criminal Police by the widow of Major Dantas Castro.)


*Maria Norah Bastos d'Almeida, teacher*:
Declares, to begin with, how revolting she considers the speculation over what is a private affair, not yet fully investigated. Pressmen are, to say the least, foul and revolting. Going for the girl like this, and why? Because she's been to bed with a married man? What do they think their precious mothers went to bed with – blameless innocents? They're a foul, frustrated bunch, afraid of the Censor even in their dreams. And what's wrong with mentioning the

Censor? Once a thing's in print it's stamped Passed by the Censor, isn't it? What infuriates her is not so much their pandering to sensationalism – they have to eat – but the way they'll belabour a blind man one minute (unless he has a decent dog, that is), and crawl on their bellies the next if anyone in authority shouts at them. And they're not alone, either, in making life a misery. This country's lousy with moralisers, preaching at you morning, noon and night. Since she could think for herself she's known it's a land for the wide boys, and the moralising chokes you. What it needs is pasteurisation; sterilising all through, as Mena used to say, with shit. Oh, yes, write it down – please. What's wrong with it? It's a perfectly normal common noun; common to every animal that lives, except the angels; they're exempt. God, this is a sickening bore. Mena – what could she tell them about her? They were childhood friends, educated together, 'if that's of any interest.' It would be more interesting to say how brave she was. You can write that down, too. A responsible girl, with courage, not the crazy fool these idiots imply she is. Their mothers were the crazy ones, bringing them into the world. In any case, we shall see. See how Mena bears up. It can't have been amusing for her, getting deeper and deeper into this ghastly mess and not a soul to help her. But courage is what she has. Witness knows her; they were at school in Lourenço Marques, then students in Lisbon, because Mena's mother died in hospital in Rhodesia, of alcoholic poisoning, with complications. Or she may have died in Johannesburg; witness is not sure. But of cirrhosis and bad temper combined. In witness's opinion, no great loss, for she – the mother – was worse than impossible and led everyone a dance, though her husband had the sense to lead his own life. Strange, incidentally, that the press hadn't made a meal of it – the mother as a castrating woman. What a topic for the moralists! Not that they haven't thought of it. She (witness) hears that two of the lowest muckrakers on the Catholic daily A Voz were to write articles – after which they would repair to the sailor-brothels at Cais do Sodré, and they and the girls could bewail the decline of Christian family life together. It was where they generally went after a Yes-Sir-No-Sir session with the editor. None of this surprises her, she says; the citizenry as a whole, having jumped to conclusions, is too pleased with itself ever to change its mind. But one question she would like to ask the journalists – them, and the rest of the shitmongers who are so obsessed with Mena, and so quick with their filthy theories: are you so desperate for a woman that you have to invent one?

*Statement by Francisco Ataíde, Civil Engineer*
Emphasises, primarily, that he is here of his own free will, to obtain information about his daughter Filomena Joana. Flew into Lisbon this morning from Johannesburg (passport produced in proof). Knows nothing more than what was in the original newspaper reports, which he heard of only when our South African embassy reached him by telephone yesterday. The suspicions hanging over his daughter he considers as evidently hasty and wrong, but is at our disposal in the interest of a full and impartial enquiry; once the facts are established, his daughter will come forward, and he trusts her legal rights will be safeguarded. Requests the return of property held by the police and the unsealing of the flat in Estrada da Luz. Sees no advantage in discussing his relations with the late major, their contacts having been neither close nor frequent since their days at the Military College. The photograph shown him for identification purposes was taken, he says, at one of their occasional meetings, probably in January or February, 1954, at a hunt in the Vale do Save, just north of the hippopotamus reserve.

As always with the oddments, Elias had reserved the Peacock Portrait to the last. Now, facing the limitless dark of the window and flanked by Reptile in his glassed-in desert to the left, he sat and stared at it – as fixedly and raptly as, when a child, he stared at the Four-Dot Saint which an old servant-maid would produce from her apron pocket.

**OBSERVANCE OF SISTER MARIA**
**OF THE SACRED HEART**
Standing in front of a white wall, fix the eyes on the four dots seen in the picture and count to twenty. Shut the eyes, open them immediately, and the Miraculous Sister Maria of the Sacred Heart, Servant of the Lord, will appear on the wall.

*(Copyright)*

If you held the photograph in shadow Mena's body seemed to move and her hair (that would become an ash-blonde wig) seemed lighter in relation to her skin; the bikini was practically invisible on rounded breasts with golden nipples, and over black pubic hair. That was startling, the blonde hair with the black. From head to foot she was a paragon. And she had worn the unobtrusive token on her ankle – the gold chain Elias handled in the shop of the grizzled pawnbroker, where it had remained since she pledged it one wet midwinter morning when the gipsies sheltered in the doorways of a rain-swept Praça da Figueira: gipsies with the aspect of smugglers, lugging rolls of material from the warehouses, and women and children trooping after, and all of them cursing the weather in gipsy jargon. Mena would walk through them, and up the half-flight of stairs to the pawnbroker's and there, without hesitation or argument, bend and take the inscribed chain from her ankle. Goodbye, golden circlet, golden love-token. Me in my bare skin now, unadorned.

In her bare skin. That lovely body in the peacock picture and no emblem of gold, nothing but Mena. Yet because of the gold chain she would lie naked on a campbed under the rafters, with sheets flung right and left as they were torn from her.

['States that she slept alone that night, as the major was constantly in and out of the bedroom and she could not sleep there. He was enraged by a discussion with the architect which continued, she thinks, until morning; about what, she cannot say, for they were in the living-room and kept their voices low. He made several trips to the locked chest-of-drawers for papers, and once she heard the words, 'Bloody list!' or, rather, 'Sodding list!'; referring, she is sure, to a list of student-friends claimed by the architect as supporters of the Movement. Confirms what she has told us of an army map, though does not know where this came from. The major's temper steadily worsened and he was invariably annoyed to find her awake; in case she heard anything, perhaps. His suspicions were, for the reasons given, imaginary, but he ordered her to the attic with the excuse that 'we shall be at this nonsense until morning'. – Official dossier.]

And in the morning Dantas, unshaven, eyes blazing, burst into the attic, ripped the sheets from her bed and lunged at her ankle. No gold chain.

'Where is it? What have you done with it?'

Mena naked. The body that bewitched Elias in the swimming-pool picture, the body he stripped in his imagination, naked; the face superimposed upon the sun, the swimming-pool, the peacocks; the face that dazzled the man who photographed her, dazzled everyone who saw it, was chalkwhite and she huddled on the makeshift bed as the sheets went sailing away like clouds.

'The chain. Where is it?'

This, to Elias, was a chilly, premeditated attack. The major must have known the chain was missing, noticed that she was always in jeans, and with what precaution she undressed; and having given no sign, he was shouting at her, savagely and unpredictably.

'You've sold it. You want to run out on me, you bitch.'

Mena defenceless, numb with fear, seeing above her, against the rafters, his contorted mouth.

'Run out on me! Double-crossing me, is that it?'

He sent the ashtray flying.

'Am I the sort of man you can do that to? A man you can betray?'

In pursuit of a sudden idea, he rushed from the room. When, almost immediately, he returned with a bucket of water and a scrubbing-brush, Mena had scrambled into a dressing-gown.

'Take that thing off!'

Roughly he pulled it from her and hurled it, with the bedding, through the door. Then he shut his eyes, muttering, 'Double-crossing little tramp!' with deep, rasping breaths, as though striving for patience.

Mena stood there hugging herself, not from cold, but absolute hopelessness. From the door Dantas regarded her as if she were some despicable traitress, past praying for.

'Double-crossing me!' (It couldn't be her he was talking to in that icy whisper.) 'How far has this gone? And how long has it gone on for? Long enough, I dare say. Betraying me to whom?' His voice rose. 'And why? No explanation, the bitch. Conceited little whore. You're a conceited little whore, above explanations. Don't speak to me! At least have the decency to keep quiet and stop lying. Don't speak to me!'

But Mena was dry and drained and beyond speech. She looked at the window. Was this when the stonemason saw her? But no, that was impossible, for the next second the major, figuratively spitting in her face, dragged her to her knees by the bucket.

'You can scrub this floor. Get on with it.'

Neither spoke, or moved. Then the door slammed, the key grated in the lock and the house shook as he stormed downstairs. After that, quiet. Sharp winter sunlight in the corners and crannies of the attic: it was the one sunny morning of that frightful winter. And there, said Elias to his lizard, is our Mata Hari as invented by the cheap-skate journalists. The stonemason, if he told the truth, saw her at noon – when he would be enjoying his solitary satisfactions during the midday break. And who's to say who else there was, among the trees in the photograph?

Elias was talking aloud, as he often did; and often, until the words echoed back to him, he did so unawares. But that was what happened if you debated between four walls in solitude at home – and especially if your solitude was shared by a creature given, as was Reptile, to extravagant and ostentatious silences. That lizard had the power to receive and retransmit what his master said, and Elias would hear the playback with astonishment, as if a stranger spoke.

Time to clean the cage – the white urine was thinner as the weather improved – and put in a fresh stock of insects: alive and kicking and attractively presented, for Reptile took some pleasing. In the local fruiterer Elias had a reliable purveyor of good-quality caterpillars, and his last foray had yielded a week's supply, though more generous rations would be needed in a baking Lisbon summer. Heat, heat. The lizard's occupation was to bask and dream of heat.

Having fed him, Elias prepared a meal for himself, in two minutes flat in the kitchen: cornflour custard with banana slices and a cup of No. 5 herb tea (thyme and other flavours) from the Intendente Health Stores. Then off to the Condes cinema.

The film was over at half-past twelve. At the door of the Arcadia night-club a Volkswagen of the Policía de Segurança Publica was depositing Captain Maia Loureiro, in his camelhair coat; he who by day, with a forbidding expression, supervised the traffic of the capital and by night resorted to the Arcadia tarts with a worse expression still. Soon there would come to divert him the two devil-may-care Counts, known as the Roustabout Brothers, who were lords of misrule in the bars and cabarets of Lisbon; champagne would flow for evermore.

Well, very nice for those who liked it. A prudent inspector did better to relax safely with a cup of herb tea. *Andante, andante.*

Tea, then at the Ribadouro, which was less a bar than a sea of spat-out skins of pickled lupine-seeds with beermugs floating in it. Workmen from Parque Mayer tucking in to crayfish, taxi-drivers arranging illegal gambling-games at some den in the Arroios or Campolide districts – private games the police knew of but left alone. There, in the pride of his achievements, was a famous fancier of chorus-girls, and there was Dona Lurdes, the abortionist. Building contractors were loudly belching. God, what a get-together!

Tea and toast were indeed a pleasant contrast, and indispensable after Imperial Russian technicolour, with the Tzars and the bala-laikas and bearded Rasputins. Dip the toast, savour the first taste; hum a phrase or two from a Tchaikovsky waltz.

Halfway through the toast the painter Arnaldo, to complete the scene, arrived on his poetic rounds, rendering odes to his lost love, his Sphinx, who had died and taken his wits with her. He did not enter. Tall and distinguished, with gloves and notebook, he recited from the street-door and retired. The building contractors, looking round to see if they were missing anything, started on more fish.

Elias was sleepy. His lids drooped, opened, drooped for another brief doze, and he was then restored and fit for hours of observation. Such, on nocturnal duty, was a policeman's lot. After his forty winks, he focused on a group in the corner: self-important-looking students – arty-crafty, one would say, and great ones for night-life. They had books stuck under their arms – what rancid literature that must generate – and were accompanied by a bevy of girls from the university who (his magic nail told him) would go nowhere unless equipped with the pill. His apparent sleepiness meant that he wasn't missing a thing. One girl, tall, partly hidden, was smoking with a cigarette-holder. Mena's friend?

He couldn't be sure. Softly he hummed the Tchaikovsky waltz with which the Tzar beguiled the charming ladies in the film at the Condes. The place reeked of malt and fermentation. Froth spilled, lupine-seeds were strewn broadcast, and beyond a bar piled with shellfish was the table where the girl was sitting. When she got up and went to the cloakroom he could recognise her: Mena's vehe-ment champion, Norah d'Almeida.

The froth on the glasses rose sky-high. For every beer you swigged at the Ribadouro, they said, you peed two and belched another. This no one would dispute, and God preserve us, Elias would have added, from such a university of pickled lupine-seeds, and all the goings-on.

He was home in bed by three, skimming *The Sea Wolf* again. Corporal Barroca had underlined, 'We're dead men. I know it': what a priest might call a *Memento Mori*. Elias closed the book and put his light out.


# V


Further, unexpected, visit, said the *Diário da Manhã*, to Casa da Vereda by the Criminal Police, accompanied on this occasion by the commandant of Military Police and by experts in mine-detection and explosives; acting, according to unofficial sources, on information recently received and sufficiently important to give a new direction to their enquiries. There is also a persistent rumour that the police have been for some time in possession of the late major's diary.

'Diary's pitching it high,' said Elias to the reporter. 'It's a very ordinary notebook.'

'Yes?' said the reporter, scribbling.

'A notebook, with "Instructions" on the cover, if that's any use to you.'

'No personal stuff?'

'In the notebook? I couldn't tell you. Ask the superintendent.'

They were on the terrace in front of the house. The inspector, as though disinterested, swung a leather briefcase by the handle. He had a wild flower in his buttonhole. The sun was shining.

'Where was it found, though?'

'Here. Hereabouts.'

Soldiers walked by, some of them with shovels, joking. A detective guarded the front door, hands in his pockets, whistling now and then to a blackbird in the pine trees.

The reporter scribbled sedulously. Working notebook, contents confined to military instructions and to the subversive Movement. OK? No politics, nothing of a personal nature, OK? No mention of the girl-friend, by any chance? That's it, then?

The biro hovered above the pad. Elias smoothed his scanty hair and gazed heavenward.

'My friend,' he said, clapping the man on the shoulder, 'between you and me, it was a game. Sort of naval snakes-and-ladders. You play it with signal-flags.'

Briefcase swinging, he headed for the house.

'Silly bugger's invented a diary, would you believe it?' he exploded to the man on the door, and hastened upstairs to the superintendent, who was escorting the Military Police commandant on a tour of the premises.

'On this floor, the bedrooms. Bathroom there, at the end of the passage, double bedroom on this side. Shall I go first, if I may? Thank you.'

At once we notice the strategic placing of this room – at the top of the stairs, away from the front entrance; and that the tree at the window might serve as an exit. Re-arrangement of furniture (deduced from position of electric plugs) to allow a simultaneous view of door and window from the bed – there could be no other reason. The main feature is the tree; freshly lopped, as we observe, the gashes not yet grown over. At the slightest alarm anyone could shin down – three, four metres, if that – into the pinewood. And these criminals were all extremely fit, not least the major's mistress. A very active girl; tennis, riding, winter sports in Spain and the Serra da Estrela.

'Very active in bed, you might say.'

'We might, yes.'

The visiting commandant looked but did not touch. He stooped to examine the pottery cat on the chest, noted a bullet-hole in the wall behind it, refrained from comment and followed on. He was purely an observer, a colonel in mufti, touring the premises.

Bedroom and strongroom had, it seemed, been combined. The colossal convex wardrobe, with dilapidated shelves, was more or less an arsenal, while the papers – the superintendent indicated the chest-of-drawers – were locked in here. Sleeping or waking, the major wanted everything under his eye.

But the commandant, rooted, had perceived some crumbled chalk on the floor. And what on earth, wondered Elias from the doorway, could the man see in half a dozen chalkmarks where the laboratory people had located bloodstains long since classified, recorded and forgotten? But a warhorse is a warhorse, and where there is blood is not to be deflected.

'The victim's blood, I take it?'

'The woman's,' said Otero, eliciting a grunt of professional comprehension. The warhorse was a ranking military policeman. 'We have reason to infer that the major was, latterly, in a disturbed state.' Otero, at nobody's suggestion, had adopted the tone of one presiding at a press-conference. ('Off we go,' thought Elias. 'Address-system as per.') 'The damage we see – this bullet on the wall, the door battered in – is the exteriorisation of a personality-crisis. A crisis connected with the almost pathological need for self-assertion.'

'Self-assertion, violence,' said the colonel. 'One explains the other.'

'Indubitably,' said Otero.

'And may have been what led him into politics.'

'The need for self-assertion? Oh, no doubt of it, no doubt. Our professor of Civil Law, I remember, would tell us that politics is the projection of frustration. Individual frustration, projected onto society.'

'Like it or not, politics will destroy the individual.'

('Two of a kind here – made for each other. You only have to look at them'.)

And speaking of politics, the visiting colonel deplored the fact that, to some, the meaning, the logic, of things was unapparent until it was too late. Though, with all the logic in the world, he could not link this brutal tragedy with the Dantas he had known.

A normal reaction, my dear colonel, and, to Otero, understandable. We can assent to natural death, not to unforeseen and violent destruction. Then, if I may enlarge, it is as if we feel ourselves threatened; threatened by a similar fate. By the way he settled his polaroids on the bridge of his nose Elias saw they were in for one of the bouts of sterile eloquence in which the superintendent was apt to indulge before selected listeners; and before a commandant of Military Police he would certainly go to town. Marooned in the domain of knife and gun Otero, the qualified lawyer, cast about constantly for allies. With allies in government departments and every branch of the police, allies civil and miltary, in politics or the Church, he sought immunity from ripple, from inflow and over-flow . . . The inspector paid no attenton and studied the pottery cat instead.

Its faults of colour and modelling were manifest in the slanting light. A poorly-executed animal, and poorly glazed; a fairground product, on a par with the gipsy fortune-tellers, the Holy Padre Cruz and shirtsleeved figures with elbows cocked suggestively. It shared their very common clay and was not a cat to grace a drawing-room. Packed, with them, in straw from fair to fair, it would be happy on a plebian bamboo table with a pot of ferns. Only the capricious destiny which rules the secret life of cats could have brought it here, to sit on a bourgeois chest-of-drawers.

The superintendent was dilating to the colonel on the murder of a priest in a candle-factory. 'Found in the cauldron where they melted the wax for church-candles.'

Two flies – a pair – buzzed above the pottery cat, flying gently upwards in intersecting curves, zooming away at speed if they happened to collide. 'In the winter,' droned the superintendent, 'so he cooled the minute they pulled him out. Might have been a wax statue.'

But the colonel was on the move. The inspector stood aside for him, and he and the superintendent continued their conversation in the corridor. As Elias said, amateurs relished crime, but they had to have it demonstrated; and at the moment, brief-case in hand, he seemed to be assisting, in disguise, a superintendent disguised as demonstrator, or cicerone. A cicerone whose lofty dissertations led, as it were, to the very lofts of the crime. 'And here,' announced Otero, as who flung wide a door to the verdict of history, 'here we have the attics!'

Attics, he said, as usual in these summer cottages. Sloping roof, rafters, piles of old magazines, and what was, probably, an old kitchen-table (this circular burn could be from the base of a frying-pan.) This ashtray advertising Convento wines and spirits. The campbed by the wall. What else? Ah yes, the window, where the woman was seen – the one the newspapers spoke of.

'Naked, wasn't she?'

'At times she was,' Otero replied. He opened the window.

The soldiers wielded spades and metal-detectors in the wood. Nearer the window they might cull more empty packets; packets that had contained SG cigarettes, or the Valium and Saridone headache-pills favoured by the major's mistress. The many containers, said Otero, were proof that she spent many hours here, in a state of deep anxiety.

The attic was musty. (To Elias, the expert, it smelled of mice.) The campbed and bare walls suggested solitary confinement, a bread-and-water diet. Winter in this dump could have been no treat for anyone. The light was dying. From the window, the colonel caught the chink of spades in the wood. The birds were roosting, and down on the left, with its red-lead paint, was the water-pump over the well, from which the stonemason must have seen the naked woman. 'The mistress, yes,' he nodded wisely.

Otero, as though he had nothing more to do, sat on a low bench, his knees more or less on his chest and his nylon socks displayed – not a wrinkle in them. Also on display were a few inches of white shin, very tender and delicate. The blackbird was singing again.

Having considered the view, the commandant turned his back to the window, leaned his elbows on the sill and considered the toes of his shoes. 'Never,' he sighed, 'never did I expect to be involved in a job like this!'

'No option, in the Service,' said Otero.

'True, true.'

'To order à la carte, you have to be in a restaurant,' said Elias, from the landing. 'And even then there could be flies in the soup.'

'I beg your pardon?' said the colonel, still looking at his feet.

'I said,' Elias replied, 'that you have to eat in a restaurant if you want to pick your orders.'

'Ah,' said the colonel; and, to the superintendent, 'We were cadets together. That one doesn't forget.'

'No, no. How could you?'

The colonel last saw Dantas Castro, as he recalled, in Mozambique in 1954.

'We have a photograph, big-game hunting, taken about then.'

'Life's a funny thing! It was at the governor's. Yes – he'd been up-country, on inspection. January or February, '54. Curious, how the memories can revive.'

'Our photograph,' said Otero, 'was taken in a hippopotamus reserve. The man with him is the father of his mistress.'

'You don't say!'

'They were friends, colonel.'

'You don't say! So Dantas must have known her by then?'

'Probably, yes.'

Wrong, but Elias let it pass. Mena in 1954 was leading a hectic

79

night-life with a circle of university students. The big affaire, she had told him, began at Christmas, 1957, when her father was in Lisbon, staying at the old Avenida Palace hotel. Happy Hour at the Avenida Palace! Elias had a vision of the venerable, columned interior, with its doddering, venerable staff – a most implausible setting for romantic encounter. However, her father invited his friends for a drink, the Devil inspired the major to accept, and that was that. But the colonel was chatting on, and Elias did not interrupt.

'Odd, but I saw a photograph, too – quite lately. I was checking something in the *Revista Nacional* and there he was, at the saluting-base at a Portuguese Youth parade, sitting like a ramrod. He may have been there as a second lieutenant, or he may have been starting out in politics; don't ask me.'

The light was fading behind him and the attic brimmed with shadow. The voices, too, were fading and melting into one another, as words drift and fade, Elias thought, when you are waiting to pay your last respects before a funeral and time trickles slowly.

'The contrast is ironical – or it is to me –' Otero intoned, 'with what he was a year ago. His idealism, his sense of justice, devotion to his men. The widow identified the body, and when they lifted the sheet from him she said, "He lived for his troops, and yet a soldier killed him". It sticks in my memory. That's what she said, more or less. As if she blamed his idealism, yet blamed the corporal – as an idealist herself. Wouldn't you agree?'

'But the corporal didn't kill him single-handed,' objected the colonel.

'Oh, definitely – definitely not. Yet for her the corporal, if I may so phrase it, personified the murder. It was the great betrayal. The soldier killing the man who cared for soldiers.'

The colonel straightened up, stuck a finger in his waistcoat pocket.

'Idealism, my dear superintendent,' he said, 'may cease to be a military virtue and become an instrument of terror. *Ipsis verbis*: terror. Any number of examples in revolutionary history – I need not quote them. And the transition – this is what I emphasise – the transition will spring from puritanism. In any form, its origins are puritanical. They were puritanical, strangely enough, in Dantas. He was an idealist. As a cadet, as a serving soldier, in his relations with women – always the element of idealism.'

'In his relations with women?'

'Oh, yes. No one has stricter standards about women than your womaniser.'

The superintendent had risen, and was running his fingertips down the crease of his trousers. He shut the window and the soldiers were no longer heard, though Elias knew they were still at work among the trees.

'Shall we go?' said the colonel.

Elias led the way. There was a dead snail on the wall by the stairs (and how had it got there?). Dead and dessicated, and at first he could not prize it loose. When he succeeded, it was a void shell, with traces of slimy membrane.

'Excessively damp, this attic,' said the superintendent, closing the door. Elias craned at the roof and sniffed. Its planks were green with insecticide, but woodworm was in the skirtingboard. There were the tell-tale heaps of sawdust; or flour. No, silkworm cocoons.

In single file they descended. Otero on the colonel's heels was saying, 'The major's puritanism, colonel.' (Very steep, the stairs were. Elias was now in the rear.) 'There was a document in here which doesn't exactly support the theory, I can tell you.'

'Oh? What document is that?'

Halt in corridor for explanation by the superintendent. A pornographic extract, preserved among the magazines and newspapers; a medley of aberrations, he might say. (He might, indeed.) Elias walked on to the bedroom where the major and Mena had slept. You could just see the shiny edge of the chest-of-drawers, and the bulky wardrobe against the darker wall. And this extract in the attic — all in a hotel lift, up and down to the seventh heaven (man-to-man laughter.) Highly lascivious, libidinous, if he might so phrase it, *ad libitum*. Cunnilingus, and other depravities. The major sent it, with a most compromising inscription, to his mistress. We have the original, there are detailed illustrations.

'Good Lord!' said the colonel. 'Illustrations?'

Elias meanwhile peered again into the bedroom: the gleaming edge of the chest-of-drawers, the pottery cat. A vestige, not of light but memory, showed him the bed, and on it, like an animal's eyes, two glowing points. The major was stretched there, firing at the cat's head with a pistol, and somewhere in the gloom was Mena, her mouth wide with horror.

81

# Orgy in the Lift

The extract in question had been torn from an 'art' magazine – the name, *Erotika*, formed the heading – and slipped between the pages of a luxury-hotel menu. In beauty of printing and paper it was typical of the genre.

On one side was an *art nouveau* drawing in Indian ink of a fashionable, crop-haired female embraced by a kneeling lover whose hat and cane were on the floor. Bending backwards, eyes closed, lips half-open in ecstasy, she held the man's glove in one hand and with the other raised her skirt to her waist over naked belly and thighs. Pubis, noted Elias, drawn in black dots. The picture was signed Jauffret/1959.

Overleaf was a text in Spanish

'. . . There's a wonderful staircase here, darling Melanie, it quite overwhelmed me when we walked in. Flowers on every step, and a bronze handrail. It fans out from the big lounge, with a pair of tall marble angels, a guard of honour left and right. You can't think what gorgeous angels, with their tulip-shaped crystal lamps; and elegant, despite topheavy wings. And speaking expressions – so melting, and not what one associates with heaven, or cherubim. *Not* angelic! There's a domed ceiling of tinted glass, with huge butterflies and fantastic fruit and flowers. Can't you see it? The angels, and the lighting, and the decoration? Bliss for both of us. That hotel, for Gaston-Philippe and me, had the refinements of taste and fancy you need for the art of living. And it was exciting to be in a foreign city, far from Paris. We were secret accomplices, nearer – if we could be – than before. We had our own little niche in the bar, the *Maja Desnuda* corner, because it had an alabaster statuette with crystal drapery on her shoulders. *Preciosísima*, as they say on the Ramblas.

'. . . And what a marvellous city Barcelona is! Most nights, after a film or concert, we went to the Bodega Bohemia, where you see a real *gauche divine* – such wicked ways! Honestly, it's unbelievable, the drunks and the deadbeats – *borrachos y pianistas muertas*, I call them – and the feminists, and people who go in for the magical bit – table-turning and things. We were pretty late in the mornings (not much sleep, darling!) but they serve the most gorgeous restorative seafood all the time in the Barrio Gotico; and of course we adored the sailor-bars on the docks; the lovely raggle-taggle you can pick up there!

'I was in that dreamy state – that delicious physical lightness and lassitude you get when you know you can do anything you want to, making love. And oh, Melanie, that lazy feeling, how deceptive it is, and what it leads to! You're exhausted, you're relaxed, you're always ready to start again! That should tell you why I haven't been writing letters . . .

'Well, I was tired. We'd been out, we'd had dinner, we were in the bar drinking brandy, and I was just sitting there – so passive it wasn't true. We were going on to the Ateneo. The consul had invited us, and I'd been to my room to change; one had to be there fairly punctually. But Gaston-Philippe, oddly enough, wasn't worried. We had the bar to ourselves, and he ordered round after round, telling me jokes and scandalous stories in the brothel-language we kept for serious subjects, as if he never wished to leave.

'Then suddenly he was silent, and he was looking at me. A stern, piercing look – it was frightening. We looked at each other. He got up. I got up. He put out a hand behind him, and led me to the lift.

'Incredible, darling, how vividly I remember. But I can see that lift as if it were yesterday. The gate was a copper grille, and the door had panels of smoked glass, engraved with vases of oriental flowers. And mirror-walls, and a velvet seat, so innocent and inviting. It was an angels' bower in white and gold, with a devil's face grinning at you in the roof. That was scary, but rather sweet – carved and gilded, with tiny horns, like a faun, and a red half-mask. The details I remember! Isn't it strange?

'Yet everything – everything, my dear – was simply out of space and time. We had hardly shut the door when Gaston-Philippe fell on me, hands all over me. He held me to him with one arm and stroked my thighs and buttocks under my dress. And when I raised it, and pressed closer, and his fingers found bare flesh, imagine his surprise!

'Yes, Melanie darling, only my dress. Don't ask me why, but in the bar I had an impulse, and I'd gone to the cloakroom and simply shed the rest. I must have been clairvoyant. And what a happy inspiration! He was enraptured. I could feel it through his fingers, so ardent, and, my dear, so grateful! The inventiveness, the things he could do! He made me soar, soar, higher than the lift was

83

climbing and when I could have fainted, it plummeted down, and I with it.

'I can't tell how often we did that five-floor ride, that stairway to paradise. Up and down; the ascent, the dive, and the ascent again. For ever, it seemed. Gaston-Philippe was one of those marvellously practical lovers with a talent for turning circumstances to advantage, and he never once let the lift stop.

'And he knelt, and buried his face in me, and forced my legs apart and he embraced them — I don't even know how. Then he was thrusting into me, big and insatiable, moving, stabbing. He pushed me apart, and he devoured me. And oh, my dear, there was more — much more! Biting me, through hair and muscle, his face hot on my belly, hands in my buttocks. Oh, much more! Standing with one leg on his shoulder I didn't recognise myself in the glass. I wasn't myself. I was free and self-forgetting, while we were in the lift.'

At the foot of the page the major had written, and underlined. 'You see — we didn't invent the elevator-game.'

He, then, must have read the pornographic extract and passed it on to Mena, who must have appreciated it, for she had kept it with her, folded carefully in a menu from the

ARISTON PALACE HOTEL
BARCELONA.

It was one of the few things she took with her to the Casa da Vereda, and she clung to it, Elias deduced, when banished to the attic: it would not have reached such a cheerless *cabinet de lecture* by accident, nor been deposited in a five-star menu. And if it were left to moulder there with the nibbled newspapers, that was because Dantas was dead, for Mena, even before the murder.

The menu: tall and narrow, 16 × 29 cm; thick, grainy paper, with a pen-drawing of the Ariston façade on the cover; a silk marker. With it, a six-page supplement, with photographs and the story of the hotel. It was the souvenir menu of a Dinner and Concert in the Buffet-Lounge on 12th September, 1958. Soloists, Elena Krautz (harp), Alfonso Ortiz (violoncello) and Cisneros (flute).

The inspector, with his unquenchable passion for photographs, dwelt on the particulars of entrance-hall and public rooms. The Pergola Room had stained-glass windows, wrought-iron pillars terminating in wrought-iron bamboo foliage, with macaws on perches; it had tinted glass lampshades, and an aproned waiter in

84

attendance. Female figures in the *art-nouveau* panels of the Salón de los Duques Cantábricos symbolised, the caption said, the seasons and months of the year; there were glass screens with large painted flowers and, flanking the entrance, two bronze Moors, life-size, each bearing a lantern.

Elias examined photographs, menu-pages and, again and again, the front cover where, crowning the arched main door was a somewhat indistinct stone face. A satyr, perhaps, or a classical god?

But no – it was a devil in a carnival mask; and had it not been stone the horns, he was sure, would have been gilded and the half-mask red.

*On 21st April, on instructions from the superintendent, Roque, with a detective-constable, proceeded to the arrest of MARTA AIRES FONTENOVA SARMENTO, widow, aged 63, of 17 (A and side-door B), Travessa da Lapa, Lisbon.*

*At 9.30 in the morning they were ushered into a small sitting-room and asked to wait. While waiting, they could see that the gardens backed onto those of more than one of the foreign embassies, and Roque had an idea that the architect, if desperate, might run for political asylum there.*

*Unmistakably, the room had the feminine touch. The pitched ceiling was decorated with painted flowers. On a round English table in the centre were twin fat volumes in French on* Treasures of the Goldsmith's Art, *and in a corner stood a mother-of-pearl chess-table and three wing-chairs. To the right of the door was a secrétaire and on the wall hung a portrait of the architect in a high-necked shirt, with a short beard, and two still-lifes signed 'Martha'.*

*The policemen assessed it all, professionally, and, though nobody was there to see, maintained an air of elaborate indifference, as if to combat this house where they were being virtually ignored. They scarcely spoke. When either had anything to say – professionally – he said it looking through the window, hands behind him, as though trees, which all might share, were pleasanter to see than the domestic luxury of the opposition. They knew, as policemen, that a studied indifference to the wealth and paraphernalia of others could be their best defence against the feeling of social inferiority. ('I like to deal with intelligent folk,' the inspector would say, having learned that the delicacy, pride and actual vanity of the intelligent is frequently their undoing. Never, to an intelligent detainee, did he reveal his own tastes, or the fact that he read books. The intellectual approach was not for him. Rather, he would appear unlettered, philistine, narrow. 'If you want to dominate them, leave your self-esteem at home,' was his maxim.)*

*Roque and his companion were thus prepared to confront the architect's mother, who entered leaning on the arm of a maid and attired in a dressing-gown. At this clear indication that she would oppose the arrest, Roque tendered his warrant at once, with no preliminaries, to show her they meant business; and as she raised her spectacles, on their silver chain, to read it, her solicitor was announced. He, obviously, was here to stonewall and to advance* objections – age, ill-health, one niggling clause after another, paragraph and sub-paragraph. Very good, very good – but Roque had his warrant, and between the claims of a warrant from the Benemérita and the pleas of a harrassed woman there ensued arguments so complicated that, as Graveyard would have said, only a learned judge with a gavel could have knocked any sense out of them. She had to give in, of course, but before Roque could make the arrest the superintendent telephoned to countermand his previous orders. She was to go into a private room, with police guard, at the Santa Maria hospital.

And so she left the house where she had passed her married life, her son's birthplace. Her late-born, only son, whom she had cradled in the soft light of these rooms, whose father had been a crack shot and a fencing champion; to whom she used to show the trophies in their cabinets, the guns and foils in positions of honour on the walls, the oils and water-colours she had painted as a girl. They would end their inspection, she and the child, hand in hand, at the big closet where the maids did the ironing. Its cupboards had belonged to his grandfather the admiral, a lover of astronomy. A glassed-in bookcase contained books in leather bindings, rolled-up maps and bundles of papers tied in tape. Above them, near the ceiling, was a plaster head – the cast of a blind, dead face, to be reproduced, in charcoal, by Beaux Arts students on papier d'Ingres. The architect's mother, as a student, had copied and re-copied it. As a widow, she planted on it her husband's fencing-mask, in which he had fought gloriously, at foil's-length with many an adversary. But the small Fontenova, in shorts and school-smock, would avoid the closet. His father was there, dead and vigilant, hiding in the fencing-mask.

All this, and the memories of years, she left that morning of 21st April, to drive across Lisbon with two detectives in a taxi, dragged by them into the ring they were drawing round her son. Most saw her as a mother enduring a horrifying experience. To others – worse horror – she was merely the woman who had carried and borne a murderer.

[Marta Sarmento was twelve days in the hospital and two in the cells of the Criminal Police. 'After the usual formalities,' we read in the record, vol. 2, 'she denied any participation, direct or indirect, in the crime, and said her son, from her knowledge of his character, is too sensitive, and too much of an intellectual, to have done it, with or without accomplices . . . Questioned again, she confirmed what she had said before. Shown an anonymous letter* saying that her car had been observed near the scene of the crime, refused to admit this, or any other evidence not properly authenticated; attributes the letter to some unknown ill-wisher, or someone who is sick and irresponsible. Says that, in her present emotional state, she cannot answer as precisely as she would wish to.']

From police headquarters, Fontenova's mother returned to the hospital, to the soft steps in the corridors, the incessant traffic of ambulances in the courtyard. Death and bloodshed had never come so near her; yet one of her servants, while she was there, had sent three exquisite April roses daily to her room.

---

* Details of which suggest that it was forged by the Criminal Police on the basis of Mena's confessions.

# Finger in Flame

Elias at this stage was prepared to wait; to sit, arms on the chairback in front of him, and ask few questions. 'Tell me,' he said. 'Begin wherever you wish.'

Mena was on the bunk, in a sleeveless sweater. She leaned against the wall, hands clasped behind her neck; there were tufts of hair in her armpits. Over the chair, he blinked at her shortsightedly.

Her breasts were taut, she had no brassière, and the hair under her arms was black, crisp and curly as the pubic hair must be, with its bitter tang. Patiently, the inspector took a nail-file from his pocket.

Silence. The prisoner said nothing. The watchful detective said nothing. We can wait, we can wait.

Elias held his hand to the light, admiring the long nail as one might admire a diamond. It occurred to him, not for the first time, that only intellectual females and peasant-women didn't shave their armpits. But the Peacock Girl, he felt, was being humiliatingly nonchalant. Or was she? Was the exhibition deliberate?

She lit yet another cigarette. That nail of his – that goulish, stiletto nail! It was ostentatious and beastly. For what grudge or humiliation was it supposed to compensate? And was the assiduous manicure a professional dodge to make himself more repulsive, or was he prettying up the nail to match the signet-ring on the same finger? You'd imagine, from the attention and the polishing, that it was some precious ornament. Cleaning it, trimming it, buffing it on his lapel . . .

In the midst of the manicure, he shot a question at her.

'Which of you disconnected the electricity that night?'

Mena smiled, wearily. Dear God, it wasn't worth the effort! The inspector bent over his nail-file and leaned on the chairback, waiting, his eye in line with a stain on the blanket and with the ankle, emerging from her blue jeans, on which she had worn a golden chain that bound her to a lover. He rocked his chair backwards and forwards.

'Do you want to hear the whole thing again?'

'I want,' he said, rocking, 'to hear whether it was the architect who switched the current off.'

'How could he? He wasn't out of our sight. I've told you and told you, the four of us were in the living-room, together, when the lights failed. How often must I tell you?'

'I'm sorry, it's necessary.'

Elias bestrode his chair. Mena, smoking, thought, God above us, when will this ever end?

'It was a good test, though.'

'A good test?'

'To see how the major would react in an emergency. Wasn't it?'

She sighed. It was unbelievable, frightening. She shook her head in despair. Positively frightening. He was a toad, goggling at her over the chair. He would goggle for hours, and say nothing. The silence was ridiculous. Why should she be swapping silences with a policeman – why? He knew all the answers from what she'd said already. Why couldn't he leave her in peace, the ugly brute? I'm going to tell him, she decided, blowing smoke. Talk or no talk, this is damn silly; as silly as his damned ugly mug. And what's the point?

'This is ridiculous,' she said. 'I see no point in sitting here and telling you the same things over and over again.'

'Nor do I,' he responded. 'But the sooner you tell me, the sooner I can complete the record.'

She shrugged her shoulders. Tell him, tell him again. Tell him about what? The electricity being cut? But it wasn't cut. It failed because it failed, nobody meddled with the fuses, nobody was testing anyone's reactions. The police were bloody awful, the sinister motives they invented. And she could not spend the night like this, she had to get rid of him, tell him anything – the whole lot again, paralysing though it was. And where to start? The bastard.

'If I start when we had supper, will that satisfy you?'

The disdain was not lost on him, though he regarded her with sorrowful tranquillity and no indication of annoyance.

'You know best,' he said.

Or take it from a little earlier, from when the major came in from his secret meeting and sat at the table in his wet clothes, drinking brandy. From then until the lights failed might have been two hours, as she had said before, and they all of them stayed in the room. Dantas removed his wet mackintosh but did not, they noticed, go up to change. He sat there, soaking wet, and drank three brandies in a row.

Yes, in the priest's costume. (Why was that important? Or

perhaps it was.) He was frozen to the marrow – you shivered to look at him – which was why he drank at that rate. And suddenly, in mid-gulp, he said, 'So you see, Fontenova, contact, when necessary, can be made without the telephone.' And Fontenova said, 'Splendid, I feel much happier.' And the major: 'Well, I'm glad of that. We're not tethered to the telephone as if it were flypaper.'

It was difficult, if not impossible, to recall the conversation over supper. This was the first time Dantas had been to a rendezvous, and they were worried. They worried because he was late back, and because he now seemed reticent.

[Here the record touches on the major's 'initial reserve': 'he progressively abandoned his initial reserve and spoke of assistance received, or not received, from "the commodore", i.e. Dr Gama e Sá.']

But Mena would not read the ultimate version of her statements, nor learn how she and her companions appeared in the condensed official documents. She continued. She had to continue, with that nail, that spur, to goad her; and she thought, 'What hell this is.'

Dantas had demolished half a bottle and was still drinking. Warm brandy dispelled the cold. His face shone, the white neckband shone, and he paced the room, cheerful and relaxed as he seldom was. The meeting he reported in cautious hints and implications. Then it was plans, and courage, and the big push: groupings, and vaster schemes, new fields of activity beyond their own, and other circles implicated; orders, communications. He was a warrior-priest on the wings of the storm, he brought them tidings of a world where gallant gentlemen and generals conspired in the midst of terror and chaos. 'We need cool heads!' he cried. 'Now, now's the time for patience!'

'And the list?'

The architect was introducing yet again the fatal topic of the list. (Dantas began calling it the Black List that night, added Mena.) Why should they not avail themselves of these friends? It was illogical not to.

The major paced the room.

'What's that you say? Illogical? Logic, Fontenova, when people haven't stopped to think, can be anything they want it to be.* You don't know, you don't care, it has never dawned on you, that others have a different logic. They don't give a damn for your list, they don't need it – and a grand mess we should be in with your bloody intellectuals. The hell with your logic, Fontenova!'

Before the words were out of his mouth – these, or something like them – the house was plunged in darkness. There were shouts of command, cigarette-lighters flaring, and the men were up the stairs two at a time, silent at their posts, guns levelled into the windy night. The police – the police had trailed the major home . . . In the silence, the telephone rang.

It rang once, a single, piercing alarm which they all heard, and which quivered, strident, in the dark as though it were part of the trap.

How long did this last? Minutes? An eternity? Mena had been standing, stockstill, with a revolver they pushed into her hand. She remembered the wind, and the flames, among pitch-blackness, on the hearth.

The light came on, as it had gone off, with no warning.

'As when a fuse is replaced,' said Elias. 'Not that it matters. Pray continue.'

No reply.

'And then?'

More obstinacy, alas, but where was the hurry? He shut his eyes and in a little while, with a dry, clicking sound, plucked his fingers, as though peeling gloves off, and cracked the joints. Click, crack. Mena bit her lip. Cracking joints, and the weird nail . . .

'And then?' he repeated, cracking one finger after another. 'You were all in the room, or did anyone stay upstairs?'

His hands were on the back of the chair. She answered, before the next click came.

'We were together, of course. To see that we were safe, and discuss what happened – why it happened, what each of us had felt and done. We analysed the tiniest detail. Except for the telephone-bell.'

---

* 'Another menace is the "intellectual" assessment of situations. I cringe to see the chicken-hearted postponement of action in the name of logic. I always remember what Rommel said – that risk or logic is the choice in battle.' From the major's notebook.

Which was odd, she thought. More than odd, disquieting, as though, by tacit agreement, they dismissed a figment of imagination bred of panic. With the telephone in front of them, they behaved as if it did not exist.

The major took pencil and paper and noted timing, distances, routes, approaches and defence-points. He was another person, Mena said; incisive, exhilerated, his old self. Weapons were to be cleaned each morning, and inventories made of clothing and emergency stores.

Clothing. This must have been Fontenova's cue to raise the – obviously vital – issue of getting the corporal out of uniform.

'Bloody hell.' The major's face clouded at once. 'We'll solve that when we have to.'

What could anyone say? Mena turned to the radio for music, anything, but he prevented her.

'Oh, stop moping, corporal. You won't go ragged-arsed, I promise you.'

'But –,' Barroca began.

'But? But? Speak out, man. Say what you have to say.'

'If we're attacked, sir?'

'Then we're attacked. What about it?'

'Only supposing, sir. How do I escape, in uniform?'

Dantas laughed at him.

'Escape? You'd be dead, my son.' A swig at the brandy, and he was serious again. 'We'll all be dead, or the other buggers will be. Eh, Fontenova?'

As if not wishing to waste words on him, the architect sat down at the other end of the room.

There was a further application to the brandy-bottle, and the major dried his shoes at the fire. Perhaps his feet were cold? He extended them alternately to the blaze, and one saw the revolver bulging in his pocket.

'Goodness, gracious me!' His back was to the listeners. 'To think the corporal's wardrobe is such an urgent problem!' He paused. 'Why the urgency, Fontenova?'

He spoke into the fire, the better to rivet his audience. 'It astounds me, truly astounds me, my dear fellow, that your pupil is so French already as to hanker for new clothes'. Renewed pause. 'Your travelling-outfit, Barroca, *pas vrai?*'

Then, in a rapid reversal of mood, he dropped the subject, Mena said, resumed his pencil and paper and bade them pay attention as he demonstrated emergency tactics on a plan of the house.

Not a situation, not a position, but was anticipated and everywhere Barroca would be busy. This area to be covered by the corporal; supporting fire from the corporal at such-and-such a spot. The corporal will be protecting Mena. The corporal here, the corporal there – the corporal for whom Paris was the Casa da Vereda and who in Casa da Vereda would remain. *Paris-sur-Tage*, that unfunny joke. But the facts were marshalled with impressive clarity and Dantas was happy, riding a wave of dramatic exhileration.

(Happy, dramatic? Were those her words? Elias pricked his ears up. 'He is living deep and high. I doubt if he has ever lived so swiftly and keenly before.' This was underlined in *The Sea Wolf*, and she was quoting, as sure as his name was Graveyard, scourge of the unwary; quoting what was said of Larsen, the sea-demon who pursued vengeance throughout the book and challenged death and power, 'raging at the summit of passion and sensibility.' The major, by her account, was equally a happy man, plotting bold strokes and cunning snares. Elias had his doubts, but kept the corporal in mind, who had not picked those passages by chance.)

Dantas expounded, with plan and diagrams at the big table, only to have his attention distracted by Barroca, who stood apart by the telephone. As if catching him in furtive and disreputable conduct, the major interrupted himself to bark,

'What's this? On telephone-duty again?'

(Ah, time that cropped up. The inevitable telephone. So what happened?)

Barroca set his teeth, and his hand, square and disproportionately huge, went slowly over his mouth. Mena saw it, and his eyes stony and undeviating above. No one dared breathe; and they all had guns. To make bad worse, they all had guns. But slowly the corporal lifted his head. Slowly the hand crept from his face and he walked, in slow motion, to the door where he stood, for a second or two, with his back to the major, offering a perfect target. Then, out of the room.

Dantas listened to the heavy tread on the stairs.

'Flies. You're a lot of bloody flies.' The corporal's boots clumped across the ceiling. 'Flies. Stick, stick, stick to the telephone.'

Next he was in the kitchen, in the pantry, into drawers and

cupboards, demanding sealing-wax. Not that they expected there would be any in the house, but as luck would have it there was, and before you could count ten the major was striding to the telephone, with a lump of red wax and his cigarette-lighter. Mumbling, 'remove temptation, no more shitting nonsense,' like a curse or a prayer, he plugged the numbers on the dial with hot wax.

'That's it, no more bloody nightmare. Deliver us from temptation.' As he finished, Mena and the architect saw the wax burning on his fingers.

The way he looked at his hand, curiously, as if it were not his, checked her instinct to rush forward and help. Then he smothered the flames, finger by finger, index-finger last – and this he held high, for them to see and note. In his black soutane and white neckband, his hand a blazing torch, he seemed the inspired celebrant of some ritual purification by fire. The telephone on the cupboard behind him shone in the glow from the hearth. To Mena it was a monstrous insect with a circle of bleeding teeth.

'There was nothing else, I think.'

Nothing else. Neither she nor the architect contributed further to the scene, and she was tired. She wanted, as she wanted now, to sleep. No more statements.

'Said nothing more,' was entered in the record.


## Even the Flies Take Off

Entered in the office diary for 22nd April was a conference with the superintendent, bright and early. They were to discuss the immediate arrest of the lawyer – how, and when.

Elias, arriving late with a bad cold, huddled in his overcoat, was annoyed to find the chief clerk from the Administration Department there. For the life of him he couldn't see why, unless to stamp the warrant and report to the commissioner. Otero, as superintendent (Homicide), referred in his introductory remarks to *homo politicus* – if he might employ the term. If not, too bad, he would explain. *Homo politicus*, as exemplified by the illustrious lawyer, was a slippery customer, with good connections in heaven and hell, not to mention the intermediate purgatory of the part-time conspirator; nor could we better the very neat saying of my colleague here, Inspector Santana, that when a corpse is political even the flies take off. The man from Administration nodded sagely, as one with access to inside information.

On the other hand, Otero said, Gama e Sá is a lawyer. He has the resources of the Law, he can manipulate rules and regulations. Law is for the enemy, friendship for ourselves, as the ancients had it, and God alone knew where such a principle might lead us. Ah, where, indeed? The chief clerk rolled his eyes; the sky might be the limit.

'Can no one tell me what he's *doing* here?' sighed Elias inwardly. He fished an atomiser from his pocket and directed three squirts into his mouth.

'Lord, man,' cried the superintendent, 'that's no good! You require a complete overhaul.'

But, as he was saying. The police, hoping their suspect would, sooner or later, throw caution to the wind, had allowed him plenty of rope, unfortunately with no success. House to office, office to house; the occasional lady, the occasional restaurant; the lawyer's life was open as the day. Calmly he pursued his business with never a foot wrong, despite the Argus-eyed Judite and a twenty-four-hour tapping of his telephone.

'You mean,' said Elias, 'we have to arrest your slippery customer and give him the works?'

'That's what I mean,' said Otero.

Elias doubted the wisdom of this. He crossed his legs and began to stroke his pate.

'And if we pull him in now, he assumes the architect's mother has been talking. He'll be malleable.'

'We shall see,' said Elias.

The superintendent looked for guidance to the administration man, but the administration man was strictly an observer, with no comment to make. Back to Elias.

'Moreover, we have the other one – the other detainee. Her statements to you could be checked by his, could they not?'

Elias divined a wink behind the superintendent's polaroids, and the Commissioner Judiciaribus behind the question. Momentarily he stopped stroking his bald head.

'We'll see. As the blind man said when he took his dark glasses off.'

A sour smile from Otero. That was to his address. Clever bugger – *touché*; but these proper technicolour polaroids were different. He retreated into his chair, feigning deafness.

The warrant, as they saw, was here; he would, however, be glad of their opinions before signing. (Would he, would he? Elias still hadn't a notion why the clerk was here, unless urgently co-opted as a special adviser.)

'I should expect a chain reaction. With the architect's mother and the lawyer both in custody, we've only two to catch. It shouldn't take us long. A chain reaction.'

Tidying what hair he had, as if trying to tidy his thoughts on the subject, the inspector found he was thinking instead of Roque and his assistants, negotiating frontier ravines and frequenting quay-side bars in their hunt for the fugitives. Tiring as the legwork was, it kept the dear boys healthy. Sleeping out with the goats and moon-ing round with seagulls was strengthening, if uncomfortable; you acquired the qualities of patience necessary to the artist as detec-tive.

The superintendent's pen was poised for a fine theatrical signa-ture. *Manuel F. Otero*, he wrote in a lightning run, with a reverse stroke to cross the t; and handed the warrant to Elias.

'A chain reaction, we shall have a chain reaction. We may as well make use of the architect's mother, since we've got her.'

'True. There's just the one of her – he wouldn't train another in a hurry.'

Otero was above acknowledging quips of this sort, but the Administration man greeted it with a face as bleak as a life-sentence. He rose, and Elias saw – what he had forgotten – that he was lame, stamping on the floor and dragging one leg. He limped into the corridor – worse every day, poor fellow. But at least he had come and gone and said nothing and left the two of them, as policemen, to their own devices.

'Why that?' enquired Elias.

'The commissioner's idea.'

'But you're the one who signs the thing.'

'To cover us, Graveyard. In ten minutes, I imagine, they'll know at the Home Office that we do not approve of this arrest. Why do you suppose we had him in?'

'The Home Office?'

Otero smiled pityingly.

'Would you say, by any chance, I was an idiot?'

From the depths of an armchair Elias saw him, barricaded with files, and Salazar on the wall. The office, for once, was quiet, bathed in morning light and free of ambulances.

Then, as if on cue, and bang on time by the inspector's watch, the corridor was a bustle of footsteps, voices, laughter, and the cast surged in, principals and extras, for the daily Dance of the Seven Veils as staged by the Criminal Police: detectives with keen noses and no illusions to speak of, capable of piecing a script together from a minimum of evidence; informers sidling through with a furtive quota of news; typists blowing bubbles of chewing-gum to encapsulate the chatter they got from *Tales of True Romance*, each sentence in its own balloon. Bless their little hearts.

'Well, I'll go and rake him in,' said Elias.

'And, Graveyard —'

The inspector turned at the door.

'— don't crowd him.'

'Dear me. Angels lending the devil a hand when the fires are stoked.

'Something of the kind,' said the superintendent.


## Evening

Even-tide, when bats, as Elias would say, flit by on silken wings.

At Criminal Police Headquarters the shades of evening fell on tumult. The news was in the late papers — or what passed for such — and the superintendent, in a frenzy, had the entire Law Society on his neck. 'Now you see the shit we're in! What the hell will happen next?'

It was no use telling him that Habeas Corpus should have been arrested weeks before; that Habeas Corpus, with his professional organisations, his couriers, connections and legal auxiliaries, would have ensured publicity in the press and elsewhere even if arrested in the public street, without witnesses; that these professional difficulties could always be solved, for — Graveyard's adage — if you have the key you can unlock the handcuffs when you want to.

But no; and next day Otero would be embroiled anew. His mania for agreeing with people was a recipe for personal disaster, and he never learned. Constantly, if a friend were the butt of a joke, he laughed until his false teeth fell out; constantly his high-flown official language necessitated a mass of corrections and erasures; and so constantly did he agree with the commissioner, the ultimate

*Director Judiciaribus*, that when a problem was at his own door he could only bang his desk, and his moustache bristled. He was in the office, banging and bristling, now.

Elias left him to it. He had a chill, and anything could start with a chill; he was off home to bed. But not before reviewing the day over a cup of lime tea.

All morning, swathed in his overcoat, he had tailed the illustrious lawyer. Down the Rua Augusta, up the Rua do Ouro. A call here and a call there. Habeas Corpus popped into the Burnay Bank, and in for a shave and a manicure. Bloody waste of time. Elias accompanied Habeas Corpus, and a police-car (its driver known as Proceed-in-Neutral) accompanied Elias block to block as, hands in his pockets, atomiser at the ready, he followed in the footsteps of Gama e Sá: who, in full sail, exchanged greetings, bowed to one side, bowed to the other, and dallied, with his Romeo and Juliet cigar, at the *tabacaria* in Rossio, just to be annoying.

At the bookshop in Rua do Carmo Elias was tempted to pounce. Patience, though, patience. The fellow was drifting with the current – why not see where the current took him? Don't crowd him, Graveyard.

Savouring his morning progress, the illustrious lawyer, with his cigar, ploughed on. As he – or, rather, they – navigated Chiado Elias, in that dazzling wake, had leisure to note the cemetery-flavour which, allowing for the character of the street, prevailed: the monumental masons, elaborate carved doorways, the churches and flowershops. The façade of Marques, the delectable *Salon de Thé*, was that of a Parisian tomb from the golden epoch of tuberculosis; and the window of a small jeweller's further on, where gems lay on velvet, was grilled like a shrine. Books, in the window that attracted the lawyer, resembled memorial tablets, and with them were portrait-medallions of defunct academics. The funeral slope culminated in a verdigrised, unremembered statue, finger raised to admonish the passer-by: Ignore me, sinner passing by, but I shall have the last laugh soon enough, when you are where I am; and *Pax tecum*.

This was Chiado, the poet, and the statue was part of Elias's childhood. The bohemian, celibate poet, the satirist – who could be more typical of Lisbon? A monk, what's more, and ideally sited in this square, between churches and bookshops, sacred and profane. He sat, smiling cynically at the world, opposite the Brasileira, *café des artistes*.

Into the Brasileira sailed the lawyer.

He sat, smoking, at a table of well-known faces. (Not that the inspector knew them; they seemed to be from the ranks of the Law and the political opposition.) A neighbouring group, of artistic appearance, were probably dancers from the São Carlos theatre. Elias took a chair at the door, with his man in sight. Women sauntered, beautifully dressed and beautifully scented, in the square; there were flower-sellers with baskets of violets and charitable ladies, with large amounts of jewellery, jingling collecting-boxes. He could look from the satiric poet to Habeas Corpus (with havana) and, as usual, the Brasileira had its patrons from the PIDE, whom he recognised from their business-visits to the Criminal Police. They were not dawdlers here – they were in and out 'on the way to the office', their establishment being round the corner – but Henrique Seixas, of the PIDE, was prominent at the table where Dr Soares da Fonseca and a selection of Deputies were accustomed to drink their morning coffee.*

The inspector must have sat there most of the morning. Most of the morning on two glasses of mineral water, with the illustrious lawyer booming at one table and Seixas looming at another, in the background. Still, he had Chiado to look at, and the statue, and the smart ladies strolling along, and Proceed-in-Neutral conveniently parked.

Chiado the poet, the old man of the statue, had shared a place in Elias's young imaginings with a toothless dotard in Elvas whom they called the Wizardy Man, o Esplérido. The Wizardy Man was filled with maggots. No, said the judge, it was only his skin. But Elias and his horrified friends, from a safe distance, saw o Esplérido squeeze wriggling white worms from his nose. Then he laughed, and the bronze poet had the same corroded cackle. Until he was quite big, Elias thought – fascinating detail – that the wizard, Lisbon edition, was seated on a chamber-pot. And now two remote figures cut across his recollections of the morning – two figures before the verdigrised statue, hand in hand.

The moment was etched in his memory. His father had brought him to Lisbon and when they came over the Tagus dolphins were

---

* Henrique Seixas had been a guard in the concentration camp at Tarrafal in the Cape Verde Islands. José Soares da Fonseca was a government Minister, Managing Director of the Colonial Steamship Company, and an adviser of Salazar.

leaping in the water round the ferryboat, whose passengers pointed and applauded, as at a natural circus. And he was taken to the Law Courts, the *Tribunal da Boa Hora* (the Happy Time, for goodness sake – the Annunciation – from the convent that had been there once; what they announced to you nowadays was time of a different sort. But that was Portuguese humour, as when *Prazeres*, the Pleasure Gardens, turned out to be a cemetery.) They saw the statue the same morning. The boy shrank from it, gnawing his finger. But this was a poet, his father said, who never hurt anyone and died long ago. Portuguese history, as he would learn, abounded in poets.

But Elias hadn't even started school then. He had no notion of what a poet was, and the statue's malevolent smile and blackened tears frightened him. The man in Elvas was the image of the bronze man in Lisbon and, an extra nightmare, the bronze toga was not unlike a judge's robes. Often and often he would examine his father's face, convinced of its hidden resemblance to that of the statue.

The local *pasteleria* in which he drank his tea and reviewed his morning in the Brasileira, *café des artistes*, was in an old house, with flowered decoration and the date of the building displayed. It was rather too high for its size, and was hushed as a reading-room, for the customers sat – had been sitting for hours – over their newspapers.

The lavatory. Elias knew where the lavatory was. Past the counter, and past a glass screen, a miniscule corridor led to a stone arch, half a dozen steep stairs, and a modest loo with a wooden lid. How proudly, he fancied, might anyone sit here, elevated as upon an altar, trousers round the ankles, and perform.

Darker and darker grew the room. Inch by inch the papers rose towards the dim light overhead. At this rate the patrons would soon be reading on their feet, with streaming eyes.

Two non-violent lunatics from the neighbouring Miguel Bombarda asylum came in: grey and cadaverous, heads shaven, too-short hospital trousers secured with lengths of cord. From table to table they mimed their request for cigarettes by puffing through their fingers. But as more and more interest was evinced in the shielding newsprint, the lunatics harvested trodden stubs from the floor instead and had a drink of water at the counter –

apathetically, in jerks, heads lowered, snuffling into the glasses. Equine, they were. Elias opened the *Diário Popular*.

Not that he could see it, however, for the proprietor, putting a pair of steps in the middle of the café, was about to renew the strip-light in the ceiling. He'd got it a size too big for the room, that was obvious. Teetering on the steps with the neon tube in his hands, swivelling from the hips, he resembled a tightrope-walker finding his balance, and for this the readers lifted their eyes from the paper. Good as a play.

The thing was in at one end; in at the other. Contact, a spark, a flood of brilliance. Lights! Music! Somebody switched the record-player on and the noise hit you with an animal bellow.

Light and noise like a madhouse, suddenly. The boy in charge of the counter contributed by hurling oranges into the liquidiser as though operating a stone-crusher. Patronise the Machine-Gun Tea Shop, thought Elias, for your cakes and cooling drinks; and yearned for warm blankets and a glass of milk and honey.

'Black eyes, black eyes,' sang Nat King Cole in Spanish on the record-player. Elias always thought that soothing chocolate voice was made for *fado*. The *fado* songs of Coimbra in tropical rhythm, Creole angels in the Old Cathedral, banana palms in the Botanical Gardens, delightful. But here and now the Black King was not a soothing sound. He rocked the roof and split the eardrums. Enough was enough, *andante, andante*. Home.

He fell into a taxi, shivering with influenza, every aching bone demanding bed. Through the dreary Intendente, Socorro, Rua dos Fanquieros. Bed all day tomorrow, which was a nuisance as, with the lawyer's arrest, there was less time left for interrogating Mena. 'I should tell you, we have arrested the lawyer.'

The driver, cap well down on the forehead, was one of those dashing apache types; a breed the inspector knew. At the next interrogation, that's what he would say; no beating about the bush. 'I should tell you, we arrested the lawyer.' Habeas Corpus, the Illustrious Doctor, with cigar. Meter ticking, tic-tac, tic-tac; shit-shit, shit-shit (thorough-bass from Otero, moustaches bristling). Tic, tac.

Tic-tac, tic-tac. The Brasileira, *café des artistes*. Seixas the Butcher, dark glasses and a cleft nose like a gun-dog's, sitting there with the legal establishment, if you please; real sweethearts, unpolluted as the day. Tic-tac, tic-tac. Tea for chest ailments, St Onofre special brand with mallow and orange-flower, obtainable at Intendente Herbal Stores. On the dashboard Our Lady of Fatima harboured a trio of children in her skirts. During the journey, and when he got out, Elias never once looked at the city. He loathed it, as if it were a blowsy tart.

One hundred and thirty steps to climb, not counting the landings, and he collapsed into bed.

## Dose of 'flu

'He has a raging temperature,' said the superintendent to his secretary when Elias, from the lizard's apartment, telephoned to say he was staying at home. At this hour — eleven o'clockish — they could have begun on the lawyer had not Graveyard, nursing a thermometer in clouds of herbal vapour, fallen by the wayside. Shit — if one might so phrase it; a comment Otero applied to inconvenience and sufferer alike. 'And you'll be better soon, I trust.'

By late afternoon Elias was out of his hothouse. With an oil-stove burning, he sat with his lizard and inhaled his herbal remedies over a large bowl of hot water. Then he played a record of *The Barber of Seville*. Victory was round the corner; a few more lozenges should see him through.

Among the eucalyptus-fumes he re-read yesterday's *Diário Popular*. Eminent Advocate Arrested was no more than a minor stop-press item, so why all the fuss from Otero? Read on. *Andante, andante*. (Elias spoke aloud, which proved that he was better; when he was ill he wasn't up to it.) Other news: National Subscription for Purchase of Destroyer, to replace that sunk by the Indians in Goa; list of subscribers headed by President Thomaz (in Admiral's uniform,) with promise that the ship be named after, and would avenge, the *Albuquerque*, the *Terribil Albuquerque*, of famous memory.

Ah, well. Elias tidied the pages and, for something to do, sat at the telephone and dialled a certain number.

'Hello, beautiful.'

'Oh, piss off!'

'But I was thinking about you.'

'Listen, I told you — I'm married.'

For months Elias had solaced his lonelier moments with these telephone calls.

'I saw you yesterday.'

'Oh, yes? Pull the other leg.'

'With your boyfriend.'

'Go on! Which one?'

'The one who gave you the clap.'

'Charming!'

The telephone was slammed down. Piqued, Elias dialled again.

'That's not very nice. Putting the telephone down, when you love me.'

'I'm married, I tell you.'

'Have you been on the bidet?'

'I washed all over, all over. But you know something? I'm not in the mood today.'

'Nor me. I'm under the weather.'

'Oh, my poor lamb. Been up your arse, have they?'

'More or less.'

'You want some soothing cream, then.'

'D'you use soothing cream?'

'Never without it. I must ring off, my husband's home.'

'Get him on the line.'

'What?'

'Get him on the line.'

'Why?'

'Ask him if he wants a striker.'

'Darling, darling, come at once! I'm on the Queen Anne bed – you remember. You've been here.'

'I had you backwards. I remember.'

'That I adore. But I don't remember.'

'Yes, you do.'

'I don't. You can't have been much good.'

'You had a see-through brown nightdress.'

'No. I'm a brunette. I don't wear brown, it doesn't do a thing for me. But yes, all right so far.'

'And little rings on your garters. I liked those.'

'I was wearing garters?'

'What are you wearing now?'

'I beg your pardon?'

'What are you wearing now, my little trollop?'

'Now? I've got Sheik on my legs, my dachshund. You know about dachshunds —'

'A dachshund? What happened to the Pom? Did the vet bite him?'

'He never was a Pom, he's always been a dachshund, and he's lying here as good as gold. And I have my purple tights on, with the silver pattern, and a silver ribbon round my neck. Nothing else. Just nothing, nothing else.'

He felt worse. His eyes ached, his bones ached, even his spectacles were killing him. Bed again, with a roaring fever and every joint a misery.

Sleep, as such, was impossible. When the early light was grey in the glass panel over the door he surfaced, half-conscious, with a nose-bleed and staggered to the bathroom.

Giddy and parched at the wash-basin, head back, arm raised, he could see himself in the glass only by squinting down his nose at the two wads of cottonwool in his nostrils. The stance was that of a blind beggar, his skimpy hair was a dishevelled crest. He saw in the mirror the shining white lavatory behind him, its chain, with a shining white china handle, cutting vertically into the reflection of the tiled wall.

Elias bathed his face under the tap. When he stood up his head reeled and he had to grip the basin. Again he tilted backwards, arm in the air, and again steadied himself in the deafening, dizzying whiteness by looking along his nose into the mirror at the tiled wall and the lavatory. On the lavatory sat Mena.

He was unsurprised, as though she had always been there, with her elbows on her knees, dissolving and rematerialising, colourless, against the gleaming tiles. Then he saw a shadow behind him, its hand lifted — was it his own defecting shadow, gliding from him? — and one finger of the hand on fire. No, bleeding. Mena, as the shadow reached her, took this bleeding finger in her mouth, as a trained animal might have done, and sucked it with a docile, slumberous rhythm.

Elias leaned forward until he was face to face with himself in the looking-glass and stared intently, though he couldn't think and could hardly see. With a final, concentrated glare, as if repudiating a twin soul, he turned to the lavatory and jetted hot, turbid urine, like a horse. Head cricked to the ceiling, hand at his nostrils, he expelled the last drops, almost painfully, into the frothing pan, as though with them he expelled some residual, unwanted memory.

## Blank Wall

But the inspector was inured to late nights and little sleep and as soon as his temperature began to fall he was in Mena's cell with his entrance-line. 'I should tell you, the lawyer has been arrested.'

The effect of this was nil. She sat on the bunk, ankles crossed, knees wide, as he had seen her through the spy-hole when he knocked, and didn't move.

He straddled his chair, head spinning, nose bunged up.

'There should be a confrontation, of course. You and him.'

A slight raising of her eyebrows, and the way she was sitting, made him vaguely uneasy. In sober truth she could not be confronted with the lawyer, since during the preliminary enquiry she was in confidential custody. But she did not – or should not – know that. She should know nothing beyond the confines of her cell. (What did she know?) Elias sprayed his throat with long squirts from the atomiser and produced a scrap of paper from his pocket.

Friday the 12th. Second visit lawyer

Fake tel. call (NB lottery day).

Complicity of architect.

'One subject at the confrontation,' he said, 'would be the trip to Lisbon on the 12th. And we should like an account of what happened when the major reported the lawyer's attitude, and of the fake telephone-call. That is correct – concerning the telephone-call?'

The scrap of paper was among the jottings from which he cast, in legal language, the ultimate version of what she told him.

[In Vol. 11 of the collected documents we read: 'That day, Friday the 12th, the major went out unexpectedly in the evening, disguised as a priest and carrying a revolver. Witness assumed he was to see "the commodore" (Dr Gama e Sá) and, from his short absence, that they met not far from the house . . . Dantas was in good spirits on his return, with no hint of what was to follow. Said at supper that he had been with "someone at the top" and that security measures were in force against various sections of the Movement. The architect said, "Which means this isolation will go on?" and the major agreed. "We have to be patient awhile with the commodore." Fontenova, criticising the commodore, was told his judgements were premature and he had no concrete evidence. "You don't know the half of it. In circumstances like this we see what men are made of." External contact forbidden "until further instructions."]

'And that,' said Elias, 'suggested your telephone-call from the village.'

There was the ghost of a resigned smile. Head bowed, hand at her breast, she said,

'Run over it again — yes?'

With the other hand she stubbed her cigarette in the tin plate. Oh, yes, she'd have to run over it again. Cradling her breast as if it hurt her, or comforted her, she repeated that she was disturbed by what Dantas had said, and left the two men arguing. She felt hopeless and helpless and could stand no more of it.

She repeated, and repeated, previous statements. That she craved air, and space, and out-of-doors; opened the window and lay down, as she was, in the darkened room; that the night was mild and quiet, with no wind and a light drizzle of rain. She heard what might have been carts on the road, hoofbeats and creaking wheels; that she closed the window, not because of cold or damp or noise, but because of the conclusions Dantas would jump to should he find her there, dressed, with it open. For some time he had been seeing signs of desertion everywhere.

Yet when he came in, about a quarter of an hour later, he was, to her astonishment, buoyant and cheerful.

'They were so scared they were peeing themselves!'

'Scared?'

'Oh, they swallowed Gama e Sá and all the poppycock — hook line and sinker.'

'What poppycock?'

She couldn't believe it. The quarrelling over the commodore was for nothing. A fraud, a fabrication.

'But why? It's paltry, it's contemptible. What were you thinking of?'

'A test. Test their behaviour. If you command men you have to test them at intervals.'

'But deceiving them — you can't, Luis, it's indecent. You've no right.'

107

Dantas by the chest-of-drawers was playing with the cat's blonde wig.

'That's your opinion. What about the virtues of the hot-and-cold douche?' He pulled the strands of blonde hair on and off the cat's face as he spoke. 'Hot-cold, that's the principle.' On, off. Hot, cold. Now you see it, now you don't. 'They'll be happy as larks tomorrow when that telephone rings. They've had their fright, and now they have their treat. They'll know it's Gama e Sá without being told twice.'

'You're sure?'

'Absolutely.'

'I mean, you're sure he'll ring?'

'It will ring. We shall have a call, don't you worry.'

Elias interrupted.

'But according to your previous statement, the fake telephone-call was a last-minute scheme?'

'It was. That is, it was next morning he told me to ring. In the bedroom, when I was doing my face to go the village. He said I was to ring from there, as if it were the lawyer.'

'He said I was to ring;' as brusquely as that. Elias saw her, not on a prison bunk but the bed at Casa da Vereda. She would have had a thick head when she woke (as always, to judge by the heavy smoking – a bucketful of stubs in the cell) and crawled to the bathroom, stupid with Valium, to wash the night away; then aged herself with make-up, plain-glass spectacles, the wig.

Was she sitting like this when the major issued his instructions? Knees wide enough for anyone to look at anything? And what the hell if anyone did, she couldn't care less. She was beautiful, she knew she was beautiful, and she must be marvellous in bed, but what did that matter here? Here she was out of her element, having to provide statements to the damn Judite as though she were any tart off the pavement, with a come-hither, tarty fringe. She had said already what Dantas told her to do, and why she obeyed him: he was the unforgiving sort. And how she walked on a country lane, between tumbledown walls and bamboo-plantations; said it in that husky, velvet voice . . .

'I was in the village by ten o'clock, I suppose.'

Village? Well, some might call it a village, perhaps. The inspector had been there, walking in her footsteps from Casa da Vereda to the tarmac highroad, and on the rock-strewn path that wound through the cane into the dolls'-house square at Fornos. In this square was a fountain and, when Elias saw it, a pensive stray bullock, standing beside a palace.

'Palace' was an exaggeration. It was a large, palatial house with a range of ogive windows, its tiled façade crowned by two colossal vases of glazed terracotta. Access there was none. The bullock, obviously the vagabond and sight-seer of the herd, stood precisely opposite the carved, canopied and blocked-in main door.

There were no other attractions in Fornos, which wasn't on the map, nor worth a detour. The square was its sum total, with post office, rows of gas-bottles at the bottled-gas depot, a panel-beater's in a former cooper's yard, and one, unnamed, café. From this café Mena made the telephone-call.

Two lads playing the football machine were the only customers. When Mena first beheld the café television-set, on a shelf slung by chromium-plated rods from the ceiling, she had thought, 'telly on a trapeze', but she didn't look at it this morning. She scarcely looked at the football enthusiasts, each of whom was being an entire team as well as the crowd − clapping and booing and whistling at the referee and doing the radio commentary, commercial breaks included. They were little more than boys, for all their firemen's blue overalls and the axes in their belts; urchins you might find marching in the band in a religious procession, with rockets whizzing overhead.

Pursued by the squalling of a child and an odour of cooking, the proprietress emerged from the back regions. Mena drank a small black coffee and bought a carton of cigarettes, two bottles of brandy, a quarter-kilo of sugar, a supply of chewing-gum, and newspapers. Then, since orders were orders, she inserted the Judas-money into the telephone-box and looked at the soft rain in the square as she dialled.

Not until she was going home did she remember the mansion with its blank wall across the square. But, plodding through the rain, she saw herself at the telephone, and the doorless house as she had seen it then. She imagined an interior with grandly severe tapestries, a table with heavy silver and a mound of fruit, richly coloured. And not a living soul. The ticking of a grandfather clock; a monster cat ensconced on cushions − an ailing patriarch with two fat crystallised tears on its nose.

'I must have been back between twelve and half-past.' The

manure-heap by the top road was steaming, she noticed.

'Then, you had a discussion?'

'Then a discussion, yes.' Actually, it was in progress, for the three of them were at the table when she put her key in the door, and the architect met her with, 'Gama e Sá! He's telephoned!'

She changed and joined them, reluctantly, in the living-room. But Dantas was in full flow, which made her entrance easier, for he waved her to a chair with the news that the commodore had rung at 11.30, and went on talking.

'Ah, implying that you were to be at the Rua do Ouro at the same time next day?'

Mena said, 'Couldn't they wash this floor? I'm sure there's a dead mouse somewhere.'

Elias twitched his nose as if to say, Fiddlesticks!

'And subsequently you had a vital conversation with the architect.'

'Again?'

She slid from the bunk, took a sweater from her suitcase and draped it over her shoulders, knotting the sleeves in front. It looked like a man's garment, loose, rough and coarsely-knit; the shade of blue, and the high neck, were those of a seaman's jersey.

She leaned against the wall facing the door, with her bunk on the left and the inspector on her right; and she saw, very distantly, the Casa da Vereda attic.

The attic; the letter; and the architect standing among the rafters, white to the lips.

'I'd been up there all afternoon,' she said slowly. 'I didn't want to see anyone, not after that hoax with the telephone.'

Fontenova found her reading on the campbed, as far away as she could get, with the radio for company. And the mice. The mice might give her no peace here, scampering round the bunk at night, and in the waterpipes, but there the attic swarmed with them — racing and fighting and mating, like mice in the garrets of any country cottage; and when they were quiet it was not true quiet, but a nerve-racking, expectant lull.

She was in the garret, isolated as in the cell, when the architect appeared.

'Mena, I've been thinking.'

His head was framed in the criss-cross of rafters propping the roof.

'That telephone-call,' he said. 'Gama e Sá was giving us the final blow, you'll see.'

The major had been told about him, and this confirmed it. He was a treacherous bastard who wanted nothing more to do with them, wanted them off his back. He knew they couldn't run – there was no one to run to. He knew they were alone. And he was making it clear as daylight that he disassociated himself. Did she intend to sit here, waiting for catastrophe?

But suppose otherwise. Suppose he had veered again and promised help – still Fontenova could not see his coming up with a red cent or an ounce of support. Promises, yes. No lack of promises.

The architect spoke in a low voice, with one eye on the door. 'After this morning, have you thought what we're in for with Dantas if that humbug goes on like this?'

'Better not to think,' she whispered.

'We must do what we can, then, any way we can.'

It was growing late, and the major might intrude on them. Most days, Mena said, the house was oppressively quiet in the late afternoon; the sort of silence in which anything could happen.

At the door, alert for a footstep on the stair, Fontenova gave her a letter.

'Read it. It's a nuisance for you and I apologise – but how else?'

She could read it now, from memory; two moving pages, imbued with love of home and childhood and written, she saw, in anticipation of death, bidding farewell to his mother and asking her for clothes and journey-money. The clothes were for the corporal, he told Mena – they had a safe hiding-place for them – and the money she was to hand to Dantas as though the lawyer sent it.

'My mother will recognise my writing. You can take my watch to show her, though.'

'Clothes and money,' Elias observed. 'But when were these clothes to be worn? Not when the major was there. Or did you not consider that?'

He stood up, instinct telling him that here was the origin and centre of the crime. For how, in view of what had passed, was the corporal to explain a new suit to the major when the dash was made for liberty and revolution? Gift to an unknown soldier from kind ladies in high society? Present from Father Christmas, deposited on the hearth? No. There was more to it. Fontenova, in obtaining the clothes, was either preparing Barroca's escape to some *bidonville* in

France, or he believed the major would not live to see them worn. 'That architect,' Elias said to himself. 'I cannot work him out. When I've nearly got him, damn the man, he slips me. An enigma.'

## Statement of a Poultry-Dealer, Landlady and Practising Christian

In the outer office, when the inspector walked through, a plump woman, smothered in shawls and jingling with gold chains, was complaining loudly to a detective at a typewriter. She had written in, it seemed, and her letter was lost in the Pending tray: complaint of Senhora So-and-So, egg and poultry-dealer in the Old Market, against Major Dantas Castro, her tenant at a house on Avenida de Roma (Flat D, 8th floor). Accusation: wilful damage and misuse of property. The tale was broadly familiar to Elias, but he had scant patience with sob-stories and proceeded to his desk.

'You speak here of moral injury,' said the detective at the typewriter. 'How do you mean, moral injury?'

'Scandals, that's what I mean. Offences to Christian morality.'

'I'm sorry, that's not an answer. Christian morality is a very general term.'

Yes, alas it was! How many self-styled Christians make the Church their alibi for sin!

'I know, *Senhor agente*, I know. I'm a Jehovah's Witness. You've heard of Jehovah's Witnesses.'

'Makes no difference to me what sort of witness you are. We are guided exclusively by the Penal Code,' he said.

'And quite right you should be – quite right. Don't you be ashamed to admit it!'

He read what he had typed. Tenant vacated flat owing rent; obscenities written on doors and walls; complainant alleges wilful damage and improper conduct. Laboriously, the complainant signed.

And the next question –

'What were the obscenities?'

To this the response was a downward, embarrassed glance and the strangled murmur, 'Words'. On her top lip was the merest fuzz of a moustache.

'Such as?'

'It said Bad Woman, all over the walls.'

'Bad woman? Whore, is that it? Accuracy, please Senhora, accuracy.'

Elias, visible through the glass panel, was brooding at his desk; head in the clouds, gaunt, stringy neck protruding from his collar, spectacles like ponds of ditchwater. He had 'gone lizard', as the department called it, and flies, in perfect quietude, might settle on him.

But now the long nail beckoned, and the constable contending with the complainant hastily steered her, shawls flying, to the inspector's office, ushered her in and fled.

Elias chose to employ another method. Hands in his pockets, coat thrust behind him, he prowled round her, coaxed her, asked a question, absorbed the answer and returned to the attack. After four or five of these circuits he knew enough to send her on her way.

Beginning from the highly offensive sentence, I AM A FILTHY WHORE, blatantly exhibited on walls and doors in the Avenida de Roma flat (and defused, for Jehovah's poulterer, into 'I am a shameless pig'), he arrived at the secrets of Mena's life at bed and board with the major: landing home at all hours, orgies with the doors locked, rumoured dinners in the nude, and booze running out of their ears. Late-night quarrels, deliciously resolved. Anything you cared to think of.

In short, there had been what the hen-wife deplored as 'discrepancies'. ('Discrepancies?' Well, debauchery; no accounting for tastes.) The girl who cleaned for them said it was beyond a joke, the shouting and bad language. They were in bed once, shouting 'you bitch this' and 'you bastard that' and, she said, with what they were at between-times it must have been, to speak plainly, for excitement.

And, frankly, some of this information was from the concièrge and some from the concièrge's brother, who collected payments for the poultry-stall.

'Aha!' said the inspector, 'concièrges! What they couldn't tell one! Little mines of information; and when their husbands were policemen, as was often the case, they were honorary policemen themselves. Or they were busy bees, buzzing from flat to flat and gleaning news in holes and corners. And most of them peasants, of course, with the peasant mentality – like housedogs, growling at the poor and wagging their tails for the rich. What a profession! Ah, but this concièrge, having worked for years at the chicken-farm, was thoroughly reliable. Years she worked there, getting on with everybody.

But, where were we? Oh, yes. Major Dantas, said the poultry-dealer, even after renting her flat (as from 7th May, 1958, see written complaint), was living with his legal wife, the one he married in church, at another address. And quite right; marriage, you can't deny, is a sacred moral institution.

Oh, quite right, Elias could see that; but for another reason, unmentioned. Mena's father was in Portugal for longer than usual in 1958, and what father would be happy to find his daughter living with a friend of his? And a friend who was an old crony and fellow-womaniser — the last straw.

But the two-establishment situation was, to the landlady, most peculiar. The major had two flats, and the girl had two flats — though in the end she was spending her days in the Avenida de Roma, smoking, waiting for him. Elias saw her, in the days of his absence, with a gold chain round her ankle, and about her the physical sense and smell of the man. No more Estrada da Luz, with windows on the sunset and the storks in the Zoo; no more Peacock Girl with high-piled hair. No more.

'If you ask me, she was crazy for him. I regret to say it but, more fool her, she was.'

To the poultry-dealer's certain knowledge, both the concièrge and a telephone-girl from Marconi's with a flat on the same floor were sick and tired of the arguments. Slanging-matches would be better. The major, blessed with iron lungs, was off at the least little thing, yelling that they were free agents outside the front door, this was liberation, this was freedom, she wasn't answerable to him. And a fat lot that meant, as we were to see. Naturally, she went for him. 'I'm fed to the teeth with liberation. Everyone's bloody mad on it. You can fuck liberation!' (Here construed as, 'Good luck to liberation'.) 'What it was, inspector, she wanted a child by him and he wouldn't oblige.'

A child? Whatever next? 'Tell me more,' said Elias.

But all single women want children! A child — the supreme physical fulfilment. It fulfills the hunger for love, it brings renewal, calm and happiness. This on the authority of *The Family Almanac*, where there'd been an article, with a very pretty border of birds, read it, and he would understand the tragedy. Oh, yes, he understood: the major singing the seducer's usual song about no strings, and the horrors of convention, social restraint and non-romance. So there she was – ah, how one understands! – saying that love was being together, and belonging, and blow liberation. (Here the concièrge and the girl from Marconi, ears to the wall as in some Gothic horror-story of murder at the wayside inn, sustained the shock of 'you can fuck liberation'.)

Solely to the police, the woman hastened to add, would she rehearse such doings, and solely in the interests of justice. And it was funny, but the cleaner said that she – the major's mistress – urged him to stay with his wife. She wanted him for herself, yet he could stay with his wife. Now, why? It might be pride, yes, but it baffled the landlady.

As for the culminating scandal, the one she had complained of, she had more than the concièrge's evidence, for the Marconi operator and the tenant in the flat below had been awakened by noise in the early hours. On what date was this? The date. After much humming and hawing, she declared for Christmas. Near enough to Christmas – say, Christmas Eve; and early in the morning, because the concièrge's husband was home from his late shift when the shindy started. Shouting and yelling, 'I am a blank-blank this' and 'I am a blank-blank that.' But there, she sighed, the inspector would know . . .

The incredible, the extraordinary, thing was that the Marconi girl swore they were quarrelling about another man and that the major was jealous. How and when she learned of this, best not to enquire. Telephonists are an erratic lot – some days all they do is listen in, and where's the privacy?

'What bothers me,' concluded this incubator of golden eggs, 'what bothers me isn't the behaviour, that's their look-out; it's the damage. It's very hard on me, inspector, having this damage and no one to apply to.'

'Try not to fret,' and 'We'll see what we can do,' said Elias, conducting her through the main office whose occupants, to a man, stabbed industriously at their machines. He then retreated to his own domain to ponder and digest, like a python after dinner. With his memory, and his policeman's antennae, he could seize the words and implications left hanging in the air. In five effortless minutes he had plucked his informant clean; sitting here, he was gathering the stray feathers and assembling the picture. Experience had taught him that with detection, as with a film, you have to see the whole before the bits cohere.

PIDE
INVESTIGATION DEPARTMENT

Report on motor vehicle reg. no. CN–14–01
*Particulars*: Ford Taunus passenger-saloon; colour, gun-metal grey. Documents and registration in order. Third-party insurance. Chassis and engine numbers as on documents.
*Owner*: Major Luis Dantas Castro, ex-Artillery.
*Remarks*: vehicle impounded by above authority in connection with current investigation of attempted mutiny in which this officer was implicated.
(Carbon copy).

This, for instance, cohered. He didn't have to re-read it. What it said matched what the hen-wife said; as in a film, everything dovetailed. She showed him one reel, of concièrge and neighbours eavesdropping, open-mouthed, in the Avenida de Roma. This was another, evoking the object of their curiosity – his car in detail, the mileage he did, the gadgets he had. The tag from the Ariston Palace Hotel, Barcelona, loose change lost under the carpet, a lipstick, it was all here; a Dior vanity-bag in the glove-compartment, with six contraceptive pills and a lucky hare's-foot. Bloodstains, none.

Excellent. But if there were no bloodstains, there was sperm. Ah. Traces of sperm. Ah, again, and the diviner's nail was glowing. On upholstery of front seats and off-side front door (Mena's side, that was); also on shutter of glove-compartment and in the vanity-bag. And, as ever, the major was a disembodied residuum, a remainder. He was a trace of semen, or a bloodstain; he was a voice, swearing, or a barrack-room legend – that was as far as you got. When discovered, disintegrating, chewed by dogs, he was a remainder only, an eye out of its socket, a skull with rags of flesh and sinew. He had taken his lineaments with him and St Peter alone could accurately describe him now. Or perhaps not. He must have been in fragments when he arrived at heaven's gate.

The diviner's nail was brilliant as the inspector read, for Mena, too, was in the document, the evidence of her conspicious as that on the walls in Avenida de Roma. What had she been doing, Elias wondered, on that penitencial night? Drinking? Blowing smoke-

116

rings, as though for a circus-act? And the shadow behind her, who was he? He must exist, the hen-wife spoke of him. The Other Man, symbolic horns on the escutcheon. Who could he be? Some playboy with a souped-up Porsche, cruising from bar to bar? An old flame from her student days?

## Same Evening

When he interviewed Mena that evening the inspector had the signed complaint of the Jehovah's Witness with him. That evening he would chat, be patient and unassertive, gain the prisoner's confidence and learn the intimate truth of what, with his addiction to Bible epics, he thought of as The Wailing Wall, a tale of sin, sex and repentance. He would listen and note, and he could suppress the obscenities and so on in the final report. What has to be uttered in confession is not essential to the transcript. *Et voilá.*

Mena read the document and handed it back to him, saying, 'Yes, that's right.'

'You agree with it?'

'The complaint? Oh, yes.'

He was by the door, she at the other side of the cell, with her arms folded.

At least that simplified matters. Complaint admitted, clearance-stamp on document, and the injured hen-wife, clucking joyfully, repairs to a magistrate for compensation. No problems. Mena could, however – and, he advised her, should – plead any extenuating circumstances.

'Extenuating circumstances!' She shrugged her shoulders.

She might have been for a country walk, in that long, loose skirt. Mena, walking in the country . . . He caught the faint fragrance of her skin.

'Unless,' she said, 'it's an extenuating circumstance to love a man. Or would that be an aggravating circumstance, do you think? There's a point you might investigate.'

She held her head up, and the light in her face was indefinable, felt rather than seen; it was nothing Elias had ever seen before. And there was that subtle, intensely personal scent, a breath of dusk and starlight; a scent that was Mena. Mena, and the world she came from.

'Aggravation, extenuation. That's for you to say.'

Only her eyes answered him. 'Is it? Is it, indeed?'

Neat as a filing-clerk, with her inattentive eyes on him, he folded the statement in half and ran his fingers over it. 'Cut and dried, then.' With a forefinger he adjusted his spectacles, but to see her, not the paper.

Standing there, as though she were a mere onlooker, and bored with what she saw, she reminded him, had she known it, of some drop-out girl in an American film, waiting for her stevedore lover on the docks. The country aura had evaporated. Some lost and outcast girl, with her man's shirt on, to keep the smell of him, waiting for the firing-squad. A woman, thought Elias; for that, and for much else, a woman.

'We must hope,' he said, 'that you don't get one of these nasty, warped judges. There shouldn't be more than a charge of material damage here.'

'Judges? So what about judges?' Mena was disinterested. Not to trust them, said Elias, even the best of them. Nicely barbered cheeks and hair in their ears, and every pore exuding bile. A vindictive crew, he was warning her, and only too delighted to nail anyone for depravities.

'Depravities!' Mena almost laughed aloud. 'You can't be serious? But I'm quite happy to tell them anything. In writing, if they prefer.'

She was opposite to him, in the corner.

'Depravities?' she said. 'That nonsense on the walls?'

The rhetorical questions tumbled out. She neither smoked nor thought of smoking as she recounted the appalling Christmas night in 1958. Are judges so infantile, she demanded, so flabbergasted if a woman says she was in bed with someone? And why does the word 'lover' unhinge them?

Such a confession, question upon question like this, Elias had never heard before. He listened and watched, filling in the gaps for himself, as she went on and on, freely, almost casually, and nearer and nearer to the Wailing Wall. 'Yesterday,' she told the major, 'I was in bed with someone else.' In broken phrases she said the same thing now, and continued in the same detached, indifferent vein.

The scent of her. Intermittently it permeated and overcame the police-and-prison-cell atmosphere.

'Silly of me.' She spoke to the major, not Elias, in the silence following her disclosure. It was a silly thing to do.' And that was all she could say, for the man was dearer than life to her now she had deceived him. He said, after a moment, 'With whom, may one ask? Anyone I know?'

Framed in the cell door, muffled in his overcoat, Elias tried to imagine the kindly tone of the enquiries. With whom? said Dantas. How often? And how was the technique? Until, her resolution and her confidence alike undermined, she threw herself at him and burst into tears.

'What have I done? My God, my darling what have I done?'

'Repentence moves people,' she was saying. 'I thought I'd tell him what happened, the whole thing, and I suppose I said too much. Why not, though? Who hasn't something to be sorry for? If a woman's sorry it would please a person, you'd think. An extenuating circumstance. But not one I should mention in court, you can forget that.'

'You' can forget it? He could? Elias suspected, yet again, that she was talking at him – at him, Graveyard – and it put him out of countenance immediately. He saw her, clinging wildly to the major, sobbing, 'My darling, my darling, what have I done?' But he also saw her in a new light; the Peacock Girl could have unfortunate affaires, and here one must be cautious. Quite another light, and do not be misled. She sheds a skin, and there beneath is Mary Magdelene, the siren tears, the lover's pardon. *Errare humanum est.* This is the real scenario.

Then, a twist to the plot. Infuriated by this drama of infidelity and remorse the major, a pastor chastising an errant lamb, hits her, hard. So hard, and so unexpectedly, that she is knocked off balance and crumples at his feet.

'You whore. In bed with some other bugger, and you come crawling to see what I'll do about it. You little shit.'

Or words to that effect. Shit and whore, certainly.

'If he hadn't hit me,' Mena said, 'I shouldn't have been in such a state. That woman complains he was shouting, and hitting me, but all that bothers her is what I wrote on the walls. What's on the wall is monstrous – the rest was only extra nuisance.'

Her vague sentences in fact contained the literal truth, though one had to pay attention and interpret. She implied more than she spoke, as was her way, and again Elias filled in, from what he knew of Dantas, and from inherent probability. Dirty whore. Shit. Bitch. Words to that effect.

For the source of the graffiti was clear, without the aid of second sight. These were the phrases which echoed in her brain when the major flung out of the room and took his grievances to bed, leaving her, with her face bruised and bleeding, hemmed in by staring walls, and things, and furniture.

It was then she rushed at those confining walls, the doors and windows, with a biro, and on every space there was wrote I AM A FILTHY WHORE, A FILTHY WHORE, where anyone could read. She wrote in the sitting-room, round the hall and in the corridor, finishing up in the bathroom, gasping and retching over the wash-basin.

Ha! Admiring herself in the glass, no doubt! Elias at his most sardonic. But Mena was in flight from herself. She had scrawled her own infamy along the walls like a madwoman, and when she raised her head a stranger looked at her. That face, streaky with blood, could not be hers. Rather than pity it, she attempted savagely to obliterate it, but the biro skidded uselessly, with a noise of grinding teeth.

'Their precious walls!' she said. 'A few scribbles on the walls, and one door, maybe, and that's what the judges, or whoever, call a pigsty?'

'I can't say. I'm not a judge.'

'As for that landlady woman, she can do what she likes. My God! I was washing walls before I had any clothes on next morning, the minute I was out of bed. I didn't want to see the mess, believe me. Well, it'll all come clean for her in court – cleaner than I could get it, apparently. Isn't that enough for her?'

'Before I had any clothes on.' Naked from the major's arms and frantically washing walls. And the major sleeping like a log, thoroughly mollified by love-making. Not that she said so, but she didn't have to. Elias knew it, because of what she was. After the storm of jealousy, the storm of passion – the sequence, it was universally acknowledged, upon which depended happiness and harmony. (Another of the inspector's mottoes: Trust in God, keep copulating, and life takes care of itself.)

Mena had finished. Looking steadily at him, she lit a cigarette and threw the match away.

'That satisfies you?'

Bitch, she was. He pulled his scarf straight.

'We have a simple complaint of damage to property,' he said. 'Other details are irrelevant.'

Still she looked at him.

Bitch, playing her bitchy games. All these intimate revelations, and her manner of telling them, were calculated insults. Damn woman with her whore's-garret scent, her femininity, humiliating him on purpose. He was to see what she thought of him, feel inadequate; which was why she slouched about practically naked in front of him, too.

'I repeat, material damage only. You are to choose a plea of guilty or not guilty. You understand?'

'Of course. I'll plead guilty. It should save you complications.' She twiddled her hair in her fingers.

'Complications! To crown everything, I've got the curse. And that's no fun, I tell you.'

## The High Yellow Walls

'I have interviewed the lawyer, Graveyard, and he was, if I say it myself, most communicative. My method at these interviews is to give a suspect plenty of rope while – if I may so phrase it – getting under his skin. And the man talked; he talked! I am convinced, after our talk, that basically he is against the major. There is a genuine aversion, I could see. Oh, God, that's three of the buggers in three minutes – if I don't change this office I cannot answer for my reason! To continue. Gama e Sá was – unknown to you, perhaps – an old, a very old, acquaintance of the major. Many years ago – with friends and connections in common. And the major's conduct stemmed, in his opinion, from what we may term destructive impulses.'

'I found a passage,' said Elias, 'in a novel the corporal was reading. "He led a lost cause, and he was not afraid of God's thunderbolts." That's a rare old muddle for you: the corporal underlines something, and somebody adopts the idea.'

Otero pressed on.

'The arrogance, the lawyer says, was a manifestation of this destructive impulse, shifting from fanatic dedication to the coldest cruelty – a classic example of the meeting of extremes. And he dearly loved to play the avenging angel. He was posted to India at the beginning of the terrorist troubles, and within days he'd put the cookhouse sergeant in jankers and disciplined one of his junior officers. First attack on home ground, with a vengeance! What's more, he loved to play Egas Moniz* on occasion. After some routine cock-up, he marches in to the CO requiring to be punished, as if it had been his fault.'

'Our history has its quota of these martyrs – which nobody can deny. He wouldn't deny it; him at the back there.'

'Who? Where?' Otero pivoted in his chair. 'Graveyard, I wish you would be serious.'

He relaxed, stroked his walrus-drooping auburn moustache, and adopted his theorising expression.

'I ask you. Fellow of – what? Fifty, was he? – enjoys a drink, always in the thick of one thing or other, very intelligent, very pleasant, they say – and he's killing himself, and knows it.'

'Lovely death, though, killing himself with that girl.' Elias was toying with an eraser on the superintendent's desk. It was marked Elephant 101. Why elephant? Rubber was from Brazil, where they had no elephants. It was alligators in Brazil.

'All you see is bed, bed, bed, as if bed were his only battlefield. But yes, the girl.' A girl like Mena was a status-symbol for a man, and Otero was a man for status-symbols. 'A superb body, to start with – not something you see every day of the week. And why?' Breeding was the answer. That combination of green eyes and black hair betokens the most intensive breeding. Pedigree it is that produces the thoroughbred. Portuguese women, short in the leg and small-minded, had no pedigree.

'Poor souls,' Elias concurred. 'When I pray, I pray for them.'

Otero, warming to the subject, said that Portuguese women were a lesson against lust; he blamed the diet, and extraneous causes. But Mena – one look was enough. He felt – purely on intuition – that Mena's attractions would be inexhaustible. The more water you drew from the well, the thirstier you got: a forced image, but it might convey his meaning. No wonder if the major – fifty, was he? jaded with years of experience, had problems. Advisedly Elias

---

* Egas Moniz, the Portuguese Regulus, stood surety for an oath to Alfonso VII of León in 1127, and when the oath was broken appeared before the King with a rope round his neck. Alfonso pardoned him.

spoke of a battlefield, but they could not assume that the battle was over the major's deficiencies, nor that these were the whole explanation. That they existed he, Otero, would unhesitatingly agree, but how seldom was the value of such failures acknowledged! He smiled a superior smile. The failure in bed – a crushing experience for a man – is extremely complicated. Well, we all know, don't we? But women, what with the maternal instinct, and the protective instinct and so on and so forth – women stay put. They don't leave you, after that. Is this the rule? you may ask. Is this invariable?

'No,' said Elias, 'I didn't ask.'

'No, but I am telling you. A man, in such circumstances, stays, not because of male pride but because his pride is lost. He'll do – if I may so phrase it – anything required of him. What woman is going to refuse?'

Elias replaced the eraser on the desk.

'So that's your Dantas theory? Out-of-commission promoted to Major Attraction?'

'Why not? She was besotted with him, wasn't she? And the sperm report proves he was firing on all cylinders. Top gear and crashing the lights, eh?'

Blue flashes, ululating siren.

'That report was the PIDE's idea of a joke,' said Elias, as the superintendent cried, 'Good God, another of them! Lisbon! Nowhere else would they put police headquarters bang next door to the bloody hospitals! Some damn prisoner will leap through that window one fine day, and we'll go crashing after him, head-on into a sodding ambulance, you see if we don't.'

'In this land of ours the traffic gets worse and its only the villains nicking cars who try to solve the problem. I have that on the authority of a most reliable traffic-cop.'

'Have you? Man with one arm, I suppose?'

'Cast in one eye. And he can't tell red from green.'

'Tchah!' said Otero, and squirmed deeper into his chair with irritation.

This office, Elias was thinking, is too bare and too empty. Maybe it was the false grandeur of two armchairs in imitation leather, but something was wrong somewhere. The chairs, and the dominant ginger moustache, suggested the waiting-room in a house of assignation, with the files and the Salazar portrait there for camouflage. The superintendent, selecting a cigarette with that studied gesture, might be killing ten minutes before the advent of a scented female, all hips, who could come swaying in. 'Oh, do forgive me, Senhor Doutor, I've been unavoidably delayed . . .'

'And if I were to tell you, Graveyard, as an item of information merely, that the major had a friend in the PIDE?'

Chin well up, the superintendent lifted a cigarette to his lips. (He'll never light it. It'll roll round in that moustache until the cows come home.)

'If I were to tell you that, when the lawyer visited him, there was among the prisoners, a man named Casimiro Monteiro – of whom you may have heard – and that this Monteiro was an old friend from the major's days in India?* True, I assure you. Gama e Sá had seen him at political trials. He was a PIDE thug – what they call a gorilla.'

Polaroids and an unlit cigarette bestowed – or so the superinten-dent hoped – panache; a relaxed sophistication. The man's anony-mity, he conceded, was the puzzle. How did this highly distinctive thug – literally a hulking great King Kong – infiltrate, and arouse no suspicion in the prisoners?

'Oh, I can see him, I can see him!' said Elias.

'How? How can anyone see anything in this complexity?'

'King Kong, in India. I can see him chopping terrorists off at the ankles, and playing Strauss waltzes on the gramophone.'

'Oh, yes?' Otero paused briefly, and continued. 'But there is another King Kong in the major's life, a different type, from another part of the jungle. Mozambique,' he added, by way of localising this new character, 'Night-clubs, smuggling; and the lawyer says he owned half the taxis in Lourenço Marques. A racketeer, a menace – and a racist, though he lived for years with a mulatto woman and never bothered with anyone else. Mulatto woman, mulatto kids, and a racist – can you imagine?'

'Say no more. The major hopped it with the woman and left him to get his brood bleached.'

'Graveyard – please.' Otero, cigarette dangling, was unamused. 'The woman had nothing to do with it. Dantas had a set-to in a bar; there were two half-castes and he wouldn't have them bullied.

* Casimiro Teles Monteiro was to be one of the assassins of General Humberto Delgado.

124

According to the lawyer, this Bandarra was leaning over the bar, trigger-happy, with a 32 pointed at the major.'

'That was King Kong?'

'King Kong. His name was Bandarra. He leaned across, with this gun at the major's forehead – and apparently he was one who shot first and asked questions afterwards. And Dantas ignored him. He may not have been in the Wild West, the major, but he had some of the gimmicks. He takes a flower from a vase on the bar – very precisely, with his finger and thumb – and puts it in his coat. I'm not exaggerating, this is what the lawyer saw. Then he taps the flower in his buttonhole and in that condescending voice they say he had, tells Bandarra, "Here, you bloody slaver, shoot at this." Doesn't it make you tingle? Two of them, eye to eye, and the gun against the flower! Talk about narrow escapes! Bandarra weakens, lowers the pistol, and the situation's saved.'

'And there I was, thinking human life was worthless in the jungle – a quick kill.'

'Quick kill? No, no. And the night wasn't over.'

Otero lit the cigarette at last and drew on it, for emphasis. As he said, the night was not over, for later on a coloured boy, a well-known local drunk, was found dead. A negro, murdered in the night with a clip of bullets in his belly, and the culprit wasn't far to seek. It had to be Bandarra. The court was satisfied of the fact, and no one doubted – Otero did not doubt – that he had been as drunk as his victim. King Kong, foiled by a flower, will drown his sorrows in rum or any strong liquor that comes to hand. In the event, however, no plea of drunkenness was necessary, for two whites from up-country testified that the negro was an inveterate pilferer and a raider of chicken-runs, and sentence was passed, with unlimited suspension. You see, Graveyard?'

'I see that if Gama e Sá were to tell us what he really knows, he'd be in for more than a suspended sentence.'

'Yes, yes.' Fish-like, the superintendent blew little smoke-rings at the ceiling. 'But we shan't be holding him. The one who has to get a move on is you.'

'Me? Why me?'

'Most certainly you.' More smoke-rings. Mena's detention could not be concealed after the lawyer's release, so – foot on the accelerator, Graveyard. The superintendent concentrated on the rings. Elias did likewise. Foot down and finish, before the PIDE collect her.

125

'Oh, look! Look how steady they are! No draughts in here, I can wave my hand without disturbing them!'

Haloes. A series of tranquil haloes, issuing from his mouth, and one small circlet immobilised before the portrait of Salazar. Just fancy, if the Dove, the Holy Ghost, were to erupt from the carpet, scattering feathers, into that smoky empyrean . . .

'Finish.' Otero spoke through pursed lips, between puffs. 'It's not in our interest to have her here any longer, you understand.'

Elias understood. Not in our interest; commissioner's orders to send her to the womens' gaol as soon as possible, for the PIDE to take charge of her, and of the case. Of course he understood, but it was not of the PIDE he was thinking. The corporal and the architect were still at liberty (there went another ambulance), yet he thought of walls already. High, yellow walls. Not the yellow walls of hospitals, but those within which female prisoners did needlework, exercised in line, passed notes. Was the Peacock Girl to be whisked away when his enquiry was so near conclusion?

'Oh, and that complaint,' Otero said. 'What about it, in the end?'

'Not much. Damage done while under the influence of alcohol. They were deep marks, though. The walls had to be replastered.'

'Well, at least the girl's a willing cleaner. Scrubbing attic floors and washing obscene words off walls, without a stitch on. What you have there, my friend, is an erotic charwoman. Cleaning and special services – it's an entirely new profession.'

'Oh, don't make me laugh, I'm in mourning.'

'Covas, you play the same old record with the needle stuck. All this time you've been drooling over her – jam yesterday, jam tomorrow – you never seem to get anywhere.'

Elias examined his long nail against the light. High, yellow walls, a prison yard, and wardress nuns. One was the actress Elga Liné, whom he had seen in a film-magazine in the rôle of Mariana Alcoforado, the Portuguese Nun, writer of the famous love-letters. But only from a distance was there a resemblance. This nun, though as poised and graceful, had a hard mouth and bristly eyebrows; she would be the dreaded Sister Librarian, said to enjoy her reading *à deux*, while indicating this and that with an instructive finger. Oh, yes, that was her. An inverted Mariana, crouching with relish above her novice-prisoner and breathing prayers up her legs. For her, Mena would be a rare morsel.

Continually the superintendent filled the office with flawless rings of smoke.

There went another ambulance.

# VI

When Elias settled at his living-room table, beside the lizard's cage and the Tagus view, it was eleven o'clock. The strokes came clanging one by one from the cathedral.

He had eaten grilled bream in the dimly-lit Estrela da Limoeiro, looking at the street-door and the bar. The company, at that disenchanted hour, consisted of two ancient ladies in a corner – napkins tucked under their chins, teeth rattling like castanets – and three canaries in a cage, swinging from the ceiling. A poster above the sideboard depicted the national emblem, a cockerel from the potteries of Barcelos.

In his briefcase was an assortment of Dantas papers, but drowsing after his meal he meditated on the fish-skeleton on his plate – whole as a museum fossil – and the miseries of influenza. Now and then he raised two fingers to his spectacles, shut his eyes and dozed off, only to wake immediately, back with the influenza; burdened with an overcoat redolent of mothballs and the wardrobe, feeling like a small turtle in an outsize shell. Then he thought of Mena, telling him about the Night of the Generals; and of other nights – cigarettes in the cell, smoke in the Casa de Vereda. He dozed again, awoke, and saw her as he had left her, with her knees wide and black flames of hair in her armpits. He saw her mouth in the white face. 'And to crown everything, I've got the curse.' Flagrant, superior bitch. She might as well have daubed him with blood from top to toe.

The dining-room juddered as trams rocketed by outside, but the canaries slept on their oscillating perches, heads beneath their wings. The old ladies chomped at the corner table and stealthily licked spoonfuls of preserves from a jar they had brought with them.

'I have no moral obligation to morality,' announced the

restaurant-owner, talking to two customers at the bar. 'It's morality has an obligation to me.' Elias signalled for his bill and had a squirt from his inhaler, gullet yawning at the slumbering canaries. When he sat up the old ladies were brandishing inhalers at him with conspiratorial smiles. 'Us too! Us too!' But theirs were enormous asthma-inhalers, modelled, it seemed, on motor-horns of 1920 vintage.

*Andante, andante.* Walking from the restaurant, he encountered members of the Portuguese Legion affixing posters in the Largo da Sé – PORTUGAL UNITED, PORTUGAL IN INDIA. They were secretive, insubstantial figures, applying paste in quick, bold strokes in the dark, with no one else about; could they be ashamed of their idiotic function?

Posters and slogans, Portuguese troops and Portuguese India: in a leaflet in his briefcase the same material was used, in reverse, to belabour corruption, dubious foreign compacts, the High Command and Salazar. This leaflet, *Corruption in the Armed Forces*, attacked high-ranking officers who betrayed military honour and tradition, who made their shady fortunes from army contracts. Its inflammatory text, to the last comma, was in his mind's eye and sentence after sentence fell into place as he walked home, with the television programme blaring from house to house.

And at home, when he emptied the briefcase, all was exactly as he had recalled it – layout, format, even the type-face. The blessed faculty of memory!

Standing at the table, he scarcely had to read the thing. Elias was proud of the filing-system he carried in the labyrinth of his brain; a system the more valuable for being unwritten and untransferable. It was his while he lived, and could not survive him, but while he lived he possessed total recall. He could recapture features and mannerisms in the camera obscura of the past and see them as though on film. More clearly, perhaps. Memory was the detective's winning card, the ace in his hand; its cultivation, the inspector would say, is the art of arts, and he himself had learned it playing poker. His memory, and the index in his head, were developed in learning to tell cards by touch, from the back, or from the tiniest defects; in noting scores and keeping check of who held what; in observing quirks of behaviour. (One gambler, he remembered, stank of urine when the cards were bad.)

'Meanwhile,' proclaimed the leaflet – and here Elias ran his long fingernail under the lines –

'meanwhile a "man of action", recently escaped from the
Fort at Elvas, has been attempting to incite civilians and
military to rebellion. His proposed armed coup is the plan
of an adventurer and he should be seen for what he is – an
*agent-provocateur* in government pay. *He must be denounced.* His coup, on the margins of the military movement proper, is designed to obstruct the impending vital
confrontation.'

From this paragraph the *Diário da Manhã* – the Daily Grind
with the faceless editors – had dredged the headline,

REBELS DENOUNCED
'A Band of Adventurers'
Say Opposition Groups in Army.

Compliant as ever, and presumably for the good of the nation, the
*Diário* had eliminated all else; the cutting was attached to the
leaflet forwarded by the PIDE, and would be cited in evidence.

It was the leaflet, not the clipping, which Elias found worthy of
attention. You could slide that flimsy sheet under a door, destroy it
in seconds with a lighted match; swallow it if you had to. To this
had come the craft of printing, to this the literature of Portugal.

The Judite had received its copy from its very own commissioner
(Director Judiciaribus), and a repentant printer, so they said,
delivered the first specimen, smelling of ink from the press, to the
PIDE (see official stamp). But who can prove these stories? And – or
so they said – the PIDE, having read it on the quiet, were then too
urgently occupied to do more than stamp it (9th Feb, 60) and stand
by for developments.

It reached the illustrious lawyer. How? From whom? And when?
That would be nice to know. Nor was it with him long, for he
handed it to Mena, who handed it to Dantas, and Dantas, at the end
of the chain, pitched it into the fire. He wasn't angry about it. He
dismissed it calmly as a Communist ploy or a piece of coat-trailing
by the PIDE. Into the fire with it.

And who's to say it wasn't the lawyer's bright idea? Elias looked
at his lizard and the insect relics in the sand at the bottom of the

cage. You'd have been a sizeable alligator by now, my lad, if you were half as bright as a lawyer.

The PIDE stamped the leaflet three days before Habeas Corpus had a copy ready for Mena. Three days. For a detective, that was something to make the whiskers quiver. Did he have it printed, to stampede the major out of the country? 'Well, perhaps he did, perhaps he didn't,' concluded Elias, aloud.

['He gave it to me with no explanation. I seriously wondered whether or not to let the major have it, but then I thought I should.' Mena's statement, in the report.]

And Dantas, luckily for her, didn't explode. He threw it on the fire and only they saw it, though the scene would have been different had she related more fully her conversation with Gama e Sá. As it was, she omitted to mention the idea of quitting the country and, thanks to the architect's doting mother, handed over a sheaf of 1000-escudo notes. How, then, demanded Elias, should Dantas guess that the lawyer was like a cat on hot bricks, anxious to be rid of them, and the sooner the better? Elias demanded, but his lizard was a creature of secrets and silence, and the night beyond the window was silent as the lizard.

He returned to piecing the jottings and notes together. 12th February, he read, 11 a.m., Mena leaves for lawyer's office.

Eleven in the morning. Eleven strokes, not from the cathedral by moonlight, but on the sunny terrace where the major saw her off. Birds were singing after the rain, she said. (Not a terribly useful detail, this, but it showed that winter was over and life stirring.) The house, the trees in sunshine; the birdsong and a scent of pines and rotting leaves where, a week or two later, policemen would be shovelling and tracker-dogs snuffling. ('Here!' 'There!' 'The major!') And Mena, with her bold, bright hair, going up the lane, through the bushes, to arrive

['. . . at approximately 1 o'clock on the 12th, in the office of Dr Gama e Sá, Rua do Ouro, Lisbon. He evinced surprise and displeasure to see her, saying he had clients with him and could do nothing about "further provision" (i.e. of money and documents), owing to the arrest of a businessman named Deveza or Beleza, involved with the Movement; there must in future be minimum contact between "associates" (his word). She could see he was on edge, for he received her with every sign of impatience and did not sit down. She was with him for twenty minutes at most, in a sort of cubby-hole or store-room for documents. Says he did not allude to any diversion of arms from a northern garrison, or elsewhere, and that she neither knew nor knows of this. That she took away no written message, and that Gama e Sá went out twice during the interview, the second time to fetch the leaflet, *Corruption in the Armed Forces* (see above). Extract from report.]

'A difficult situation, very difficult. The major must realise, the major must decide . . .' Habeas Corpus pushing her, resisting, towards the door. 'They must get out, they must get out; it can be arranged. Explain to him. Off you go, now. We have our friends abroad, the struggle can be carried on.'

Elias read, piecing the narrative together. The Night of the Generals, when the lawyer was entered on the major's death-list, would be in the next instalment. He was still on the preliminaries.

[Report: 'Pressed as to what she told the architect Fontenova, witness replied that, in a natural desire to reduce the tension, she concealed part of her conversation with the lawyer; as, for similar reasons, she concealed it from the major, thinking the proposal to leave the country would alarm them. The major told her not to mention the leaflet to the others. When telling the major that Beleza or Deveza (see above) had been arrested she did, however, manage to convey the lawyer's reluctance.']

Elias fancied a cup of warm milk. In the corridor the hum of the refrigerator was so loud that he wondered why he hadn't heard it from the sitting-room, and when he put the kitchen light on the thing jigged about as though smitten with D.T.s, or struck by lightning. He paid no attention and lit the gas.

In the weighing-scales on the table were a fifty-escudo note, a key, and a communication from the daily woman, which he deciphered as the milk boiled. 'Sr santana, cant com monday hospital Day tell you latter Lucinda.'

Under a stool by the hearth was a large mousetrap, sprung but empty (he didn't even bother to look) and, on the tiles above the oven, a large dead fly. Or was it a lump of grease? At a touch of his nail it fell straight down the wall.

(Documents studied by him that evening:
– newspaper cutting referring to activities of *agents provocateurs* in Armed Forces
– report on Ford Taunus, registered number CN–14–01, property of Major Dantas Castro (carbon copy)
– five-page summary of statement by Dr Gama e Sá
– notes and report concerning Filomena Joana Van Niel de Athaíde.)

## The Mice

Mice in the cathedral roof; mice skittering in shrouded furniture; a bedroom light burning, and an open book on the sheet.

'I wandered all these years among
A world of women, seeking you.'

Here in *The Sea Wolf* were echoes from the Casa da Vereda, but how had a near-illiterate plough-boy grasped them? How did Barroca identify and mark out passages which might have been express warnings to the major? 'I wandered all these years' – with the addition of the word 'death', Dantas himself could have written that.

'Death, I have wandered all these years among
A world of women, seeking you.'

It might stand for his last confession, unrecorded in the notes, but underlined already by the corporal.

Elias, hand idle on the bedclothes, thought of an acid-scarred skull, its platinum wig streaming in the wind. And, 'a child,' he thought; and, 'You can fuck liberation, I'm fed up with it.' That's what Mena said.

He saw her knees, raised and wide like the prows of two boats. The room dissolved into walls of rough cement, and there he saw her face. But was it Mena? Before he was sure, her loose dressing-gown parted to reveal the voluptuous body of a blonde with black pubic hair, and he knew – or thought he knew – the summons of caressing fingers, and an intent, even breathing over him, over his loins. Against the erect penis, he knew, was a woman's face. Eyes fixed and blank as when, a child, he had stared at the Four-Dot Saint until he was blind with staring, he abandoned himself to the ascending, descending, ascending rhythm.

Masturbating, he saw with the blind unfocussed vision of someone who is willingly led. Her hand, her face, her mouth, were on him. There was nothing else. He was lightheaded, free and self-forgetting, in a small cabin walled with mirrors; his body a taut arc, the intoxicating, insistent rhythm coursing in the backward-curving penis. The glass walls changed to a transparent windscreen with a driving-mirror and a label with a name on it. Driving up, driving down, springs of a car-seat answering rhythm for rhythm. Mechanically, rhythmically; for ever.

Then he was still. The name floated before him – Ariston Hotel, Barcelona. Name in gold, on a windscreen sticker, on a menu cover. The Ariston Palace. Mena, Melanie. Highly lascivious. Libidinous, if I may so phrase it, *ad libitum*.

Hell, thought Elias on the brink of sleep, that's what Otero said.

Among the dust-sheets sensitive whiskers tested the darkness and quiet for the smallest tremor; then, confident the night was theirs, the mice made a concerted dash into the corridor. As in a shadow-play, they poured up the walls – it was fantastic how they climbed, and how high – and glided on the skirting-boards to invade the room where Reptile, in his glassed-in desert, lived his mystery-life. A huge moon over the Tagus shed an artificial brilliance on the window-frames and sent the elongated shapes of table and barley-sugar-carved cabinet reaching in among the cane-bottomed chairs and sofa. The ceiling, with plaster flowers and central chandelier, had a moon-white dazzle. Next door, his breathing deep and regular, Elias slept.

In the morning, when he awoke to the family photographs – lamented sister, lamented parents – and toured the mousetraps to find each one mortifyingly vacant and his family furniture mortifyingly bestrewn with droppings; when he visited Reptile in his miniature kingdom and greeted the view of the river, the sole reminder of the night was a dried smear on his pyjamas; and this he washed out under the tap.

# Night of the Generals

Mena, in a cloud of cigarette-smoke, described the Night of the Generals.

After confirming what was in the notes so far, she said that on the first or second Saturday of March – she couldn't be certain – her companion (this she corrected to 'the major'), had an appointment somewhere; something to do with politics. Early in the evening, when she and the architect were talking and listening to the radio downstairs, he let himself into the house noiselessly – which was unlike him – and accosted them with,

'Oh, go on – pray go on! I shall be charmed to join the conversation.'

This had been his third or fourth secret meeting, and though she had tried to recall the date she knew only that it was on a Saturday. A Saturday evening; and he came in, said that and started looking round in an odd way. Then, as usual, went to the drinks cupboard where the telephone stood.

'And where's our boy?' he enquired, filling a glass of brandy.

The corporal was in his room, they said.

'Oh, that's nice, very nice.' He looked round again. There was a beauty-box on the floor by Mena's chair.

'What fun! You're planning a party, I declare!'

Item by item he scrutinised the contents, which were more or less as Elias saw them on the shelf above the wash-basin and by no means exotic, though the major chose to regard them as such. He took the Scandale face-pack ('Or it is Standale? No, Stendhal'), smelled it, squeezed the cream onto his finger, and read the instructions, repeating 'mask', 'face-mask', with heavy sarcasm, before putting the tube down in the box.

'Better results with sulphuric acid, my dear.'

He began to stride up and down.

'I'll give you a real face-mask, one of these days. And you won't get it off, either.'

When he was in this mood it was not wise to interfere. He paced and paced, unstoppable; then remembered the corporal, and blew cigarette-smoke at the ceiling. 'And that's convenient, my God it is! Send the bugger to his exercise-books and have the place to yourselves!' But neither she nor the architect rose to the bait.

Dantas, as though at bursting-point, strode like a caged animal. When Mena said she felt ill and was going to bed with a hot-water bottle he wouldn't hear of it. He'd come back too soon, that was all that was wrong with her.

'That's not fair!' protested Fontenova, only to be reprimanded for unfairly deluding the corporal for so long as to his – the corporal's – fate; which was to remain where he was ('not to desert'), unless wishing to attend his own obsequies. But the corporal was the least of the major's worries. To hell with the corporal. 'It's the masks.'

'What are you talking about – masks?'

'Masks, masks. Everyone in this house is thinking of a mask. She is' – indicating Mena. 'She thinks of nothing else, with her war-paint and her fairy-stories. Not that I don't see through her lies. I shall have to be thinking of a mask myself, shall I not?'

To and fro he stalked, trailing smoke.

'Well, I'm preparing my mask. And hers. Wait – wait till my patience really goes!'

Having finished one bottle of brandy, he threw it into the fire and opened another, at prodigious speed. His gestures and utterances were violent and alarming and, to the witness, incomprehensible. An onlooker would have judged him demented – an automaton, rambling hoarsely through clenched teeth about masks and altered faces. Not until he stood over her hissing, 'A new face. I shall need a new face,' did it dawn on Mena that this was not a recent idea, and the face he talked of was his own.

['He in fact spoke of plastic surgery. Merely to test my reaction, as I thought.' Dr Gama e Sá to the police. 9th Nov, 1960.]

'A new face!' he grimaced, bending so closely above her that she was hot and giddy, catching the metallic pungency he had at times. But as suddenly as he had approached her, he pushed her into the chair and resumed his striding. It was fearful, she said, this pound-ing back and forth, back and forth, and the contrasting silence was audible; was visible in their expressions, hers and the architect's.

'Bloody hell!' He wheeled on Fontenova. 'You should have told that oaf what's what. Why didn't you? Where's the problem?'

Fontenova paused before he answered. Problems or not, he said, there were reasons.

'May I be frank, Dantas?'

It was not he, Fontenova, who had enticed the corporal with prospects of crossing the frontier and – intentionally or otherwise – duped him. Nor, as absolutely nothing had happened since, was this the happiest moment for converting him to the Movement. All too probably Barroca, being deceived, would cut and run, or do something as stupid.

Mena said 'deceived', though Fontenova, who watched his words when talking to the major, and that evening was especially careful – said 'coerced'.

Dantas strode and listened, unpersuaded that the other was not, once more, sheltering Barroca, exercising once more the crappy, Daddy's-Boy ethics that made him sick. He, the responsible military leader, had no patience with this milk-and-water nonsense. 'I could shit on it.'

'And I'll tell you what, Fontenova. In your heart of hearts you think – you hope – he'll run. I'm not such a fool I can't see that – or why do you go on cramming French into him? Am I right, Fontenova? Am I right?'

In silence the architect collected his cigarettes and his book, and was almost out of the room when the major added, loudly and distinctly,

'I was with the commodore this afternoon.'

The shock, for Mena, was as though the floor had folded beneath her feet. There was no escape. He must know everything – how could he not? That she had lied to him over the money and the messages, concealed the suggestion that they should leave the country. Everything.

She could remember only her stunned confusion, and the major's voice, from a long way off, announcing that the commodore had provisionally withdrawn. Provisionally? At any second the thunderbolt would fall. 'And you,' he would say. 'Now we come to you.'

But there was no thunderbolt. Of course – Dantas, unaware that Fontenova had a hand in it, would not discuss the deception in his presence. No undermining of morale, that was the rule. The chain of why-and-wherefore was unending.

He talked of politics, and more politics, of contacts postponed and supporters frozen (this seemed to be the term) on orders from the Movement which, for security's sake, must be obeyed. Among those frozen was the lawyer-commodore, who had passed the tidings personally. And there was a general in it somewhere. His name she had forgotten but the fault, whoever he was, was his. He wouldn't give the go-ahead to other officers, and wrecked the scheme.

He was no surprise, this general, for Dantas hated generals. They were a bloody rabble, all the bloody same. Nor had the commodore made a good showing, with his excuses and his 'important secrets', but the major had insisted, had prevailed, and put the fear of God into him. 'Finally he said he'd think again – the crawling bloody tortoise, hiding in his shell.'

'I should doubt it,' was the architect's comment.

'So should I, but he has to make his mind up. Either he stays with us, or he'll be meeting a nasty accident.'

'The fact remains, we're isolated. We have no contacts at all.'

Mena was more or less positive that Dantas spoke, then or later that night, of 'a nasty accident'. No names were bad enough for Gama e Sá, who was a bloody eunuch, a bloody traitor, a capitalist lackey, and much besides.

'And the hours – the hours I've wasted in the bastard's office!'

[From the notes: 'Denial by Dr Gama e Sá. Major Dantas Castro, he says, visited the office on a single occasion, telling the secretary he was a priest on furlough with news of a common friend in Africa. He had no appointment. A short and disagreeable colloquy led to the severing of relations. This in mid-March last. It could not have been on a Saturday, since at weekends he – the lawyer – was at his quinta at Ramal do Ribatejo, as anyone would testify; his wife was convalescing there after a severe illness.']

'And us?'

'Us, Fontenova?' The major clenched his teeth again until the cheek-muscles swelled. 'We are surviving, and he'll have his punishment. He'll have his punishment.'

Definitely, she said, punishment was the word he used, both then and later, when he got round to the generals. Generals, brigadiers – swine and pigs. 'They might impress a blind man with the bloody stars they wear – nobody else.' She had heard it all before.

Ranting on against lily-livered fat-bellies, he filled the smoky room, for her, with a rout of mangy generals, arthritic staff-officers and jumped-up field-marshals who never saw a shot fired in anger.

What she mistook for disparaging laughter now and then was pure revulsion. He was nearer vomiting than laughter.

(Perfidy of Generals.
a) cowardice, e.g. Marshal Carmona, President of the Republic, commits himself to a *coup d'état* to overthrow Salazar, and changes his mind next day,
   cowardice, e.g. Commandant Abrantes Silva, while on active service, halts his troops on the march, assembles them about him and orders them to their knees, saying, 'My children, let us pray!'
b) corruption, e.g. General Pereira Lourenço and his brother, a co-director of the PIDE, purchased the Lisbon printing-firm of Fernandes and cornered contracts for political and government printing.
   corruption, e.g. 'For a million and a half escudos I support your revolt. Otherwise, no.' General Ramires to Captain Fernando Queiroga (1945).
c) practice of denunciation, e.g. General Fernando de Oliveira had 5000 escudos a month, as an informer, from the PIDE. This on top of army pay and his emoluments as Managing Director of the National Soap Company.
   denunciation, e.g. General of the Air Force Alfredo Sintra was an informer for Hitler's Foreign Office.
   denunciation, e.g. General Galvão de Melo engaged in anti-government conspiracy with the connivance of Salazar.

The compliance of Portuguese generals exposes them to mockery and disgrace.' (General Humberto Delgado, in his *Letter to the Generals*.)
   'Generals and brigadiers, equally bad, equally rotten.'
   'Their stars not guiding stars but absolute delusions.'
   – From the major's notebook.)

When Mena went to bed at last the two men, it seemed, were to battle through sleepless hours with a host of generals. The major's voice grew less and less distinct as she lay, open-eyed, between the nightmare and the night.
'Where was that money from, you little cow?'

Her throat was in his grip, his face above her. It was here, the thunderbolt. He wrenched the lamp from the bedside table and shone it at her.

'Tell me – where from? How much have you hung on to? Where is it. Quick – or I'll smash this in your eyes.'

The details of this scene escaped Elias, but he knew what the final transcript said: 'Accused, unable to defend herself, gave him an exact account of what had happened.'

This exact account she had repeated, in expurgation of the past. The architect requested money from his mother for their expenses, to relieve the tension they were under, and for no other purpose. She, Mena, neither kept nor spent any of it; ask him, he would say the same. She could not have added worse fuel to the flames. 'Ask him? Christ, are you both children, do you think I can't see you're in this together?' The lamp was near her skin. He was foaming at the mouth and grinning horribly. It was indescribable.

Then, at an imagined noise, he leapt to the door, in case the others were listening, and Mena, naked as she was, ran past him and into the bathroom. For half an hour she stayed there. Her face was burning and swollen, she was close to fainting and had to sit on the lavatory.

Until the shot. Yes, she heard a shot. He might have killed himself, or be settling scores with the architect. No, she never thought of the corporal, only the architect. But he was lying, wreathed in tobacco-smoke, on the bed in their room, pistol aimed at her blonde wig on the chest-of-drawers; the bullet had grazed the pottery cat and lodged in the wall.

'No cause for alarm,' he said with a smile like ice. 'I shan't be killing you. A bottle of acid, that'll do for you.'

It was then that the corporal and the architect came to the bedroom door, but left without speaking.

'And there you are,' Mena concluded. She corrected the words 'companion', 'Scandale' and 'Standale'. Having no more to add, she stubbed her cigarette in the tin plate and said she would sign the statement.

Elias flapped a hand to disperse the clinging smoke.

## Off to the Brothel, Mamma

The moon shone bright on Criminal Police headquarters (or, as the poem had it, 'was high in the mansion of death'), when Elias walked homeward. Lapped in quiet – with no prostitutes about, and certainly no police, you wouldn't know the district at this time of night – men with welders' masks and acetylene torches conjured sparks from tramless lines in Rua Gomes Freire.

The habitual, hackneyed route was through the Largo Martim Noniz and the Rua da Madalena, with its Appliances, to the Sé – the old cathedral – and so to the flat, and Reptile, the river view, the photographs of beloved parents and sister. Latterly, though, he had been making a stop in the Socorro quarter, at the Bolero Bar: an angled door and ogrish doorman, and beer-fumes within to galvanise the dead. All you descried was an oscillation of accordions, each instrument lettered in spangled silver to spell out HARMONY.

'The Bolero Bar? Never heard of it,' said Otero.

'A low, low dive. Syphilitics only. I found it quite by chance.'

In the course of the Dantas investigations the inspector, as we now know, did much more than appears in the documents, and covered a lot more ground. The Bolero, as he told the superintendent, was where he saw Mena's friend and fellow-student, Norah. 'Quite by chance' is a matter of opinion.

'That's him – that clown from the Bolero,' Norah said to the defence counsel on the first day of the hearing. Elias had taken her original statement at headquarters ('Thank the Lord,' she must have thought, 'I don't have to see him again'), and she recognised him when, to her annoyance, he began to frequent the bar she and her coterie patronised in the evenings; shadowing her, obviously, though why was anybody's guess. Did the idiot expect Mena – of whose detention Norah was ignorant – to be hiding in the Bolero Bar, for heaven's sake? Or was he plaguing her simply because she was Mena's friend.

His arrival had been telegraphed from table to table when he bumbled myopically through the door and cannoned against a whore with a foaming glass of beer at the bar. This whore, a good hater with a long memory, had once tangled with the Judite over a stabbing affray, and immediately she signalled to her sisters and their protectors. But Elias looked fish-eyed and dim, as though he hadn't noticed, and stood observing the table shared by Norah and her group. They were progressive drop-outs, one supposed: girls dressed anyhow and dissident young men from decent families, in company with the statutary frank and honest strumpet as star guest, and the more dissipated of the two underworld characters known as the Brothers Karamazov. The accordions spelled *HARMONY* in silver letters; emotionally the blind accordionists rendered *Only You*.

'The motive,' pronounced Otero, 'is retaliation. When these classy bitches socialise with whores, they're reacting against their respectable mothers at home.'

Over her whisky, Norah rapidly spotted the inspector among the lost sheep in this unlovely den. One night, two nights, she saw him there. On the third night he received a look of withering disgust. You *ghastly* man, it said.

Dreary and comatose, he drooped by the bar like an exhausted mosquito at rest, while near him a couple of street-walkers pawed each other – to provoke him, perhaps. One was pregnant. The other patted her on the belly.

'It'll be a girl, and it'll be the image of me.'

The pregnant street-walker looked down and answered solemnly.

'You're right, there, love, you're right.'

God, what a life! Elias was thinking.

From Norah's table the waves of antipathy were overwhelming. For her and her friends he was the *flic*, the bad news, the bastard who was after Mena, sleuthing round to see what he could see. They froze and excluded him as an obnoxious interloper; as though, inoffensive and distant as he was, he stank. They – Norah and her friends – smelled, as Mena did, of Balmain and *Sauvage*, and their scents blended happily with the whores' deodorants and the sour reek of the drunks. The message was that whores and drunks were more authentic, and more interesting, than any drudging factotum of outraged morality. That was the message, that the notice served, as mutinous youth defied the unpretentious man-on-duty and the accordions vibrated. The heartening logo, *HARMONY*, seemed more like a lamentation, the music from the rostrum a wailing of blind Apostles, of players contemplating eternity with sightless eyes.

'Norah d'Almeida,' reported Elias, 'is a fallen woman. Almost one of the sisterhood. Teaches all day and on the town all night. Culture on an endless belt, as you might say.'

'Culture nothing, Graveyard. It's a cleansing process. They indulge in low life because they're ashamed of the life their parents lead.'

The superintendent had not been to the Bolero, but the Texas and the Grego, which he knew, were similar. The same cineclub clientèle, the same little whores with their anecdotes of repetitious adventure. And there's no limit to their undertakings, he said. The Magdalen's a saint, isn't she?

Elias agreed, reflectively, as to the cleansing process.

' "Cleansing by filth" is what she said – Norah. "Pasteurise the place with shit". It's in her statement. And I can't see that she either objected, or was for doing it by proxy.'

Otero laughed.

'Mothers of Portugal, your daughters are in the whorehouse – why not go and join them? Wouldn't you say, Graveyard?'

*Admitted to the Penitenciary in Lisbon, 2nd May, 11.30 a.m.:*
*RENATO MANUEL FONTENOVA SARMENTO, 25, profes-*
*sion, architect; and BERNARDINO BARROCA, 22, corporal,*
*army number 3976/57. Both unmarried, both deserters from the*
*Portuguese Army. Accompanied by Detective-Sergeant Silvino*
*Saraiva Roque of the Criminal Police, with two constables; war-*
*rants exhibited. In compliance with regulations, prisoners were*
*dispossessed of clothing and belongings, had their heads shaved,*
*and were put in solitary confinement.*

They had been arrested early that morning at the Marina Motel
at Praia Azul, in the Algarve, by a GNR detachment under Lt
Roma. In a dawn like something out of a Pacific Islands travelogue
– one star paling in the sky, beach glimmering honey-gold, and a
satin-smooth sea – the GNR occupied the approaches to the
building. Roque and his constables were in position with a police-
waggon. You could hear the farmyard cocks crowing.

Gradually the whitewashed walls of the Motel took the increasing light; the shutters of slatted, varnished wood emerged, the
dwarf-palm fans, the sapphire-blue tiles of an empty swimming-
pool. And Roque glimpsed other, hitherto concealed, features of
the landscape, such as soldiers crawling beyond the ragged agave
plants, a walkie-talkie between the carob trees, a dog's pricked
ears.

The Motel was shut (May was too early for the cheaper tourist-
trade) but a burst of machine-gun fire signalling the attack brought
the manager to the doorway with his hands up and his wife behind
him, and it was plain sailing thereafter. The two men, who must
have slept in their clothes, came out onto the terrace fully dressed
and shouting that they were unarmed.

Mission accomplished. On what Elias would call the underlying
negotiations history is dumb; they are secrets of the Criminal
Police, and heaven help anyone who tattles. It is, however, known
that the architect was awaiting money from a friend in Lisbon, and
that the hotel manager was in a smuggling-ring and had a police
record. It is known he dabbled in currency and the sale of land, and
ran such minor tourist-attractions as a fleet of donkeys for rural
expeditions; and that he passed off his two refugees as casual help,
hired to clean the rooms and do the garden. He was arrested with
them, said what he had to say to the police, and was home in
twenty-four hours. The circumstances are known. Also to be noted

is the fact that May the First was Labour Day, when the PIDE and the GNR had their eye on the fish-canneries. There were strikes, and too many policemen about, and too little money.

The smuggler's trade is neither patriotic nor scrupulous. Roque was able to talk to somebody. The Judite gave somebody its blessing, and that somebody had a word with someone else. The Motel was rid of its undesirable guests. And all on gentleman's agreement; a detective need not sign these things over an official stamp ...

. . . and a smuggler's word, said Roque, is a smuggler's bond. His – Roque's – lifelong motto, was Play your fish and reward the penitent informer, and in transactions with smugglers and offenders by the seashore he had proved there was no better policy. He had quartered the territory from the rugged Spanish frontier to land's end and the Western Ocean (to quote a very fancy poet whose eye was fixed exclusively on the western ocean). He followed the Algarve coast by the fleecy, rippling waves, from bar to bar; small bars where you bought marijuana, and bars where haggard ladies peddled heroin. (Detection widened your horizons and taught you the way around, never say it didn't.) He had moved about. He was seen to move about. And in God's good time he was presented with the architect and the corporal on a plate.

No figure of speech, this, for on a plated salver the maidservant in a pension had offered them, as a surprise packet, with his bill one evening. Weeks he had wasted by the rippling waves, and as he sat at leisure on a balcony there came an envelope addressed to The Criminal Police (By Hand), and the search was over. Corporal and architect entered the pension, two butterflies pinned to an anonymous letter, delivered on a lordly dish.

'You're babbling, my boy,' said Elias. 'Is something worrying you?'

From the tone of the letter, Roque continued, it must have been from several co-operating smugglers, not a loner with a grudge. No civilised kangaroo will go frontier-hopping by itself, and certainly not without giving a friend a lift in its pouch; his knowledge of the smuggling fraternity was limited, but that much he knew. Yet why had they turned to him, and not to the local customs officers?

'You, with your rose-coloured spectacles. Who says they didn't turn to the local officers, before you had their little note?'

'May,' said Roque, 'and the clover needs cutting already.'

'Clover? What do you mean, clover?'

'It was the corporal. Mile after mile to Lisbon he kept on – they ought to cut the clover.'

'As I said, you're babbling. Verbal diarrhoea. You have verbal diarrhoea because they've pinched your prisoners.'

'Me? Verbal diarrhoea? I tell you what, Chief – sod the PIDE. Sons of bitches. Sod the bitches, too.'

'Tall order, my boy. There are hundreds of 'em.'

'I hope they have their bloody hands full with prisoners; and I hope they have a ball with the two I've produced for them.'

'On a plate, remember.'

Roque shrugged. 'Bugger it,' he said.

'Now, now. It's been first-class experience. It's extended your horizons.'

'Well, yes. The women in the Algarve, Chief —! And the almond-blossom's incredible; and the snacks they eat, and that medlar liqueur — you should taste it! Tourists are the target, of course. Even the donkey-dung is worth its weight in gold, due to tourism. Different from the Alentejo. Nothing there that I could see, though the corporal saw these fields of clover. How he could sit there, on his way to prison, nattering about farm work!'

On the inspector's desk was the PIDE report about the Ford Taunus, but instead of reading it he looked through his thick glasses at Roque.

'Jealousy as a motive for the crime,' he said. 'The architect was jealous. Where did you get that notion? Anything you heard on the journey?'

## Day's End. 10.30 p.m.

Elias was co-ordinating his notes, though some of the dates were still unverified. Slotting dates together is the detective's supreme satisfaction; and how else can we see whether the Minerva Wardrobes priest is in or out of step with this misguided girl?

Let's try again. Check the days and wrestle with the calendar while we have time and opportunity.

The first unverified date was that of the Night of the Generals, a Saturday.

The Night of the Generals perplexed Elias. Dantas was away all afternoon, and in the evening said he had met the lawyer. Something wrong there, for the lawyer was in the Ribatejo at the weekends, with his wife. And though the major spoke of several meetings ('the hours I've wasted in the bastard's office'), he had seen Gama e Sá no more than once since the escape from Elvas. Yet he did go somewhere, dressed as a priest, with a revolver in his pocket, and must have had some purpose. But where did he go, and whom did he see? The inspector could only think that these confessional errands were perhaps not such as Father Dantas would willingly confess to.

Second unverified date: that of his actual meeting with Habeas Corpus.

Indisputably, there was one, but the major had not mentioned it, nor its unsatisfactory results. He was saving all that for the grand Saturday showdown when he lumped the lawyer and the generals together as traitors and hammered them till the sparks flew. The jackal Santos Costa, Botelho Moniz, Craveiro Lopes – to each his just deserts. (And each, with his evil deeds, was listed in the notebook.)

Half-past ten by the pocket-watch, and the Parque Mayer girls would be entertaining the second wave of customers. In a few moments, a visit to the Peacock Girl in her cell . . . That was a shrewd notion Roque had – jealousy.

Third date undecided: when did the major say, 'That's where she'll be going?'

When Fontenova told her this she shook from head to foot. Dantas had planned her grave. 'There, that's where she'll be going,' he said, walking in the wood on, so Fontenova claimed, the day before the murder. But Mena herself now doubted it. The major spent his last days in the sitting-room, playing cards – patience and *crapaud* – alone, and the conversation in the pinewood was improbable. So was there an intended grave, or had Fontenova imagined it? Yet why should he lie, unless further to excuse the crime? She knew only that the major, in the last days, played cards in the sitting-room, alone.

Elias shut his door, his mind on Roque and the jealousy theory.

No one in the corridors, cleaning-women in the offices; a cavalcade of vacuums, charging across the carpets. To the basement, to the confessional, at an hour when reasonable folk were in their beds. Tonight he knocked on the door with the flat of his hand and called 'Get up!' as though bringing her urgent news. A gigantic yawn, as he waited, threatened to dislocate his jaw. Blank cell-doors to the left, no one on the right. He put his eye to the spy-hole.

There she was. She had pushed the blankets down and knelt, in a pair of briefs, hiding her breasts with her rolled night-dress. (She feared the spy-hole, as all prisoners did.) With the other hand she reached for a shirt and slipped it over her head; then swung her feet to the floor and sat for a second, as if to gain control.

She stood, very straight, in her bare feet and he saw the magnificent thighs, and buttocks that were not inert, but as much alive as the rest of her. She stooped, and the long hair swept from the firm springing curve of her neck. She turned, sideways to him, lifting her jeans to eye-level against the light, and pulled them on. The little sisters – buttocks in prison-language – rose and fell, and her spine was supple and flowing.

Elias, clamped to the spy-hole, had her in a tiny circle of vision. He had her there, he saw her as she was: asking, with a body like that, for the deep, sinking thrust, for spurting semen, thick and heavy. Scorching and saturating from her eyes to her arse, that's what she wanted, penetrating to the backbone until she yelled for her mother – More, more, and Yes, yes, and so on and so forth. Even in the distant, tiny circle the bitch, the bitch, assailed you.

She had her jeans on; was bigger as she neared the door (Elias, outside, stepped back from it), then sat again on the bunk with one foot on the coverlet, as if she were prodding a thorn, or a blister or something. That would do. He turned the key and came in.

'We've caught them,' he announced from his chair by the washbasin.

She hugged her leg, chin on her knee, and said nothing.

'We had no trouble with them, no violence. The PIDE have them in custody. I can't tell you any more.'

Water was dripping feebly into the basin. He tightened the tap, to no avail.

'A case must go through the normal channels, so yours, too, will now go to the PIDE.'

'Channels.' Mena felt behind her for cigarettes and matches. 'Ridiculous way to put it.'

'You are prepared, I trust, for certain questions from them?'

He crossed one leg over the other. Lumpy socks, drab grey and due for a wash, sagged onto his shoes. He uncrossed his legs.

Mena smoked, and hugged her knee.

'It won't be much – personal questions, mainly. Mud-slinging, to discredit you.'

He had a paper to show her.

'This sort of thing. The major's car.'

'The car?'

'They ordered a report. You can see the line they'll take.'

'Heavens above,' she said, 'what are you talking about? What about the car?'

'Traces of sperm,' said Elias. 'They have a fair amount of

compromising evidence. Compromising for you. Here you are – read this.'

She waved it away, hugging her knees more tightly.

'Listen. He and I were lovers. Lovers – you understand?'

She was still and inward-looking, speaking in a low voice, slowly, with the whispy smoke curling from her cigarette.

'Lovers,' she repeated, freeing her leg and sitting upright on her bunk against the wall, as if defying the two thick, vigilant lenses; and the whole atmosphere altered.

The inspector clicked his nail, ran it over his bald head, and changed the subject.

'Norah. Norah d'Almeida?' he said.

'A friend of mine, yes. She's not in their report?'

'She might be, she might be. If she were in his car, she would be. Was she in his car?'

Wearily, Mena replied, 'A report! My God, they knew the terms we were on!'

She faced him, as though she wished to see, and be seen by, him yet more directly.

'Lovers, you can tell them. He and I were lovers, if that's what they want to hear. And we made love all ways, you can tell them that. In the car and out of the car, if they're interested.'

Cool, detached, she was talking, at a far remove, to someone who didn't matter.

'All ways.' And she went on, in the same contemptuous whisper. This catalogue, from the queenly girl of the peacock picture! That she could say such things, in such a tranquil voice, and with that innocent face!

He fidgeted in his chair, but Mena would not be interrupted. Whoever wrote your report, she said, they're living in a world of their own. They haven't a clue what happens in this town, in cars, and lifts. Oh, yes, lifts! They'd never imagine! And restaurants. No, she said, I didn't believe it either, what happens at restaurant tables. And that goes for museums, too, and under staircases, and I know people – nice people – who behave like this. They couldn't be nicer, or more normal, but that's what they fancy. And on the beach, too. Early-morning mist, with fishermen at work, and bathers and whatnot, and making love in water up to their waists. Yes, yes, I'll come to your questions in a minute. Now it's this report I'm answering, since you have it with you.

149

'Please,' said Elias, 'please. If you think it's in the least relevant.'

'Relevant? It's more than relevant. Anything you want to know – where, and how, and anything. Hell, it might be useful for those little beasts with their report. Once we took a prostitute in the car, what about that? A whore off the beat. And she sat in the car and I sat behind, in my dark glasses. And whether it was a threesome or whether it wasn't couldn't matter less. But I do hope I'm clarifying the report.'

Behind his forbidding spectacles Elias envisaged the connivance, the intimate contacts, the manipulation. In cinemas and restaurants and luxury hotels, on dirty weekends in Barcelona. The naked foot that sought another foot beneath the table; the dive for the lost napkin and the mouth, primed with wine, that met the ready penis – a mere swoop among the napery, but unerringly on target. These, and other manoeuvres, she hinted at; the thousand and one stratagems of lovers hell-bent on destruction.

He listened. The bitch, with her cool, poised manner and the velvet in her voice. Only later did he perceive that this Mena – Melanie, the Peacock Girl with high-piled hair, was evoking an image of the major. That the orgiastic lunacy mirrored his macho self-glorification, his 'Do this, do that,' and her Yes, yes, to everything; his inordinate appetite. She stopped, and looked at the inspector calmly.

'Is that it?' he asked.

She glanced round the cell.

'Those tablets on the shelf. Would you pass them, please?'

He hesitated, then passed the aspirin from the shelf over the wash-basin. There was no acknowledgement.

'Thank-you,' he prompted.

'Oh, sorry – yes. Thank-you.'

She folded her arms, glanced at the walls again, and at the ceiling; pressed a hand to her temple, and stood up.

'Might I ask you to leave? Then I could go to bed. I have an awful migraine.'

Elias stroked his scanty hair. Migraine; oh, yes, that would be her excuse to the major. Neverthless, he went.

His dream that night haunted him to the day he died.

# Dream

Long corridors, glacial brilliance, and walls of merchandise, as in a supermarket. A hospital; gloss on the floors, and drifting, silent crowds. Silent and slow, with supermarket trolleys. No – empty perambulators. A procession of bereaved parents, traversing the long museum corridors.

Unsure at first what he was doing there, Elias found he was following a woman with blue-tinted hair. She wasn't a shopper (nobody was shopping; they all sauntered by, eyes front), and her bag, with AIRPORT written on it, was unique among the burnished perambulators. The walls, stacked with boxes, went on for ever, curving and converging as they do in the elevated observation-mirrors of a supermarket, and the boxes were labelled BRONCHITIS DETERGENT, BRONCHITIS DETERGENT, BRONCHITIS DETERGENT. Ridiculous way to put it, he was telling himself in his sleep, when the corridor became a subway platform, shelves on one side and on the other a train going through, with faces at the windows; transfixed, framed in rectangles of glass, an interminable gallery of police-photographs on the move.

The woman walked between the train and the shelves. Shelves of pigs' heads, yellow and smiling. Elias had seen such heads – glazed with egg-yolk, he assumed – in a Chinese butcher's window in a crime-film. Had he not been here in an old dream, he wondered? The woman stopped short by the wall of pigs' heads and he lurked out of sight, knowing she would turn. Her hair wasn't blue, he noticed, but had steely lights in it, like metal, or the moon. Now – now, very slowly, she made a tiny turn left, then right, to see if she were spied on, and covertly took something from the plastic carrier.

As she walked back towards him he pretended to blow his nose, to avoid recognition, but she passed him with her head high, and was Mena. Mena, amusedly aware of being followed. He was unsurprised at this.

Hastening to where she had left whatever it was, he saw at once, among the pigs' heads, a pottery cat with a curl of hair. He touched the curl, and it was human hair. He hurried after Mena, but she was out of sight and the further he sought the more deserted grew this cold, brilliant world of vacant passages and glassy, blinding floor. In the warren of lights and reflexions he lost his sense of distance and direction, but hurried on until, in an unpeopled courtyard, he saw an escalator snaking upwards and a booth for automatic photographs. He saw what this was, and that, beyond its dimly illuminated window, Mena sat motionless, as though posing for the camera, with an open book on her lap.

On again, riding the almost perpendicular escalator to a moonlit grove of dwarf pines with rags fluttering on the branches. There was a gate, and a shed through whose door was revealed a gilded chest on which stood a pottery cat. No, he thought, the cat doesn't suit the furniture.

The entire shed — a spacious public lavatory, perhaps? — was lined with gleaming tiles and a bucket in the middle brimmed with worm-like cigarette-butts. Or were they worms? Before he could check, he felt there was someone behind him and turned to see his sister, naked, dignified, and earnestly staring at him. Stark naked and very tall, much taller than he would have said she was. Her hair was a faded silvery aluminium colour, and the pubis jetblack — a black flame quivering on a waxen body.

'Just look,' she said, gyrating placidly. 'We're all like this at the Bolero Bar.' From neck to haunches ran a line of scaly white scars.

These scars appalled Elias, He could not see what they were, whether warts or ulcerations, but they suggested witchcraft, the resigned acceptance of ritual torment. That fatalism, and the whiteness, chilled and horrified him.

. . . he was a dead man, forgotten in his bed, yet he had woken with a shock of shame and remorse. His sister would not leave him. She guarded him in the night and the dream continued, or recurred, with neither rhyme nor reason, fitfully. 'We're all like this at the Bolero.' Again the cabin for automatic photographs. 'All, we're all of us like this.' And the window over his door was the much-magnified portrait of the cabin's occupant. He knew it for his sister before he was near enough to identify her gentle expression, or the kiss-curl.

Then she came gliding, still naked, from the cabin, with a long, measured pace, as though she were dancing, and she had grown to a stupefying size. She undulated her broad back, with its ridged line of scars. He thought of her as untamed and beautiful, a girl who galloped through the woods like a Valkyrie, in a haze of light.

At last he saw another bright, empty corridor, walled with accordions. It twinkled and scintillated, full of white keys and irridescent glitter. There was nothing in it but accordions, and the name *HARMONY* stamped each instrument with discord.


## Out of the Blue, One Morning

There came the royal command. Boots and Saddle. 'Prisoner to be transferred immediately. Signed: F. Otero. Superintendent (p.p. Commissioner).'

When this *billet-doux* appeared on Elias's desk it was too early to do much about it. No one was yet in the office. Otero was not yet on station, moustache well to the fore, beneath his portrait of Salazar, in earshot of hospital traffic. This was going to be complicated.

'Get me the superintendent on his private number, please.'

No reply. (Astonishing.)

'I think the superintendent must have left, sir.'

That's as may be. Elias replaced the receiver. He may have left, and then again he may not have arrived. More probably stirring from slumber in an adulterous couch, beside a perfumed charmer. If I may so phrase it. Yes, indeed. And heartily Graveyard wished him total non-success.

In the desk-drawer, on the last page of the Book of the Dead, was the last section of notes for Mena to sign before she went. God might know – he, Elias, did not – where they would transfer her, but transferred she was to be, and he had to complete the documents. He rang to have her brought from the cells.

At the windowpane he subdued the dishevelled strands of hair on his glistening dome, arranged the grey pear-dop tiepin and, hands in his pockets, surveyed the bustle below. Shops were still shuttered, but a detachment of the mounted Republican Guard clattered by, the trams passed, and sleepy hands bore folded morning papers office-wards. The two Black Marias on the other side of the street had been there overnight, but he imagined them packed with women derisively demonstrating their sexual attractions to the guards. 'Hey, look what I've got!' and a boastful indicative slap.

He turned. Mena was in the room with the chief warder, a fat, pockmarked man exuding an odour of stale food. Elias indicated the chair in front of the desk and sat down. Prisoner and detective, face to face. Let's tidy things up.

The warder was seen through the glass panel, dawdling among

the tables in the outer office. Two shiny rounds highlighted the fat bottom and he rubbed his hands together. Life was a picnic, evidently.

But the staff were trickling in, and the inspector's attention was on Mena opposite, in a low-necked sweater with her arms crossed.

'Shall we begin?'

He read the familiar transcript as if it were quite new, pausing and repeating where necessary. Witness said this, witness that; Lisbon, police headquarters, such and such a date. Now and then he stopped, to remind her that corrections could be made. Yes, so she understood. He read on. And of course this is definitive. No more statements after this, we can have no mistakes and no omissions, for she was to be transferred.

'Be transferred?'

'Surely you expected it?'

She tightened her arms against her chest as if she were cold. Dread of the PIDE, he thought, and thought of the Black Marias parked in the street and the bedlam of harridans pulling their pubic hair out.

'The normal procedure would be to put you in a women's prison.'

'Put me?' She was staring at the palm of her hand. 'Anyhow, I shall see people,' she said in a small voice. She stared at her palm, at the back of her hand, and into the palm again.

'Yes – well –' Elias mumbled. Witness said, witness confirmed, or wished to alter. She listened to the condemnatory transcript, compressed and revised from what she had told him. Would he please re-read that bit?

'. . . says that after the crime was committed, on learning that the major intended to kill her and had shown him – the architect – where he would bury her, had taken his words as a warning, not to her, but to the architect.'

'No,' she amended. 'Reconsidering, I see he would have killed me.'

'Reconsidering? Why was that?'

'Tortures. It was worse every time. He'd have killed me in the end.'

She stood, and rolled her sweater above her brassière at the back; and Elias saw, incredulous, that from waist to neck her skin was patterned with the silver-grey raised scars of cigarette-burns. They were neat, and they were numerous – scales in a fishbone pattern the length of her spine.

'He'd become impotent,' she said.

# Reconstruction of the Crime
## 8th August, 1960

Elias had very little to do with the architect and Barroca beyond reading their confessions in a clean copy of the PIDE dossier. This comprised reports, injunctions and charges. The interrogators, a PIDE agent named Mortágua, who transcribed the statements, and a superintendent signing himself Falcão, had not been idly chosen for their task. Unmentioned were the beatings, the statue torture, the sleep torture, but these you could take for granted. Essentials only were included, and even politics omitted as far as possible. 'Facts concerning crimes against state security have been deleted.'

Nothing new, that is, and everything regular in what Elias read about the pair. Later, he interviewed them; better, he interviewed them together, after which they were returned to sender. Thank-you very much, he said, and *au revoir*. The PIDE could have them, he would revert to normal.

Not until 8th August did he see them again, and then at the Casa da Vereda itself. At two that afternoon Fontenova and Barroca were decanted, dazed, into the sunshine from a prison-van, both in handcuffs. The corporal, head still cropped, was in prison uniform, the architect in flannels and a tweed jacket.

'My goodness, look who's here!' exclaimed Roque, halting on the terrace.

## Locations (1)

'It was here he said he'd bury her.'

Elias and the architect were by a narrow ditch that traversed the pinewood. Thorny brambles arched above it and the depth was hard to judge. Some of the berries were black and juicy, others thin and shrivelled already.

'He really meant to kill her, you think?'

Fontenova groped vainly with manacled hands for his cigarettes. Elias helped him, lit the cigarette for him.

'Thank-you,' Fontenova filled his lungs with smoke as though with the scent of pines.

'He meant to kill her? I wouldn't say he didn't. She, more than any of us, was a problem for him.'

Elias peered into the bushes.

'The impotence, yes.'

Heavy wings were thrashing somewhere near. It might be a jackdaw in the brambles. But why jackdaws in a ditch?

'He fetched me out to see. "That's where she'll be going," he said.'

Elias pictured Dantas, playing patience and working out schemes with cards at the table, alone, standing up to study his game; and simultaneously saw him under the trees, in his dressing-gown, followed by the architect. 'There – that's where she'll be going!' Fontenova was saying something about army training. His father's? 'Soldiers invariably take a situation to extremes,' he said.

This had the oratorical ring of a speech, by the overgrown grave. He spoke of boyhood, Military College, of the father who served as a captain in the Medical Corps in the Great War, was thrice decorated and held the French Legion of Honour; who, a fencing-champion since his cadet days, wore uniform, at the government's request, to receive his Olympic trophy.

The brambles were dense as barbed wire, and wasps whined angrily, unseen. Elias cut the reminiscences short, scraping at the ground with his foot. 'You couldn't bury anyone here,' he said, 'it's solid rock. He must have known that.'

Above the rock in this corner of the wood was no more than a layer of pine-needles from which the roots writhed, some of them for yards.

'Impotence, that would upset him.' The inspector kicked at a treetrunk. 'Worst thing there is for making a man suspicious.'

He was ambling comfortably on in front, shirt open at the neck, coat on his shoulders. No fear of Fontenova's straying.

(Points discussed by Inspector Santana and the accused, Fontenova, in pinewood on occasion of the reconstruction of the crime:
– burial of Mena.
– tortures inflicted on her by the major (other than blows and cigarette-burns?)
– Fontenova's grandfather (the admiral) and father (fencing-champion). Why did he speak of them?

– underlinings in *The Sea Wolf*. Had he read the book after Mena? Was it underlined when he read it? No, to both questions.
– Ah!' commented the inspector.)

Crossing a patch of bracken on the path to the house, they met Roque and the corporal, descending.

'Ships,' said Elias, 'that pass in the night. Your pilot is reliable, I trust?'

'He's managing.'

The corporal was showing the way to the major's retreat. 'If he remembers it!' (Joke).

'Oh, yes, the retreat. Is it far? I said, is it far? Have you lost your tongue, man?'

Realising this was for him, Barroca gestured vaguely with his head.

'Down there.'

'Down there.' He looked scruffy, poor devil, in his cotton garb, with his cropped hair and handcuffs. Lacklustre. 'OK. Down we go.'

The wood was sparser on the slope, the trees bent in one direction (prevailing wind, Elias noted) and the undergrowth of heather and cistus was thicker (wind again, the seed-carrier). Another step or two, and the prospect widened to the sea.

Of course Barroca remembered the way. He had chanced on the place the first afternoon that the major was off at a secret rendez-vous. 'It was a nice change,' he said. The tedium of four walls must have been intolerable.

Elias smiled. 'A nice change!' More change than the corporal bargained for when he strolled by this heap of logs, and to that heap of stones below, which might be a well. Yes, at a nearer approach it was a well, recently dug, with a scatter of soil lying about and a small zinc canopy bright in the sun. And there, said the corporal, from a second log-pile, slightly to the right, he observed, with a shock of dismay, the major. A priest, sitting on the rim of the well, alone.

'You bet he was alone,' agreed Elias. 'Hatching his one-man plots.'

Here, beyond the trees, there were only heather and cistus, stones and sun; sun which drew from the polished cistus leaves a scent like that of close, warm flesh.

'So, you're behind this firewood.' Correct. 'The major's at his secret meetings, and you drop in and rumble him. Three times, was it?'

'Twice. One time he really went to Lisbon.'

Elias urinated in the bushes. 'And that once,' he said, over his shoulder, 'you knew he'd gone to Lisbon – but the other twice you didn't say he hadn't. Yet you knew, perfectly well.'

He came back, fastening his trousers.

'You left the others in the dark. A fine thing, I must say.'

Barroca kept his eyes stolidly on the view.

'Roque!' exclaimed Elias, 'this isn't an enquiry, it's a bloody masked ball.' He laughed mirthlessly. 'I lie, thou liest, he lies – they were all bloody lying!'


## Locations (2)

On the main road were two parked Landrovers and a GNR picket with slung rifles. A curious crowd gawped at a few visible inches of roof and a path to the terrace.

Neither Mena nor Otero was yet here. The latter was doubtless with the Big Cheese, assenting madly to every proposition; or, worse, had been summoned for private instructions from the PIDE. (Not astonishing.) 'Each in its proper sphere' – immortal phrase – 'the forces of the Law must pull together.' Et voilà! Elias, with the dossier under his arm, took a turn on the terrace.

Roque was there too, whittling a cistus twig with his penknife. The prisoners sat, until further orders, each in his pool of shadow, under the pine trees and the photographer teased a bad-tempered puppy nearby. The man, an odd-looking, ageless albino, had a fluff of white-cotton hair and naked eyes drained of colour; when he laughed he resembled an elderly child, his teeth as small as the puppy's. A blackbird somewhere was singing its heart out.

The delay, and the book of words, transported Elias to his youth and the long intervals during dress-rehearsals of the Estefânia Amateur Dramatic Society. They would do Ramada Curto's play, The Recompense – Dr Ramada Curto, popular dramatist, and lawyer – with its tear-jerking flights of rhetoric; and Elias advanced

to the footlights trolling Offenbach's *Barcarolle*, inserted, on a whim, by the producer:
'*Time will pass and joy will fade,*
*For love is ne'er undying.*'
Infallible memory played it to him now.

He went indoors and down to the garage where the body had lain, then to the scene of the crime, the living-room. From a plan attached to the dossier he checked the position of the furniture and the fatal weapons on the table – a Parabellum pistol, calibre 7.75, a Walter 6.35, a Smith .32 revolver. And there had been plenty of ammunition in the house. Hanging his jacket on a chair, he sat on the sofa by the hearth. It was cool here. The telephone was on the cupboard opposite.

He riffled through the papers.

'. . . woke to the noise of the major shouting in the living-room. "I shall denounce them! I shall denounce them all!" ' Thus the corporal, when questioned together with the architect.

'. . . this was when he first spoke unequivocally of executing named supporters of both government and opposition.' (The architect, on the same occasion.)

The Night of the Generals, obviously. Elias flicked the pages. More clamour, more details, more about the major's intentions. 'Denounce them all!' he shouted, but the voice was Mena's. And the architect: 'He spoke of attacking individual police-officers, and of raiding police-posts for arms and ammunition. Other targets, such as arsenals, were unspecified.'

The inspector consulted his watch. Had the reconstruction been postponed? Owing to Unforeseen Circumstances, Programme Cancelled by the Management; what a disappointment. Instinctively he glanced at the telephone.

'Asked what he knew of the victim's plans and objectives, said he first heard of them the night before the murder, when he and the major talked in the living-room. Said that the major, on the sofa, scowled in a menacing manner at the telephone. That he did this, and nursed the long-barrelled pistol, from which he was now inseparable, as deliberate intimidation.' (Fontenova).

'He's mad. He'll kill the three of us!' (Fontenova again, waking the corporal during the night of 25th March.)

'They were to rouse the country initially with a series of "political" fires, arson being spectacular and easy, with no training needed.

The São Luis cinema, adjoining PIDE headquarters, was one target; also the *Diário da Manhã* building (inflammable materials), and the Military Courts (an old fabric, mainly used for the storage of archives). He did not say how he would execute individuals.' (Fontenova.)

Next page. The telephone? No. And no sound of cars in the sleepy afternoon; nor any sound save that of the blackbird, who had renewed his flood, his delirium, of music.

'None of your idealism, Fontenova. Either they support me, or I denounce them to the police.' Liquid arabesques of birdsong accompanied the reading. 'In line, or I denounce them!' And this, and that, and more and more, and the scorching menace at the telephone ('I only have to pick it up –'); and Fontenova, perturbed at the other's increasingly furious aspect, attempting dissuasion. 'Witness,' said the transcript, 'could not believe it of the major.'

'Could not believe it.' Elias had marked the sentence. 'I shall denounce the lot of them – and I include your little friends, don't think I don't.' To this witness, though angry, made a conciliatory reply, saying he respected the major too much to believe him capable of such an action, and that he had confided the list to him in good faith.'

Elias could weigh what was in the PIDE transcript against what was not. This was the version For External Use Only. Do Not Shake or Contents May Explode. It referred to persons to be executed, but did not say who they were. It ignored the major's notebook, from which the names could have been copied without difficulty. The architect's list was mentioned, not the names. In it Dantas banged on the butt of the Parabellum and bawled, 'I have their names, Fontenova, I have their names, remember!' Then hastily the PIDE skidded away from politics and kept to blood and shooting.

And so the three prisoners were here, as though they were average, ordinary murderers, to enact the killing they had carried out together.

## Action Replay

'Your attention, please,' said the inspector, when the superintendent was seated.

A GNR corporal was on the door, Roque with his Smith portable typewriter at the table, his back to the terrace window. The flaxen photographer arranged his camera. The prisoners, in handcuffs, were by the fireplace wall.

'We are to imagine ourselves at the night of 26 March, 1960.' The police driver entered, with red stains on his shirt. (Blackberry juice.)

'Here, you can be the body,' Roque told him. 'Lord, man, you're bleeding, and they haven't shot you yet!'

'Twenty-sixth of March, 1960.' Elias had the dossier in his hand. 'On the previous day, in this room, he (indicating the architect) had an argument with the victim. A political argument, was it not?'

Fontenova hesitated. God, here we go! sighed Elias. Impediments, as per; trifles and trivial fuss, to clog the proceedings. But the criminal at this juncture, was preoccupied with truth. Not for reasons of scruple nor, as a rule, of vanity, but because he wanted to have done with his crime. He wanted to inter it, in every particular, exactly where it was committed; expunge it and leave no trace. Resigned to loss of freedom, he desired to be free of the crime, and this was his last opportunity.

'Yes?' said Elias. 'Go on.'

Fontenova looked fixedly ahead, as did his companions. Chiefly, he wished to add that it had been in no proper sense a discussion. Dantas was excited, and quick to lose his temper at the slightest difference.

'Is that all? I will therefore,' continued Elias, 'read a statement of 15th May, signed by the architect Renato Manuel Fontenova Sarmento: "We have to kill him, he isn't sane. God knows what happens to us if we don't." The corporal acquiesced, saying he had seen it coming and that the major had spent his life humiliating him.'

'Had spent his life.' Elias turned the page. When the corporal said that, the major was, for him, a dead man. 'Spent his life.'

'One plan had been for witness and Barroca, with the girl Filomena, to apply for asylum in a foreign embassy, but it was rejected as the major would then have denounced to us (that is, the PIDE, said Elias), various anti-government supporters; certainly would have denounced those on a list the witness had given him and which – in the language of a blackmailer – he called the Black List. This statement is confirmed and signed by Corporal Barroca, present with the witness at the confrontation.'

After his speech, or reading, the inspector had a word over the dossier with the superintendent, left it with him, and stepped round the table for a word with Roque at the typewriter. Roque stepped over to the prisoners, released the handcuffs and distributed firearms.

He had typed the first sheet of the official account.

RECONSTRUCTION OF CRIME

*Casa da Vereda, 8th August, 1960. Reconstruction of the murder of Major Luis Dantas Castro. Dr. Manuel F. Otero, superintendent, presiding. Present: Detective-Sergeant Silvino Roque and police-photographer Albino; the three accused (v. documents) under police supervision. Victim impersonated by Silvério Baeta (driver of police-car).* Victim was *seated* 'on the sofa over there,' Elias directed. 'You're playing patience, with the cards on the floor. The major was alone, in slippers and a woollen dressing-gown, in the pocket of which (Roque passed the Parabellum) was a gun.'

'Other pocket,' said Barroca, in a low voice.

'Oh, yes. Roque – he was left-handed.'

Seeing the driver sitting where Dantas died, Elias thought of the solitary card-player. He'd start here, at this very table, standing where I'm standing, setting out his deck; and end up on that sofa as the game, or whatever he was working out, fined down. A man with fewer trumps in his hand, and fewer cards to play. A man who played himself into a tight corner.

'Fined down,' had brought him immediately back to the superintendent, leafing through the dossier with the fastidious touch he reserved for any legal document. He finished, and Roque transmitted the volume to Elias, who opened it flat at the room-plan.

Positions and movements were marked. To his right was the major, as he was when he was shot, playing cards by himself; and as he played, the others too were cornered by their fear – the corporal and the architect in their rooms, Mena caged in the attic. Now the three stood, unmanacled, by the fireplace, the men with guns in their fingers, Mena barelegged between them, in a linen suit and high-heeled sandals; three assassins, here to re-enact their deed. OK, Elias told Roque, let's get on with it.

'The two men come down to supper,' he said to the room at large, leaning, arms extended, on the table's edge. 'The victim takes no notice of them. The girl (he indicated Mena) is in the kitchen. The table (everyone studied the table) has not been set for the meal; it was not set that night, as we shall see. It is seven o'clock, according to the statements, and the lights are on. He (the architect) and the corporal, each with a gun in his pocket, are in their agreed positions.

'Between the table and the terrace-window Barroca is at an angle of 45° to the victim's left, thus covering the side from which the major, who was left-handed, might shoot. The architect goes to the cabinet, as if for a drink. The corporal, pistol cocked in his pocket, then crosses nearer to the major, as if making for the door. The major is ostentatiously absorbed in his cards and ignores the two of them. He could not know that Barroca would swing round and level a gun at his head from less than a yard away. When he realised, it was too late, and the architect was aiming at him from the right.'

The inspector motioned to the photographer and a flashbulb exploded. (Photograph no. 1.)

Elias went to the fireplace wall; two paces from Mena.

'The first shot, the corporal's, penetrates the left parietal bone. The corporal fires the second shot also, Fontenova's revolver having jammed. Your revolver jams (*crescendo*) and what do you do?)

'You cast about, seize the poker from the hearth, and you strike the major on the back of the neck.' (Photograph No. 2.)

Photograph no. 3, illustrating her own statements to Elias, was of Mena beside the body.

'Witness ran in, alarmed by the shots, then fled in horror to the kitchen. In perhaps ten minutes – she cannot say – the corporal came for her. Says the architect was kneeling by the body, listening for a heartbeat. That he rose slowly and, with an arm on her shoulder, said, "We had no choice. We had no choice." In an access of compassion, and of comradely feeling, witness embraced him.'

'And you saw, over his shoulder, that the major was moving.'

Mena nodded. She had screamed, 'My God, he's still alive!' Blood was gushing from his mouth, the head was clotted with hair and flesh, and a dull globe hung from one eye-socket.

Again Barroca levelled his pistol, but before he could decide between head and chest, the architect grabbed his wrist.

'No. No, Barroca. I haven't fired yet. We must be in this together.'

Photograph no. 4: Fontenova with the corporal's pistol at the driver's heart. Driver squints in consternation at the barrel.

Photograph no. 5. The architect said, 'You, Mena', and gave her the gun. She experienced neither revulsion nor incredulity, but obeyed, either from that same impulse of comradeship, of being in it together, or because the idea of death had grown familiar. She would be firing into a corpse for the sake of two living people – three, for she counted equally. The architect had one hand on her wrist, aiming the gun for her, and the other over hers, pressing her trigger-finger. She did not look where she fired, but at his hand, whose light, soft chill on her fingers she never afterwards forgot. A man's hand, yet it could have been the skin of a dead hand made into a glove, curiously dead itself, and weightless.

'That will do, I think.' Before Otero had risen from his chair the driver, unable to believe his ears, was out of the room like greased lightning, leaving his cap behind.

But Elias wasn't happy. A detail, as he chewed his Rennie's tablet, bothered him.

'There's something not quite right,' he said.

The superintendent was with Roque, reading over the typescript and stealthily admiring Mena's bottom.

'Mm? Not right? What's not right?'

Elias rubbed his head.

'She says she saw the dead man's mouth as she embraced the architect. It's in the notes. She saw his lips move and blood gushing. She couldn't have done, not from where she was. From the way the corpse fell, she could have seen his mouth only from this side.'

Mena said, 'He was facing this way.'

'That's true,' said the architect.

'This way? How peculiar.' Elias polished his spectacles and examined them at arm's length. 'Have we lost that driver?'

'He needed fresh air,' said Roque. 'Can't endure the smell of blood.'

Feeble jests from Roque were as provoking as the fact that the light was now fading from this tree-encircled house. In the driver's absence, Elias would be the major on the floor. 'Come on, come on,' he bade Mena and the architect. 'Where you were for the embrace, please.'

Prone on his back in the requisite position, head hanging like that of a slaughtered animal, he saw their feet, Mena's and Fontenova's, inching, inching nearer. They stopped. There were her ankles, unadorned by the golden chain. He saw them with the greatest clarity, almost on top of him. He was closer to them than he had ever been; slim, beautiful ankles, whose contour ran to the arching instep from the scented depths of her body. And her sandals, he saw, were lizard-skin.

'Photograph,' he commanded, speaking into his shoulder. 'I want their positions accurate in relation to the body.'

Photograph no. 6; to be endorsed, 'Corresponds to statement by female prisoner.'

When he was again vertical, he had the wildflower fragrance in his nostrils, though it might have been no more than a trick of memory, or the subconscious.

He was alone with the prisoners. Otero and Roque were on the terrace – had just gone past the window – and the cameraman Albino – Whitey – was out there with them, frail and pathetic as ever, blown along by his cloud of thistledown hair.

Elias sat at the table. Under his hand was the final record, from the typewriter; and here, at the scene of the crime, were the confessed criminals and the detective on duty. He fastened his collar; he was on duty. Got up, and turned to lay Roque's pencil, pen, penknife and eraser as he had found them. The GNR corporal remained on guard, as though the murder were newly committed and the room a shambles, with playing-cards all over the floor and the dead man – well and truly dead – were spouting blood. 'We had to stuff a towel in his mouth,' the typescript said.

The photographer, seen through the window, shielded his pink eyes with one hand and whistled into the trees, hoping the puppy-dog would respond. Elias had not previously noticed that Whitey grew no older. He remembered him – flaxen, ethereal, a trans-parency – on his first assignment; remembered saying, 'Bugger me, it's a negative!' And the man was a negative still, martyred by the light of day.

But the blackbird? Had you finished your song, Caruso?


## 'We will now resume,' said Otero

'Resuming the reconstruction of the murder, prisoners were escorted to the room above, that occupied by the major and his mistress.'

166

It was here that she and the two men talked, after seeing to the body.

They had struggled to wrap it in a blanket, with the head in the plastic cloth from the sitting-room table – tied securely with string to keep the blood in; and Mena had gone for his shoes. It baffled everyone, this aversion to burying him in his socks. Why they put his shoes on, neither Mena nor the architect could explain, much less the corporal, who merely looked down and had nothing to say. Events, succeeding one another automatically, were chaotic and beyond control; objects surfaced as though clamouring for integration and unreal incidents were dealt with hurriedly, as they presented themselves. Mena brought his shoes, there were his shoes, and they had to be put on – forcibly, because, or so it seemed, the corpse was stiffening and resistent. Not until they read the newspapers did the three learn of the left-right reversal.

There came a point when Mena could not stay in the room.

'When was this?' the inspector asked.

'Later,' replied the architect. They were washing the floor and the body seemed to bleed again. She ran upstairs, in panic or despair, and was lying on the bed – there, where the inspector sat – when he and the corporal followed; which must have been an hour afterwards. ('I was knocked senseless,' she had told Elias. 'I was in a stupor, numb.')

Light from the window fell on the two men in front of the mammoth junkshop wardrobe, and curious partners they made, the corporal with his prison stubble, the architect in the everyday clothes he was permitted to wear. Yet a partnership it was, though no look was exchanged; as though they were bound together, and apparently unperturbed.

But on the night of the crime they were statues, dehumanised, scarcely breathing. Mena turned to the wall when they entered, wishing neither to see them nor to imagine her own face. They stood there, livid, mute and frightened, companioned by a ghost from the bellying antique behind them.

After a while – a neutral, non-existent interval – Mena said, 'It was his fault. It was all his fault.' The words, muffled in her pillow, shocked her. Had she uttered them aloud?

'What else could we do?' said the architect.

'We might have poisoned him.'

'Poisoned him.' The inspector looked at her, leaning by the

window, indifferent to what was going on. Linen suit; legs a little apart – the more tantalising, more inviting – and the high instep in the lizard-skin sandals. What she had was style. Born with it. She lit a cigarette with the gold lighter he had held in his hand at the pawnbroker's, that gipsy morning in the Praça da Figueira. Her father would have redeemed the pledges at once, the gold chain among them. But she wasn't wearing the gold chain.

'Approximately how long were you here?' said Otero, at the chest-of-drawers with a scribbling-pad.

They could not tell him. 'How long' was neutral, non-existent. There were vivid flashes of sight and sound, as on the night itself, but the time in this room was nebulous, out of context. They knew that, gradually, Mena revived, and sat up, and that they talked, jerkily at first, then in a confessional flood, and always of the dead man. Always of him. Not in vindication, but to be sure that they were free of him and living still. In the pinewood, said Fontenova: 'that's where she'll be going.' By the well, said Barroca – no one had met him there. Mena said, what she had not said before, that he had tortured her. Their faces as they spoke, and as they had told the police, were ugly, disfigured beyond recognition.

Freedom through a killing; the idea was underlined in *The Sea Wolf*. 'It would be a most moral act to rid the world of such a monster': this monster, glowering at them with a long-barrelled pistol on his knee. Underlined and, by Elias, unforgotten. But in ignorance of that prophetic condemnation, they enumerated the major's lies, the major's threats, example on example, until they drove him further and further from them; until his very features were indistinct and he might have been someone in a history-book.

Never had they themselves been so united, or so unconstrained.

'And next,' said Elias (don't lose sight of facts), 'you went to the living-room and telephoned the architect's mother.'

To telephone? No. They went into the kitchen.

They had as yet no notion of ringing the architect's mother, for the pinewood had seemed, to Fontenova and the corporal, the obvious burial-place, though Mena was horrified. He would be there, and it might be days or weeks before they could leave . . . Nor had they thought of tools, and there was not a spade or a hoe in the house – nothing to dig with.

It was then the solution occurred to them: the seashore, a sandy beach. The men carried the body, in its blanket, to the garage, with Mena behind them, mopping blood.

'You put him on the ping-pong table and came back to the kitchen.'

Correct. It had been an awkward descent of the narrow internal stairs; and they could not guess that the major's notebook was under the trees by the garage, with Fontenova's list copied in it.

'Then, back to the kitchen.'

To the kitchen, yes.

'And you ate,' said Elias.

They ate, but first they telephoned. Or rather, Mena telephoned, and then they ate; though why, they did not know, unless from habit and a desire for normality. In the kitchen, Fontenova said, Mena was obsessively tidying. As they talked she was touching the taps, moving a glass, brushing, wiping, opening and shutting drawers. And when she spoke to his mother she was dusting the top of the sideboard, fiddling with the ornaments by the telephone.

'You spoke in French?'

In French. And the call was a short one.

'It's a party,' she said. 'Do come. Here are the directions.' There was a protracted silence, then 'D'accord,' and a click as the line cleared. An hour later the architect, from the shadow of a wall, saw his mother park her Citröen at the next crossroads before the Casa da Vereda lane.

'I have to borrow the car. Something's happened.'

'In my notes,' said the inspector, 'this was about 11.30.'

Yes, thereabouts; and raining heavily. The architect's mother did not see the major. She sat in the living-room with Mena while the car was away.

'Two hours you were away. According to her statement it was three before she started for home.'

Three? The prisoners could not be exact, but yes, probably three. The men had had difficulty in finding anywhere that would be safe from the winter tides; and the rain, while it kept traffic off the roads and lessened the chance of being seen, also cut down visibility. They sought for miles along the coast, with the body crammed in the rear seat, and resolved on Praia do Mastro the second time round. Driving some 300 metres past the bathing-beach, nearly to the big TAP hoarding by the road, they finally took the body into the sand-dunes, where the dogs were to scent it in a week.

The superintendent was writing flowery signatures on his scribbling-pad. *Otero*, he wrote, *Manuel F. Otero*. was a calligraphic maze, the *O* bedecked with coils and curlicues. His cigarette was out. His face was out, eclipsed by the brown-tinted polaroids. Head nearly touching that of the pottery cat, he was faceless, expressionless, enthralled by curlicues.

'And after this – after that night – you and the architect slept in here together,' he said, as though reading aloud what he was writing.

Mena looked at him.

'I slept that night in the attic. I slept for ten solid hours.'

Elias said nothing – but, ten hours! Annihilating, terror-induced sleep. When she awoke the others had noticed and scraped clean the blood-splashes on the ceiling, and that morning there was a frenzied search for the major's notebook. Anything of his they burned – clothes, papers, personal possessions. Elias recalled an old crime-article in the *Século Ilustrado* – suspects who gave themselves up to the sheriff of Jacksonville, 'exhausted by their efforts to obliterate all trace of their victim.'

Otero, intent on the calligraphy, continued, 'Sleeping in this bed, and you left the cassock in the wardrobe. Why, will you tell me?'

No reply.

'Then I'll tell you.' He elaborated a pleasing pattern. 'The cassock stayed in the wardrobe to prove the man was dead. Indubitably. No other reason I can think of.'

The inspector allowed his attention to wander. One had heard more than enough of the priestly costume. It was, of course, an unnerving discovery on the first day. It had unnerved him, for one; he had gone down and gulped, 'There's a hanged priest in the wardrobe,' to the superintendent. But that was the first day and the mystery had ceased to be a mystery when they had the prosaic explanation – that Fontenova planned to escape in this disguise. And a sensible plan, too, in Elias's opinion, remarkable only for the duplication; the architect would be masquerading as the major masquerading as a priest. Kill a man and assume his second self – there was an amusing nuance in it. But that was why soutane and dog-collar were saved from the flames to be, with the notebook, the sole relics of Major Dantas Castro. The fire had the rest; the illuminating, purifying fire, as they say. Not even the pack of cards was spared. Cards: and Elias saw sinister characters in an ancient film-cartoon, playing poker for beans, and an ace of hearts which bled at the touch of Jack the Ripper.

Otero pushed aside his scribbling-pad, screwed the top on his creative fountain-pen and became the heavy policeman. He observed each prisoner from head to foot. He shot the point-blank question,

'And the flight to the hotel?'

Fontenova stepped forward. There was no flight, he said. Mena quitted the Casa da Vereda with the agreement, after thorough discussion, of all of them.

The superintendent would query the 'all' but for now was more interested in filling the gaps. A week after the body was discovered they were yelling for help. They had money enough, thanks to the architect's mother, but they must get out of Portugal, and who was to organise that?

'Ah,' said Elias. 'A telegram to Mozambique would solve the problem?'

'One way or another, yes,' Fontenova answered. 'But it was a shared decision.'

Otero rolled the cigarette in his fingers. An SOS to her father in Africa, when the police had tabs on everything! Or had they not thought? She would be arrested before the message was off the teleprinter at the other end. And worse if she telephoned; they'd be there before she could hang up. Unless the PIDE preferred to use her father as a ferret, to lead them to the house.

But Mena insisted, seeing no alternative. It was a risk she had to take, and she would take it alone. She would await her father in an obscure hotel, and ring the Casa da Vereda at given times. The others would thus be out of danger, and if the police intercepted her telegram – well, that was her risk. There was no salvation in sitting with your arms folded. With this she packed her bag and was off. 'Quite simple,' she said.

Mena at the Novo Residencial, hair in a ponytail and loose slippers, as when she arrived at police headquarters; her father lazing in Mozambique with the hippopotami, and she sitting glued to an airline time-table . . .

In the event, it wasn't a long wait. There next morning, with the compliments of the *Benemérita*, were Otero and the indefatigable Roque. She had taken her risk. The two men, hearing nothing from

171

her, bolted for their lives. 'Simple,' she had said, and simple it was –
all done by 9.30 a.m. on 10th April last.

But to the superintendent it was less simple. Rolling his cigarette,
he enquired whether Mena had no 'other reasons' – if he might so
phrase it? More explicitly, reasons to do with her and the architect
alone?

Mena's eyebrows arched. Whether in incomprehension or absolute disinterest, who could say?

'You were sleeping together. I want an answer. Why did you
wish to leave him?'

He gave the pottery cat a shove. Unexpectedly, he felt his temper
going (he could talk himself into a fury, as policemen can), and he
took a deep breath, trying to be calm.

'Will you read this!' He snatched the dossier from Elias. ' "Complete intimacy" is what it says; is what you said, remember?' He
was simmering again, shaking the dossier at her. 'On terms of
complete intimacy with him – the architect – after the major's
death. That's what you told the PIDE, or had it slipped your mind?
Why the PIDE? Why not us? We were too decent, I suppose. Not
enough pressure. And because we were decent you saw no need to
mention it?'

For a second or two he glared at her, his moustache oozing
contempt.

'You bunch of putrid shits,' he said, and stalked out.

Hands on his knees, the inspector sat on the edge of the bed,
looking down, saying nothing. He glanced now and again at the
pottery cat, or heard a voice – his own – humming, not much above
a whisper. The tune faltered and frayed in the twilight and the
prisoners thought they had imagined it; but it had been there, the
transient shadow of a tune.

Elias stopped humming. He shrugged his shoulders, and spread
his hands towards the three, as if to say, 'That's it. Buggered. Can't
do any more.' At the door he signalled them, absently, to precede
him.

Then it was just routine. Roque at the foot of the stairs with
the handcuffs, the GNR corporal on the terrace, thumb hitched in
his rifle-sling. The prisoners went outside one by one, Mena last.
The inspector gripped her arm.

'You. It was you who underlined that book!' His words were
barely audible. He pushed her after the others.

She trod, firmly and gracefully, behind them.

Behind her came Roque with the typewriter; he, too, was watching the way she walked.

Yet another visit to *Imperial Violets*, now showing at the Capitol. Ascending steep streets from the cinema – Rua do Telhal, Travessa do Torel – Elias paused for a snack in the Campo Santana. Dreamy with Russian waltzes, humming softly and a little sharp, he was making for his favourite public garden.

In the dimly lit bar were a trollop or two on their way to work and a man doing his football pools. The inspector swallowed his milky coffee and left, passing at the door a police-informer whom he pretended not to recognise.

Campo Santana and the Jardim dos Mártires. He hugged the café-wall, humming his private tunes. Here, at night, all was quiet as a provincial town. Façades of dressed stone and tiles, a glassed-in balcony on a corner house, a mansion among palms and camellias – these were the legacy of a vanished republican bourgeoisie. You could smell grass, and the trees of the Martyrs' Garden, with their fleshy, archaic-looking leaves, pervaded the dark, almost hiding, from where he stood, the statue of the ever-popular and continuously effective Dr Sousa Martins, on whose pedestal guttered the candles of pious spiritualists. The doctor was constantly supplied with candles.

A cluster of whores approached, surprisingly, from the obscurity, but Elias did not loiter with a serenade.

*'You pretty moths, you butterflies,*
*You pearls that pierce my heart.'*

(Not from *Imperial Violets*, this; he was improvising.) On they flew, out of the chrysalis, away from their slummy streets and into the bright lights, to the perfumed glitter, the reverberating hive, of Town. Pretty, pretty butterflies, with brassières a-flutter. Goodnight ladies, goodnight sweet ladies.

Against the wall, he was alternately seen and unseen as clouds scudded over the moon. He would smooth the dome of his head and then, with limp hands and dead eyes, blend, like a lizard, with the background. The super-policeman will adopt a still, reptilian patience and dart, without warning, at the fly. Elias the lizard, when he moved, moved fractionally and fast and was again immobile. The tiny, sibilant noise he made seemed to emanate from the stones.

Suddenly, he darted: from the wall, over the road and into the garden where, halting or flitting on, he toured the flowerbeds and his purpose was revealed. He was hunting, with a storage-bottle and a flashlight, to see what he could find. He found a rich booty. Shining his torch in the grass, he could unearth worms and beetles, dislodge a locust, catch a praying mantis on the hop.

Bottom-up in a Lisbon flowerbed, the detective was a secret hunter; and as a hunter, even of such small deer, gifted and persevering. In half a dozen sorties he had filled his game-bag and was free to enjoy the night-air, in solitary meditation, on a bench; on any of the empty benches.

He sat, with the bottle and its captives in his pocket, by the statue of Sousa Martins – a surgeon dead but still in active practise. The monument was more of a shrine, with its lighted candles, ex-votos and letters of medical advice from the spirit-world. Elias patted his bottle of insects and thought of this apostle-doctor, incarnate in bronze, a saint on the side, embowered in humble offerings and wreaths from funerals; or else he thought of Reptile, asleep in a glass box by a window over the Tagus.

Unheralded, from nowhere, appeared a paratrooper; dropped from the skies with no intrusion on the moonlight, no rustle of the black-and-silver leaves, to sit on the same bench.

'Got a match?' Got a cigarette? was what he meant. No, said Elias, he didn't smoke; and could feel the top-to-toe survey that lingered at his crotch. A comfort that the shrine was near, and guaranteed expert advice per spirit-post. He could not actually discern the heaps of thank-you-notes on the magic table, but they were there; also wax models (the globular breast, the child's hand), and walking-sticks, a mouldering surgical boot, jars of gallstones or slices of somebody's stomach. A thousand and one testimonials, perpetually renewed before the Wise Doctor in mystic obedience to an unseen ebb and flow. This was the realm of the occult, and the attitude of Elias to the inexplicable was that some things are inexplicable. Science, however, existed to explain them, and in this conflict lay the key to Progress.

The paratrooper had a match, after all. He lit a cigarette, puffed it with a cryptic smile and spoke, in choppy phrases, into space. He was a man, he said, with a great sex-drive.

At no season of the year had Elias known the statue bereft of its faithful complement of faulty human fragments, and he was thinking how Reptile had discarded a fragment of his tail. Another mystery – and mysteriously done, with teeth and claws. God, it must have hurt him! Left as attestation in the sand, the severed segment withered and blackened as the mutilated tail grew stronger and more vigorous.

The soldier rambled on into space. What a night, he was saying, for a Night Out. But Elias was in Homicide, social behaviour was not his province. He unwrapped a Rennie's, having heartburn and a bad taste in his mouth. It was his belief that the juices ruled the disposition, and what, oh Sainted Surgeon, can you send us for the juices? One's humour depended on the digestive juices, and on the handy remedy. He chewed his tablet. A good tablet taketh away the sins of the gizzard. A consecrated host which enabled one to belch, moreover, and thus eject the racking afflictions of acidity.

The paratrooper continued to unburden himself. It was no part of his plan, he said, to sleep in any stinking barracks. He wanted to see life and sleep around. And as for satisfaction, he could promise the whole repertoire, what with equipment like his, and no inhibitions – a real privateer – as present company would doubtless appreciate. Was he right?

'Thank-you. Another time, perhaps,' said Elias mildly, in farewell.

His homeward course, whether by the Avenida da Liberdade to Rossio, or through the Intendente, was meditative and regular as a pack-mule's, punctuated by the stops and landmarks which were his signposts, north or south.

Behind him were the parachutist dropped from heaven and the surgeon soaring thither ('only connect' – a counsel of perfection in this life), and he had reached a vast and brilliant showroom of stepladders. It had no counter, no shelves, nothing on the walls, but in the centre, face to face, were four open metal stepladders – actors in some everlasting, ever-incomprehensible tableau. This was the Socorro district landmark.

Grimy buildings; the leprous exterior of the morgue, then the Mouraria, in whose bars knives were concealed in stocking-tops (though infection was not, as at the Bolero, mandatory), and where the Judite scooped the drunken prostitutes into its Black

Marias more than once a night. No stop here, but on, up Rua Madalena — appliances, aviational wheelchairs and artificial limbs — to the oldest quarter, to the glass den and the wide sight of the Tagus and a lizard anticipating rations. There were no trams, though taxis cruised quietly, without haste, their green lights like transient fireflies.

Humming faintly, he examined the insects at a travel-agent's window. Under the fluorescence and distorted by the shape of the bottle, they were obscure and nightmarish. Armoured beetles in their shells, the pure green menacing mantis, locusts with serrated legs and leaden beady eyes — they kicked and wriggled and struggled, a shut-in jumble of knees and wings and elbows. In the window a poster proclaimed PORTUGAL, EUROPE'S BEST-KEPT SECRET. FLY TAP. Or, FLY KLM: Holland with a feather sabot, took to the air. Busy-Bee-Tours-and-the-World-is-Yours.

Three travelling cages passed him, and where could they be coming from? Long miles, certainly, on the main road from the north; in by the Avenida do Aeroporto, and across the city. Three railed circus-vans, travelling in the small hours — circus-vans, with no animals in them, only the keepers sprawling half-awake as they traversed deserted streets in the small hours, faces between bars and legs stuck out.

Elias sang no more, preoccupied, for the remainder of the walk, with these wild-beast keepers voyaging in cages through the night. Most striking, he thought, was the fact that there was really nowhere they could be going to.

(During his walk the inspector had hummed:
    Spanish tunes from *The Violet-Seller* and *The Last Melody*
    Tunes from Bizet's *Carmen*
    O, *Sole Mio*
    Tunes from *Les Cloches de Corneville*.)

# Appendix

p. 6) 'Inspector Santana died in Angola, where he was employed as assistant inspector by the Companhia de Diamantes, in January or February, 1974. Our news of him was infrequent, but we gathered that he had, to some extent, gone native. Graveyard gone native, with a gaggle of dark-skinned infants! His death was never properly explained. He was found, they say, in a sort of store-shed, where he had a collection of idols and other native stuff, which naturally attracted police enquiries. No result, though, beyond evidence of poisoning (the body was entirely decomposed), and this indicated that he had taken witch-doctor medicines.' (Inspector Silvino Roque to author, May, 1979.)

p. 34) Maltês Soares, 'the infamous Maltês', as Otelo Saraiva de Carvalho calls him in his book, *Alvorado em Abril*, commanded the riot police, known for their brutality in Lisbon and their absolute subservience to the PIDE. At the revolution, says Saraiva de Carvalho, Soares came crawling to the liberating forces, proposing himself as traffic-controller for the capital.

p. 55) 'the monocled major': later General Antonio de Spinola.

p. 111) Here, as for other details, I am indebted to the architect Fontenova. He asked his mother for clothes and money for the reasons given in the text, and as a precaution in case of a police attack on the Casa da Vereda. He had no intention of deserting the major until the latter's behaviour 'became such that it would have been disastrous to stay with him.' Secretly, Fontenova then worked out a plan to be implemented on one of Mena's shopping-days in the village.

Two conditions were essential: that neither Mena nor the corporal should be left at the major's mercy, and that his reprisals – that is, denunciation of those on what he termed the Black List – were prevented or annulled. Mena, therefore, instead of shopping in Fornos, was to go for refuge to Father Miguel Barahona,

Fontenova's boyhood friend; and Fontenova would join them, with the corporal, the same day. From Father Miguel's house they would contact and warn the five people – there were only five – on the list. None was closely connected with the Movement and it should have been easy for them to reject any accusation. 'Should have been,' Fontenova emphasised.

For the danger was that one or more of them might be involved with other opposition organisations. If this were so, even an unproved denunciation could furnish a lead to the police and do more damage than he, Fontenova, could possibly calculate. That, he said, was why he abandoned this plan.

p. 124) The major's presumed links with the PIDE were obviously non-existent. He had, on the contrary, been for some time under PIDE observation, as is proved by records found after the April revolution.

As did many servicemen stationed in Portuguese India, Dantas Castro there met Inspector Casimiro Monteiro of the Special Police, whose job was to suppress the independence agitators.

Monteiro, who had Indian blood, was tried soon afterwards for crimes committed in the district where he was born (see *O Caso Delgado*, by M. Garcia and L. Mauricio). Sentence was commuted and, through the influence of extremist supporters of Salazar, he entered the upper echelons of the PIDE, where he was known as the Leopard. The Catholic daily *A Voz de Chaves*, on 24th July, 1958, congratulated him publicly as 'one of the worthiest representatives of Portugal, in this or any age.'

p. 138) The account of The Night of the Generals is based on Fontenova's personal recollections, as well as on police records. For the major's repeated references to corruption in the Armed Forces, see:
a) on cowardice: *Portugal Oprimado* (pub. O. Século. Lisbon, 1974), and *Alvorada em Abril* (pub. Bertrand, Lisbon, 1977), both by Fernando Queiroga.
b) on bribery: Queiroga, op. cit; *Memórias do Capitão*, by Sarmento Pimental (pub. Felman Rego, Sao Paulo, 1962).
c) on corruption: *Documentos Secretos da Pide*, by Nuno Vasco (pub. Bertrand, Lisbon, 1976); *Relatório Stohrer do III Reich*, (in *Documents Secrets*, pub. Paul Dupont, Paris).

General Galvão de Melo was a Presidential candidate in 1980. Interviewed by the *Diário de Lisboa* (1st Sept 1982), Colonel Varela Gomes stated that the paper had printed, some time previously, a letter from Galvão de Melo to Salazar, 'giving details of a plot against the Fascist régime and saying that he had himself joined the conspirators, in order to discover as much as possible.' Delgado's *Letter to the Generals* (i.e. Lopes da Silva, Beleza Ferraz, Jorge Botelho Moniz and Costa Macedo) was published in *Missão em Portugal*, by Álvaro Lins (Rio de Janeiro, 1963).

p. 156) Assistant-Superintendent José Aurélio Boim Falcão was an old and trusted interrogator for the PIDE. Silvio da Costa Mortágua also owed his success in the PIDE to the brutality of his methods.

p. 161) 'Fear, I believe, is a dramatisation of solitude. It is also constricting, since one's equilibrium is shattered and one is no longer in balance with one's external circumstances. Worst of all, this rupture will eventually make one's reasoning entirely defensive; or for me it did. The reasoning of fear will undermine normal values until fear brings one to the point of murder.' (Fontenova, in conversation with author, summer, 1980.)

## Concluding Note

1) It was during the autumn of 1961 that I received from L.V., then a political refugee in the Brazilian embassy, a 22-page document written by a young man sentenced some months before to penal servitude for complicity in a murder. It was an account, lucid and direct, of a crime which had profoundly disturbed public opinion; simple, I thought, and objective. One saw into the conscience, heard the voice, of a courageous man.

Later re-reading of the two dossiers – of the Criminal Police and of the PIDE – confirmed my belief in the accuracy and directness of his document; but when I came to know the writer after his release these qualities took on a new dimension. For here was someone sensitive, creative and imaginative; who, in examining this chapter of his life, had imposed upon himself – almost depersonalised himself by – the strictest obsession with truth and accuracy.

He was, and is, aware of how much his crime is that of society as a whole; that a society founded on terror, and therefore embodying social crime, will seek its justification by castigating the crimes of the individual; and that for each and every individual crime it is itself responsible. But though he knew this – who better? – he would not speak of it, much less plead on such grounds for sympathy or compassion. If people understand, he said, you cherish their understanding without making calls on it. The terrible thing has been, and is, the knowledge of his crime, because with that he is inescapably alone.

2) Over twenty years after these events, his personal loneliness regarding them is, I think, the counterpart of the solitude he shared then. Alone, he looks the experience of terror in the face, accepts it, and is reconciled to fear because, as he said, 'it is the acting-out of solitude.'

3) Fear, the acting-out, the limit, of solitude: are the words his or those of my character, the architect Fontenova? Or even of someone else entirely? Or could I have invented them, to make him seem more real?

Some elements in some lives – in all lives, I would say – will raise the individual to general significance; something that will repay study, and transform him into the material of history or fiction. And we probe this material because it probes us, each one of us, to the depths – which is why I conceived this book as a novel. My 'architect Fontenova' is a literary creation. So is the major. Mena and the corporal are literary creations. They are imaginary: that is, they are distilled, imaginatively, from real people.

Thus fact and fiction, at every step, divide and come together, independent when parallel, conflicting when they meet; and no resemblance between truth and conjecture is purely coincidental.

J.C.P.
September, 1982.